ALSO BY BENJAMIN NUGENT

American Nerd

Good Kids

A NOVEL

Benjamin Nugent

SCRIBNER

New York   London   Toronto   Sydney   New Delhi

SCRIBNER
A Division of Simon & Schuster, Inc.
1230 Avenue of the Americas
New York, NY 10020

First Scribner hardcover edition January 2013

SCRIBNER and design are registered trademarks of The Gale Group, Inc.,
used under license by Simon & Schuster, Inc., the publisher of this work.

For information about special discounts for bulk purchases,
please contact Simon & Schuster Special Sales at 1-866-506-1949
or business@simonandschuster.com.

The Simon & Schuster Speakers Bureau can bring authors to your live event.
For more information or to book an event, contact the Simon & Schuster Speakers
Bureau at 1-866-248-3049 or visit our website at www.simonspeakers.com.

Manufactured in the United States of America

1   3   5   7   9   10   8   6   4   2

Library of Congress Control Number: 2012027692

ISBN 978-1-4391-3660-7
ISBN 978-1-4391-5433-5 (ebook)

For Bobie, Zeidi, and Polly

1994

1.

We're Not Going
to Get Thrown in a Van

The Dads were a man and a woman. They were my father, Linus, and Khadijah's mother, Nancy. Khadijah called them the Dads because, in her family, Nancy played the traditional paternal role. She spent more time at work than Khadijah's father, she made more money, she was harder to talk to. She was a Dad. And my father was a Dad.

To explain why we needed a name for the pair of them, I'll start with the Friday that Khadijah and I, with our respective Dads, ran into each other at Gaia Foods. The Day of the Dads.

It was early March, Language Day at Wattsbury Regional. As sophomores active in language clubs—I, Russian; Khadijah, French—we both manned tables, selling borscht and mousse outside the cafeteria after school. We never spoke during Language Day, although our tables stood five feet apart. All I knew about Khadijah was that she was third-tier popular, all academics, no sports, no theater, no newspaper, an organized girl who recorded homework assignments in apple green pen in high-quality notebooks, and that her deceptively black-sounding name, pronounced Kah-DEE-jah, was a product of Nancy's Sufi years.

My father picked me up after we collapsed the tables at five, and we stopped at Gaia on the way home, for dinner essentials, wine, and ice cream. After Nancy picked up Khadijah, they stopped at Gaia too. While I was trying to show my father how smart I was by making an argument about how many pears he should buy versus how many grapes for a fruit salad, I saw Nancy and Khadijah hovering by bananas.

An astute observer probably would have seen there was something weird between Nancy and my father right away. But I was only fifteen. I was stupid when it came to interpreting the behavior of the Dads. It's strange: When you're trying to impress a person, you can't see that person well. And Khadijah and I, we longed to impress the Dads.

I noticed nothing unusual in the Dads' body language or in their faces. My father reached out and laid his hand on the pears peeking from Nancy's wicker basket, looked her in the eye, and said, "They're fresh today."

The gesture did not strike me as remarkable. I found it mysterious, but my father was a sophisticated person. Everything he did was mysterious.

"Sometimes," he hastened to explain, looking at Khadijah and me, stroking his beard, "the fruit at Gaia is slightly rotten. That's the dark side of organic. Everything isn't spritzed with poisons to make it look neat."

I was, myself, as odorous as aging fruit. My parents were hippies. They had not spritzed me with poisons to make me look neat. My blond, shoulder-length hair was triangular, because while I knew there was a hair product called conditioner, I didn't know that conditioner was what people used to make hair lie down. I hadn't acquired the habit of shaving my ghost mustache or wiping the fingerprints off the lenses of my glasses. I wanted to be like my father, who taught political science, who knew how to talk about capitalism in such a way that people either agreed heartily with him or looked personally affronted and concerned for their safety. I wanted his air of rebellion and authority, his shaggy, dark hair and revolutionary beard. But I didn't know how to turn myself into him. I was wearing one of his blousy, long-sleeved shirts from the early seventies that I'd discovered in our attic, green with wooden buttons, and the consequence was that I smelled as if I were kept in an attic.

Khadijah, by contrast, had the grooming and bearing of a girl with a hands-on mother. She stood straight and still. The burgundy scrunchie that held her brown ponytail matched the trim of her Esprit socks. But for all the inorganic, detail-oriented parenting lavished on her, she was almost as awkward as I was, no surer of how to start a conversation. When the Dads asked for some time to chat by themselves, she tensed at the prospect of being left alone with me. We both doubted, I think, that we could find something to talk about.

"You hooligans won't cudgel each other, if we wander a little?" My father thumped a box of Finnish crackers against his palm. "You can keep yourselves entertained?"

"Five minutes?" Nancy asked us, edging toward my father. "Maybe ten? You see, my chickens, a mutual friend of ours is in the hospital." Nancy had managed to tame her hair, I noticed, the way I longed to tame mine—it formed a neat, soft bell behind her face, like Tom Petty's. She batted aside one strand with impatient, bony fingers.

"Go, Mom, it's Gaia," said Khadijah, picking at her cuticles. "We're not going to get thrown in a van and sold into sex slavery."

The Dads shot around a corner and vanished. At first there was only silence. But eventually, Khadijah turned to face me with a solution to our not knowing what to do with each other, using semipopular girl instincts I lacked: "Should we spy on them?"

I said yes. "I'm so bored," we both said. But I think the reason we spied on them, aside from the need to kill awkwardness with action, was that we suspected something. We were in tenth grade; it was strange they'd felt the need to ask us if we'd be okay while they spoke in private. We just didn't suspect that we suspected something.

Trolling the aisles, we sighted the grown-ups in Candy. Nancy was slouching in order to better inspect an item on a chest-high shelf. My father was scratching his beard as if he was looking at art.

"What we need is a hiding place," said Khadijah. She snapped her fingers. "The African-American History Month thing."

5

The African-American History Month display sat at the aisle's mouth, fifteen feet from where my father stood speaking with Nancy. It consisted of two tables pushed together and covered with kente cloths. February was over; like the produce, the display had been kept out too long. The tables were poorly aligned, and the cloths sagged in the gap between them. A traditional African-American cookbook and an Ethiopian cookbook remained upright, but a third volume had toppled over. There was something foreboding about this structure. Something told me that, if Khadijah and I hid inside it, like children in a fairy tale, we would have a hard time getting back out, would require a trail of crumbs. Before we could discuss the pros and cons, Khadijah crept. She slipped between the kente cloths and vanished beneath the tables, and I had no honorable choice but to follow.

We were on our hands and knees in the dark, cheek to cheek, almost touching. I smelled Khadijah's vanilla shampoo, and my own stale shirt. I made a promise to myself: *I will never emit this scent again.* We peered through the gap between the maroon kente cloth and the green kente cloth, drawing them aside like stage curtains. My father and Nancy faced each other in the candy aisle, oblivious. We watched the show.

My father did something astonishing. He took a candy bar and slipped it in the pocket of his quilted corduroy barn jacket. He was going to steal it. Nancy whacked him on the shoulder with the back of her hand, and he put the candy bar back on the shelf. Next he took a large, glistening gift bag of chocolate and shoved it halfway into the same pocket. Nancy whacked him harder; he put it back.

Then he took a paper bag of cookies down from the shelf as Nancy dealt little blows to his shoulder. He made a show of trying to stuff the bag into the pocket, until it ripped open at the corner, and bled cookies on the floor. Nancy crossed her arms. My father tried to gather the cookies and hold the broken bag at the same time.

"Linus," said Nancy, "you clumsy outlaw."

My father arranged the fallen cookies in a little pile on the shelf and slid the mutilated bag back into place. After he'd brushed the crumbs from his fingers, he reached down and tipped up Nancy's chin. I could only assume that he would restore the chin to its original position, as he had everything else he had taken in his hands. He would put Nancy back, just as he had put back the chocolate and the cookies. Nancy stared up at him and dropped her hands to her sides like a child. That was when he kissed her, full on the lips. She kissed back, hungry. It was probably because of the sweets all around them, but one of my first thoughts was that they were eating each other.

Khadijah and I said nothing. Our faces were almost touching in the dark. We jerked away from the gap in the kente cloths, and my head struck the underside of the metal table.

"Why would your dad do that?" she demanded, finally. She was breathing hard. "My mom is married to my dad."

"My dad is married too, to my mom," I pointed out. "Your mom kissed him back."

"I'm going to go out there and ask them what's going on."

"I predict that question will prove unacceptable to them." Even in this moment of father-related crisis, I tried to speak with my father's gravitas.

"My poor dad," Khadijah said. There were tears in her round brown eyes.

"Just because your mom kissed my dad doesn't mean, necessarily, that they're screwing." This was my idea, at the time, of being comforting. I sent a thought out to my father: *If you are screwing, I will cut off your dick and give it to Mom on a sword.* Then, immediately afterward: *I'm sure there is a good reason for this.* It's only a kiss, I thought. Nothing else.

"I hate your dad," Khadijah said.

"This isn't necessarily anything." In truth I felt it was beyond doubt that my father, who had held me on his shoulders on marches he'd organized for divestment from South Africa, had a more nuanced moral understanding of the situation than we did, and was doing the right thing, even if it looked wrong. "I repeat, all they're doing is kissing. Why should we make an assumption?"

The kente cloths lifted slightly when a brisk walker passed by. I knew from the acknowledgment of Kwanzaa at school that the cloths were used for sacred rites, by the Akan people.

"I wouldn't want to kiss that beard," Khadijah said, her face pressed against her legs.

"Your mom dresses Republican," I responded. "That's one of those lady blazers."

"Your dad dresses like a homeless person." She was actually sobbing now. "He's in public but he's wearing sweatpants."

"Don't cry," I said. "It's going to be okay." It was something I had learned to say from movies, but I meant it.

Khadijah was always pretty, but crying, she was so beautiful my face was going to burn off. I found the discovery that tears enhanced beauty nearly as disorienting as everything else that was going on. At any rate, I realized it might be acceptable to reach out and touch Khadijah, now that I had told her not to cry. I laid my hand on her head. When she didn't object I stroked her hair slowly. I liked the feeling of doing this too much to stop.

She jerked her head back. "I think that maybe I should tell my dad and you should tell your mom."

"That's out of line. It's kissing."

"True." She thought for a moment, calmer now. "Whatever they're doing, if we told on them, it would make it bigger."

With nothing to do, my hand, the one that had been stroking her hair, was shaking. I sat on it.

"We can't leap to conclusions," I said. "I don't want my father's reputation to suffer. My parents have an excellent marriage." *A kiss,* I thought, hearing a new voice in my head that I hoped was the voice of adulthood, *means nothing at all.*

We sat and watched through the gap in the cloth as the Dads walked away and turned a corner. We found them where they'd left us, in Produce.

"Did you survive our absence, darlings?" Nancy asked. She and my father were peering at us, I realized, to make sure we hadn't seen them. "Did anything bad happen?"

There was a soldierly expression on Khadijah's face, an expression you already saw on Hillary Clinton sometimes, in 1994. Her eyes were pink, but her face was dry. She shrugged. Smiles dawned on the faces of the grown-ups. They were concluding they hadn't been caught.

"Mom, please don't be paranoid," said Khadijah. "We're fine."

2.

Thank You for Saying That

When my father and I came home from Gaia Foods, he kissed my mother on the mouth and sliced the pears. I watched him to see if he looked guilty, but I couldn't see his face as he stood at the kitchen counter chopping. My mother slid a pizza from the oven, spun the greens, and asked about his day in her low, steady therapist's voice, the way she always did. If she knew anything, it didn't show on her face.

"Did the anthro guy try to get his new courses in the major?" She dialed down the volume on *All Things Considered* to give her full attention to his answer.

"He tried, and then he asked us to articulate our needs. He's a whore." My father plucked the grapes from their stems and dropped them on the pears. A grape fell to the linoleum, and he stepped on it without noticing.

"Does he make you angry?"

"Do I seem angry? Not particularly. He's a nice whore."

"So nothing's wrong?"

"I'd like to banish him to a comfortable island before he kidnaps more of my students and conscripts them, that's all."

My mother nodded as she fanned the steaming pizza with a mitt. She'd sensed something was off about him—did she know? Was there more to know than what I'd seen? She called my little sister, Rachel, who shuffled in with her library book about an Arab girl forced into marriage, her hair wild with static from reading in the corduroy beanbag. I didn't want it to be dinnertime. I was usually ravenous all hours of the day, but now I was too jumpy to eat. I drummed my fingers against the fridge, the radiator, the bowl of greens.

As we sat at the table, my mother, my father, Rachel, and I, I stood my mother next to Nancy.

Nancy, like my father, taught at Wattsbury College, a small liberal arts school whose campus sprawled a square half-mile between the Wattsbury town common and the lumberyard. From the common you could see its glassy library, from the yard its columned gymnasium. It had redbrick dormitories jacketed in ivy, but it was smaller than any school in the Ivy League, and sported a color scheme I'd never seen elsewhere: The stucco business school and the observatory were lemon, the administrative buildings sherbet orange. It was as if a more whimsical civilization had ruled Massachusetts in days beyond remembering, and fallen, stranding a colony in our midst. Whereas my mother taught psych at a college twenty minutes west, in the shadow of the Berkshire Hills. It was my high school duplicated five times over, beige blocks, concrete.

"You look glum, Joshua," my mother said. "What's wrong?" She flashed me clown faces: a cartoon frown, a madman smile, the gape-mouthed stare of a person struck with a pie.

Was it that my father thought Nancy was hotter? "Your outfit's strange, Mom," I said.

My mother's clown face disappeared. She looked at me probingly, twisted a lock of her long brown hair. She wore a denim button-down over a pleated denim dress. "It's not really an outfit," she noted.

"In this family," my father said, "we permit women freedom of dress." He reached into my mother's hair and rubbed her earlobe between his fingers. "Your mom looks nice."

"Notice he didn't actually defend what I was wearing," said my mother. But she was smiling. There was something about this, her smiling at my father, after he'd kissed Nancy, that was intolerable to me.

"We ran into Nancy Dunn and Khadijah at Gaia today," I said. My father glanced at me and resumed chewing.

"Khadijah Silverglate-Dunn," said Rachel. She had memorized the names of all the girls and most of the boys in my class, knew our social hierarchies better than those of her own grade. "She's pretty, unconventionally." My father waggled his eyebrows. "I bet Josh liked *her* outfit." Rachel made the sound like the crescendo of a police siren that to seventh graders signifies the detection of lust. I blushed and dropped the subject.

When we were done eating, my father cleared the table while my mother headed for the stairs. Every evening, immediately after dinner, she performed her rituals: a hundred prostrations, a seated meditation, the pouring of water into twin orange cups. "Why do you do that stuff?" I called to her. It was the first time I'd raised the subject in years; she never spoke of it. I looked to see if my question had provoked a telling reaction from my father, but he had his head in the cabinet over the sink, where we kept the wine. "Does it ever bother you that the rest of us don't believe in it?"

"No," she said, turning on a step, crossing her arms. "It would be worse for you to become a Buddhist because I'm a Buddhist than for you to not be a Buddhist." It was the same answer she'd given when I was in junior high. "I do it because if I didn't do it I'd be"—she lifted her hands and wailed like a ghost—"crazy."

I knew what she meant. Nine years ago, there had been a period of experimentation with violence. When Rachel was in toilet training, my mother had made her potty fly. The kick was more fluid, more natural, than the ones I'd seen her execute when she picked me up at soccer practice. It was a surge of strength from her heart to her leg. The potty leapt across the living room with its lid open and landed upright at my father's feet, splashed pee on his sandals. She apologized to me, because I'd seen it, and I pretended to be upset because I felt it was expected. But I liked my parents' fighting, even when it frightened me. When I saw it I could feel that they needed each other, sharpened each other. I felt some of what they felt, the fear of getting hit mixed with joy that somebody might give enough of a shit about what you were saying to hit you.

What I wanted right now was for them to scream at each other. "Dad," I said, as my mother disappeared upstairs, "don't you get sick of Mom doing insane groveling in the bedroom? Doesn't it annoy you?" My mother paused on the landing and listened. My father spun a bottle of wine against his palm. "No, Joshy," he said. My mother continued her ascent. "It's restorative. The equivalent is when I watch baseball, or read popular history."

The thump of my mother's prostrations sounded rhythmically from the master bedroom. My father uncorked his bottle of red and took it to his study. Rachel went to the phone to call one of her friends—it was Friday night. I stood and sat down, stood and sat down again.

"Why are you being weird?" Rachel asked.

"This is what I do when I'm thinking about a Russian paper."

I went out to the yard and lay on my back in cold grass and stale snow. The gray branch of a sapling shivered. What I'd seen in Gaia might have been a dream, to judge from the way the world marched on. Had my senses tricked me? Was I one of those adolescent males my mother talked about who had manic breaks, who lost their minds forever in episodes of grand hallucination?

I yanked grass out of the ground, my arms stretched to either side, and filled my hands with snow. I pounded the earth. "I saw it," I said.

I rose and walked inside, through the kitchen to the closet in the hall. My father's barn jacket hung from a chipped white hook. I stepped into the closet and closed the door. It was dark. I pulled on the quilted jacket, warm and capacious, like a bed. I ran my hand over the corduroy on the right side until I found what I was looking for, stuck in the grooved cloth, and tasted them for sweetness, to make sure they derived from cookies: crumbs.

The next day, when the phone rang, I was taking close-ups of the kitchen radiator for photography class. I was pouring small amounts of water on the radiator, trying to make it look like one of the ominous steaming props I'd seen in a Nine Inch Nails video.

My mother answered. I knew from her face that a person of significance was on the line; in moments of drama she assumed a meditative reticence. As a general rule, the events that caused my father to go bombastic caused my mother to go still.

"It's for you," she said.

I took the receiver and said hello.

"This is Khadijah," came a small, effortful voice. "How are you doing?"

So that was what my mother's portentous blankness had meant: *It's a girl.* This was unprecedented. My mother made a face I had never seen her make, a mix of triumph and amusement, and jogged upstairs.

"It's really good to hear from you," I said. I punched myself in the back of the neck, three times, as the words came out.

Khadijah asked how the Russian Club had fared on Language Day. I gave a nuanced account. She provided an overview of the French Club's fiscal woes. When she fell silent, I looked outside, trying to think of a way to say, Why did you call me?

"The snow appears to be melting." I slurred the words, to sound casual.

"What?" she said.

"Snow is melting," I enunciated, enraged at myself.

"True." She drew a breath. "Maybe you'd like to meet. Maybe you'd like to meet up, downtown, and discuss that thing that we saw happen."

"Yes." I took the cordless into the bathroom and shut the door. "Yes. I feel insane. I am becoming an insane person."

"That," she said, "is exactly what I hoped you would say."

I sloshed uphill, past the common, the Bank of Boston, the head shop, Al Bum's Records, the fire station, the townie bar. In half an hour I was kicking the muck off my Doc Martens, on my way to the back table at Classé Café, where she was already seated, homework spread before her.

"I have proof it's not just kissing," she said, after we'd ordered carrot cake and herbal tea, and she'd put away her binder. "They're in love." She said this in a perfunctory manner, looking out the window at an incense salesman on the sidewalk who moved as if he'd had three strokes. I asked her how she knew.

She reached into her backpack and unrolled a charcoal still life: a pineapple. "Grotesque, right? I draw like an ape."

"All the pineapples are like that," I said. It was true. Ms. Chumly had made everyone do a charcoal drawing of a pineapple, and no pineapple had been an unqualified success. The halls were blackened with grenade-like fruit. The effect was austere. It made you think about how every student who drew a pineapple was someday going to die.

"Even so, my pineapple particularly sucks," Khadijah said. "So last night, after we put away the groceries, I show it to my mom so she can see I got an A—she has a rule that she has to see all my grades on everything—and my dad walks in and laughs at my pineapple and then he leaves."

I sipped from my cup of Lemon Zinger. I looked directly at her with my eyebrows raised, something I'd seen male love interests do in romantic comedies.

"My mom looks at him like she's going to throw a knife at his back. She picks up my pineapple and goes, 'There's a friend of mine who's seen your work, who told me you'd be a great artist if you had the proper training.'" Khadijah paused for effect. "She was talking about your dad. Isn't it obvious, when you think about it?"

I stared at her, trying to figure out if she was right.

"Do you think I'm overdramatic? My parents say I'm overdramatic."

"No way."

"Oh my god, thank you for saying that." She threw her arms across the table and laid her head beside her plate, to signal a lifting of a great burden from her shoulders.

The bad news: It was possible that Nancy and my father were committing a crime against our families. The silver lining: There was a conspiratorial feeling growing between Khadijah and me. We were being drawn together in a game.

That night, I walked through the last snowstorm of the year to

CVS and bought a Gillette Sensor Excel razor. I studied the pictures of hair on bottles until I began to comprehend conditioner and pomade, how each might amplify the benefits of the other. I bought a Neutrogena antiacne scrub, a witch hazel toner. The next afternoon, I asked my mother to take me to the JCPenney in the all but gutted Mountain Farms Mall, known locally as the Dead Mall, where I picked three rugby shirts, and to Payless, at the nameless, less thoroughly eviscerated mall farther down Route 9, known as the Live Mall, where she bought me a pair of running shoes. As the fresh snow melted on the springy new track at the college, I went for the first run of my life.

When I came back, my lungs full of silver air, my skin red and warm, I looked at my father with wonder, reading in his chair. How could he look the way he always had, even though he had kissed a person not his wife? I wanted to scoop up a snowball and throw it at his head, if only to catch him off guard, dent his shell. I needed to know: Were he and Nancy Dunn screwing?

No matter what he had done, he had a talent for secrecy. He sat with a bowl of ice cream, his first glass of wine for the evening, his eighth or ninth military history of the year—he never tired of wars, though he hadn't been in one and professed hatred of them. He saw me staring. "If I keep eating like this, and you keep working out, I won't be able to murder you, once I start to feel threatened by you," he said. He smiled, warmly. "You'll just outrun me." He returned to *Scourge of Dunkirk*.

I climbed the two stories to my renovated room in the attic, showered with conditioner, cranked out four push-ups, and took my clothes off in front of the mirror. I felt I could see myself become less revolting as I became more and more interested in being devoted to someone. And now that there was something unrevolting to give, I wanted to give it. I stretched my arms out in either direction and lolled my head to one side, imagining myself on a cross.

I wanted to give what I had to Khadijah, of course. Part of it was the way she looked and the way she carried herself. But it was also that a small piece of me was close to a small piece of her in a way I had never been close to someone, because of what we had seen.

Satisfied my father was stationary for the evening, I slunk to his study, in my pajamas, and rifled through his desk. It was the nicest piece of furniture we had. We didn't have a lot of money; we'd been to Europe once, to Paris, and my father had cursed every time the bill came for lunch. The desk was a gift from an entertainment lawyer he knew from the Harvard Lampoon. Made of black wood, it worked like a drawbridge; you turned a little brass key and eased the work surface down on brass hinges, revealing six black drawers, each brass-knobbed and coated on the inside with mauve felt.

There was nothing of significance in any of them. A magnifying glass, an unopened letter from the Democratic Socialists of America, a roll of tape with no tape left on it, little mauve strands clinging to the translucent circle. In one drawer that was otherwise empty, there was an unused postcard. I flipped it over; the picture side was a photograph of Emily Dickinson's house, in nearby Amherst, taken from the street. I thought about this a little while, and slipped the postcard in my pocket.

On Monday, during study hall, I wrote Khadijah Silverglate-Dunn a note on the postcard. "My dad HATES the Emily Dickinson house. He says it's an ahistorical tourist fetish. Does your MOM like it?" The capitalization of *hates* might have been hyperbole, but he *had* called it a tourist fetish once, and though he hadn't really called it ahistorical, *ahistorical* was a word he applied with derision to many things other people liked, like *Schindler's List* and Mel Gibson's version of *Hamlet*. I slipped the postcard through the gills of Khadijah's locker.

It materialized in my own locker the next day. A message was written on it in a large, loopy script that must have been Khadijah's: "Found in my mom's office @ work." A twice-folded sheet of graph paper was attached with an apple green paper clip.

I'd deduced that Nancy Dunn was an art historian of some talent from the fact that my father deigned to kiss her, but I was still awed by what I saw. On the graph paper was a time line, untitled, drawn with a fine, black pen, ferociously graceful, the cursive you'd think would flow from one of Nancy's dark hands, with their skeletal fingers. It might as well have traced the development of pottery in Mesopotamia, or perspective in European painting. But its subject was a series of local outings.

At the beginning, on the left edge of the black horizontal line, there was a perfect miniature architectural drawing of a greenhouse. Beneath it, a caption: "Botanic Garden of Smith College." The next item, two inches to the right, was a little millstone, filled in with black and perfectly round. Beneath the millstone, in the same indestructible, filament-thin block letters of the caption previous: "Book Mill Used Books, Montague, MA." Next was the Sunderland Pet Shelter, illustrated with a litter of lithe kittens, who bared claws at each other in Darwinian conflict as they tumbled across the bottom of the page; then, a movie screen that emitted thick, black rays of light and displayed a title I didn't understand: *La règle du jeu*. It was at the terminus of the line that Nancy had drawn a picture of the Emily Dickinson Homestead, its balcony framed by identical trees.

Outside the social studies classroom, I caught Khadijah's shoulder. For a moment, our eyes met and we passed something back and forth, a mix of elation and panic. Then we remembered we were surrounded by our peers and assumed postures of ironic detachment and bemusement.

"For what it's worth," I said, "I'm still not persuaded. But thank you."

"Neither am I," said Khadijah. "So." We turned in opposite directions and walked away, backpacks bouncing, stupidly fast.

The time line became the keystone of our investigation. It turned otherwise innocuous objects into proof; it was what allowed us to settle the matter in our minds.

"Dad," Rachel called from the kitchen that evening, "are we getting a sweet-natured, mixed-breed sheepdog whose behavior shows very mild signs of puppyhood trauma, but who will blossom under the care of a firm but gentle master?"

"Who wouldn't blossom under one of those, honey?" My

father swiped the Sunderland Pet Shelter flyer from her hands. "Daddy was using that as a bookmark. Why did you take it from Daddy's book? You should try to keep a respectful distance from your daddy's things. My own daddy, good Irishman, would have gone somewhat apoplectic if you had appropriated a bookmark like that."

"I just wanted to see if the book had Holocaust pictures." She was at the peak of a one-sided carnage phase.

"Your old dad went to Sunderland for a bike ride and stopped to look at the dogs. You know how much I'd love to get you one, but we have to consider your mother's allergies."

At school the next morning, I ran to Khadijah as she hopped off the bus. "My dad took home a picture of a dog from the shelter," I said. "You were right. It's a definite thing."

What we'd been doing had come to resemble a game so closely that I was surprised when Khadijah's face collapsed and she covered her eyes with her hands. When she withdrew them, she was twitching. Her brow wrinkled. Her mouth puckered. Her cheeks assumed an alien roundness. She was trying to hold it together, like she had a broken wrist.

"Sorry," I said. "I didn't mean to say it like it was good news." But it was too late. She signaled forgiveness with a wave and spun into the crowd marching through the green double doors.

We were in almost the same location that afternoon, just after the final bell, when she appeared at my side. Her eyes were red, her face was calm.

"Come with me," she said. "We're going to the Thing in the Woods."

The Thing in the Woods was a rusted wheel that must have once belonged to a landscaping vehicle. It sat in a fairy ring of mashed cigarettes and glittering bottle glass. Residual snow lay in patches on the brown grass, like mold on bread.

Khadijah drew two sheets of paper, the same graph paper her mother had used for the illustrated time line, from a pocket of her three-ring binder. I considered for a second whether the chart could have been a forgery of Khadijah's, but I knew that her draftsmanship was not as delicate as Nancy's; the person who could make those inky kittens dart and swipe would not have drawn as geologic a pineapple as Khadijah's. Khadijah's handwriting, too, was different from the handwriting on her mother's time line, larger, loopier, more arabesque.

She'd written: "I, Khadijah Silverglate-Dunn, will never cheat on anyone. If I'm in a relationship and I want to be with someone else, I will either wait and see if it changes or I will break up with the person I'm with before I do anything. I will not be an asshole and just cheat on them. If I think about doing it, I will remember this moment, now." The other sheet of graph paper had the same vow written on it, only with my name at the beginning instead of hers.

She took the sheet with her name, knelt in the grass, and held it to the side of the rusted wheel. She took a blue ballpoint pen from her pocket and signed. Watching me closely, she offered the pen.

I knelt beside her in the grass. I pressed the paper against the rough surface of the wheel and put down my name in stilted, overly slanted cursive, the first time I signed my name rather than wrote it. Facing each other on our knees, we shook hands.

"Here's my question," I said, dusting off my shins as we walked away. "If they're into each other, if they make each other so happy, why don't they get divorced and be with each other? People don't hold it against you if you get divorced in Wattsbury."

She folded the sheets of graph paper, creased the fold, and handed me mine. "Because we exist."

3.

They Just Try
to Make Things Prettier

In the days after the vow at the Thing in the Woods, I thought of the darkness under the table at Gaia, with the light that snuck under the kente cloths. I wanted more of Khadijah. I especially wanted more of Khadijah in hiding places. But I thought it might be better to wait to initiate further contact until after I had made myself less ugly. I ran every night, and lifted my father's boxed, multivolume Churchill biography over my head, watching my insect forearms in the mirror, waiting for them to change.

I monitored Khadijah in class. We had other star students, but Khadijah was a person conditioned exclusively for school, for this activity and no other. When she raised herself from her desk and took the floor to deliver a presentation, she came into an intellectual inheritance. She became a person who was not who she usually was. She became, I now understood, her mother.

She must have given her speech about ancient writing to Nancy several times, rehearsed it to excess, before she gave it to our class.

"Before the development of the alphabet," she almost shouted, in Nancy's clear, high voice, "a particular logogram had to depict a particular object, a particular object always signified the same concept. Alphabets enabled the meaning of characters to shift, depending on context." She seemed to have memorized every sentence, every syntactical gambit.

It was unusual for a tenth grader at Wattsbury Regional to speak like this. Most academic parents nodded to the idea of meritocracy by concealing their handiwork, helping their children translate the ideas they'd given them for their schoolwork into plebeian English. The baldness of the parental involvement here was notable. But the truly remarkable thing was Khadijah's composure. It was as if Nancy had not only dictated the content of her presentation but inhabited her the moment she rose to speak.

". . . and therefore the creation of new words, an entirely new means of communication. Characters that had once been static in their meaning gained the ability to shift, taking on different meanings depending on their location among other characters."

The visual aids she'd constructed were larger, I suspected, than cuneiform tablets. With the madness of an artist, she had created an exhibit that reached beyond the demands of the assignment. She'd decided that Egyptian hieroglyphs and Greek lettering each deserved a monolith made from four conjoined sheets of extra-large black poster board. When she was done speaking like her mother, she shouldered the massive charts and returned to her seat, her arms full, her head obscured. She leaned the time lines against her desk, and I studied them from across the room. At each notch, there was an empire's outline, or a glyph, or the sketched face of an ancient despot. They were dark and chunky with effort. They were imitations of Nancy's art, drawn by a hand that couldn't move like Nancy's hand.

The following Thursday, we had the day off from school to participate in the ABC Walk, which benefited the ABC House. *ABC* stood for A Better Chance. The ABC House was an old Victorian in downtown Wattsbury where poor black and Latino boys from New York City came and lived for four years, so that they could attend Wattsbury Regional. The method of collecting donations was to go door to door pledging to walk ten kilometers through the woods if your neighbor would give you ten dollars. Sophomores wound through the Robert Frost Conservation Center as a cold rain sprinkled the birches. Khadijah walked with two other girls fifty feet ahead of me and my friends—I could see her scrunchie, apricot today, through white branches.

I was walking with my father's backpack held in front of me, bouncing against my knees. I'd left my own backpack at school the day before, so my father had told me to take his from the floor of the bedroom closet. Halfway through the hike, the social studies teacher placed in charge of us cupped his hands around his mouth and announced lunch. Rooting for a bottle of water, my hand closed around a minibar bottle of Sutter Home wine.

Burbling, abundant love for my father flooded my heart. I unscrewed the top as we sat on stones.

"You can have some of the wine my father gave me," I whispered to my two friends, the straight-backed, dark-haired son of a Spanish literature professor in immaculate corduroys and the slightly obese son of an acupuncturist. "Just be cool about it, or people will freak out and tell on us."

They each took a substantial gulp. We had a conversation about whose father was chiller about wine. After I'd wolfed my meatball marinara from Subway, I searched all the pockets and compartments in the backpack clinging to the hope my father had included a Subway cookie. In a pocket within a pocket, my hand closed around an unfamiliar form.

I drew out what looked like a hard candy imported from Europe. It was a round object in thick golden wrapping, with tiny writings on the side and the gleam of an elite continental sweet. I was even prouder of my father now; here was further evidence of his good taste.

I interrupted my friends and asked if they knew what kind of candy it was.

"I can't open it," I said, which was true. "Maybe you guys can figure out how to get this fancy foreign wrapping off. It's most likely from France or Italy, or Prague, where they just try to make things prettier."

The Spanish literature professor's son held it first. Having lived in Barcelona, he liked to tell us of the superiority of things European, so when he bit away the golden wrapper, and his eyes opened wide, and his jaw snapped open and shut, I believed I had just revealed an object of great rarity and preciousness. He looked at my other friend, the acupuncturist's son. "Is this what I think it is?" he asked him.

"No," said the acupuncturist's son. "It's too good."

Dread coiled through my happiness. They scrutinized the fine print on the wrapper.

"It is," said the acupuncturist's son. "It really is." He raised it skyward in the palm of his hand, to honor it.

"Want to eat it, Josh?" There was a gentleness in their voices, an ambivalence. A note of *I must immediately give you shit or it will be worse.*

I shoved between them and snatched it. Cradling it in one hand, I inspected it with the other, trying to understand what I saw. This was not a dessert, as I had believed, but nor was it a condom—this much I knew. At any rate, it was not like any condom I had ever seen. It was a soft plastic ring, off-white, with a small spherical appendage. Inside the appendage there was a tiny, dark egg. Beside the egg there was a soft plastic switch, set to Off.

The acupuncturist's son finally turned to me and placed a paternal hand on my shoulder. "It's called a cock ring."

With two fingers, I traced its contours, full of wonder. A strange thing happened: It leapt from my fingers, emitting a loud, steady, midrange buzz. I had hit the switch.

The former Barcelonan plucked it from the mud at our feet. He held it, still vibrating, behind his back with one hand, as he held me at bay with the other. He and the acupuncturist's son passed it back and forth, under the wet pines, scholars.

As a circle of my classmates mustered around us, the acupuncturist's son bent toward me and folded his arms. Our social studies teacher was studying the bark of a tree. Khadijah left her friends and came over to watch, from a respectful distance.

"Your parents are married, aren't they?" the acupuncturist's son asked me.

"Yes," I said.

"Then your dad"—he walked the student through the obvious lesson, for the benefit of the class—"has been trying to spice things up with your mom, or he's got some hot ass on the side."

"Clearly the former." I strove to control my voice, to deflate significance.

The acupuncturist's son, angry I had shoved him, held the toy in one hand, in the other its golden packaging. He climbed onto a boulder. The audience clucked at the immaturity of what was going on, but continued to watch. In order to free his hand and insert his fingers through the ring itself, he tossed the wrapper to the wind. The rain had stopped, and the clouds had begun to float away. As the buzz filled the air, the little square of foil drifted on the breeze, caught sunlight, and became a tiny golden bird.

4.

The Harp Player

"I want to extend an invitation," my father said to me that night. He paused the videotape, *Ma nuit chez Maud*. My mother and sister had pronounced themselves tired ten minutes ago and left us, the Paquette men, to consume two pints of Häagen-Dazs ourselves. "Nancy Dunn and I got to talking at the office, and we thought it might be a nice excursion for you and Khadijah if we all went to see the Pre-Raphaelite exhibition in Boston, at the MFA." He was wearing gym clothes, because he had just worked out on the rowing machine. In a white, sweat-stained T-shirt and short, purple Wattsbury College track shorts, he was regally unwashed, his already formidable air of authority strengthened by his immodesty. The sweat in his straight, dark hair made it stand in unpredictable spikes. "Do you have any plans for Sunday? Your mother is going to be taking Rachel to some Yiddish Book Center thing. I thought this might appeal to you more." At leisure, he waited for my reply.

"Sounds cool," I said, after a moment of frenzied reflection.

"Some hesitation, Son?" He swirled the melted ice cream in his bowl. "Do you harbor some ambivalence toward the Pre-Raphaelites?"

You owned a cock ring, I thought. *My friends buried it beneath a copse of pines.* But I raised my eyebrows and made a civilized response. "I love the ancient Italians."

He winced. "Oof, Wattsbury High School. Oof, PC education. Teach the nuances of H. Rap Brown, but the Pre-Raphaelites . . .

Sorry. I don't mean to be snotty with you, your mother's been on me about that." He put down his bowl and massaged his temples. "Would you like some wine?"

I was barely able to contain my joy. "Don't get up, Dad," I said. "I'll go to the kitchen and get a glass."

When I returned he was lost in thought. He barely looked at my glass as he filled it, letting a little of the Argentine Malbec cry down the side. "Did you know Nancy was a far more radical youth than your mother and me?" He grinned. "Nancy was a hippie to be reckoned with. When the rest of us were practicing Buddhism, she was in this gaggle of non-Islamic Sufis, Emersonian Sufis. They sang and danced by Walden Pond until a different bunch of Thoreau-Whitman grad student types drove them off the territory through guilt-tripping. They argued they were destroying the silence, whereas the Sufis believed they were creating a microcosm of a peaceful society. Nancy was the appointed artist, very talented. She would draw these geometric patterns that corresponded to the peace dances. But once Khadijah was in the mix she got bit by the neocon bug. It was the times, you know; she rediscovered the middle-class work ethic. It's like a little death that must come for us all someday." He reached out and pushed Play on the VCR. We sank back into the black-and-white netherworld that was France.

Having a father who had a crush on the mother of an interesting girl was actually kind of awesome. In some sense, it didn't matter what the Dads were up to, what mechanisms they were using on each other. They were taking Khadijah and me to Boston, to stroll through a museum at their heels. I knew that using us as cover would work. My parents had mentioned the Silverglate-Dunns in passing any number of times, so there must have been some friendliness between our families; my mother would see nothing objectionable in a trip to Boston with kids in tow. The Dads would stand with heads cocked dreamily to one side and whisper intelligent things to each other about non-Italian paintings, never suspecting that Khadijah and I would whisper intelligent things to each other about them.

The next morning, after homeroom, I made for the hall where Khadijah took French. She whirled around the corner a moment after I arrived and reflected my look of amazement back at me. "Sorry about your dad's . . ." She formed a ring with her hands. She made the ring vibrate.

"We're all going to a museum. Like a family."

"Come with me." We twisted through the crowd, never touching, never speaking, never drawing so close that anyone would think us in league. She took a sharp right in the midst of the hard science hallway, and we were in a short passage with a blue door at its end. She banged through it, and I followed her into a closet of retired Apples. Their cords dangled like viscera from the shelves. She had a nose for corners, recesses, empty spaces.

"Are they insane?" I asked her. I could see in her face that she felt what I felt: the thrill at discovering the Dads' misbehavior, the fear of losing them.

"The brazenness of it, Josh."

I considered that *brazen* was probably an SAT word.

"It looks so much more wholesome if we come," she continued. "We're like a disguise. It's obvious. The Pre-Raphaelites are baby unicorns and shit. And of course they picked the big Yiddish Book Center Open House day, because it puts my dad and your mom out of commission."

"Why would you go see baby unicorns with somebody you have a thing with?" I asked.

"You know the painting on the cover of *Reviving Ophelia*? That's the Pre-Raphaelites."

I thought of the mad, cream-skinned girl lying prone in the river. "Superbrazen," I agreed.

She made her hands into triumphant claws and shook them at her sides. "So fucking brazen."

"I feel bad for my mom," I said. "And I hate your mom."

Something warm passed between us. "I hate your dad," she breathed, almost whispering. "As always." She reinstated her backpack on her shoulders, and we parted.

• • •

It might have been the way Khadijah and I had begun to speak to each other, but the Pre-Raphaelites seemed to me to make pretty art. After we'd wandered fifteen minutes in beauty-nauseous silence, my father brought our party to a halt by a little Rossetti, in which a woman in her mid-twenties plucked a harp. She stared away from the instrument at an apparently sublime object out of frame, her eyes narrow, her mouth open. She was in love or lust or religious rapture, or all three. Down the hall, people swirled like water moccasins around the drowning girl in a brown and green dress, so we had a little row of non-Ophelian Rossettis to ourselves. I counted four long-haired harp-girls.

"Feminist Art Historian," said my father to Nancy, "what say you? Is he remotely palatable? Or is his thing with pretty young muses just too creepo?"

My father wore an art outfit: a loose black jacket, a black T-shirt, gray jeans, his white Converse sneakers. Nancy cocked her head to one side, as I'd imagined she would. All I knew about the term *neocon* was that it denoted a new kind of conservative, but it nonetheless seemed clear to me that Nancy was neocon in matters of dress, if not in matters of state. She wore a loose white sweater over a purple collared shirt that looked like it could only be dry-cleaned, a string of pearls barely visible against the long neck Khadijah had inherited. Her beige, boot-cut slacks were creased. She was old-fashioned with no frills, old-fashioned gone efficient, like the word *con,* which was *conservative* with the extraneous cloth sliced away.

"When people think of Rossetti," she replied, "they think of the scenes from Shakespeare, from *Le Morte d'Arthur,* tragic angels, enchantresses. And he must answer for any number of those. He painted Elizabeth Siddal as an idealized sprite, not quite human. But take this one." She directed us to *The Harp Player, A Study of Annie Miller.* "It's demystified, for me, it's better. She's just a woman playing an instrument. She's got the epic hair, and the instrument is a harp—which is angelic. But her *face* isn't angelic. She's not consumed with lust, she's not abject, like the star of the show over there." Nancy gestured with her head toward the

Ophelia crowd. "I like this one because he hasn't plunked her in medieval times, or in a river. He lets her be awkward, stare at the floor. She's not part of a story he needs to tell."

When we pulled away in the Subaru, Nancy sighed so forlornly I could see her straighten in her seat as she took in breath and slump as she let air leave her body. My father asked her what was wrong.

"I just don't know how my life came to be located so far from these beautiful things."

My father's arm flashed out to stroke her hair. She leaned into him, willing to be consoled. And then they remembered that Khadijah and I were sitting behind them. My father yanked back his hand as if Nancy had bitten it. Nancy jolted in her seat as if she'd been punched.

In the back, I tried to hold Khadijah's gaze, to exchange a meaningful look, but she was gazing out the window, at the rain. The Dads glowered at the road. No one spoke as we waited at the tollbooth emblazoned with the Mass Pike insignia, a sapphire pilgrim hat tipped at a jaunty angle.

Khadijah nudged my sneaker with her clog. Using her index finger, she wrote in the moisture that had accumulated on the interior surface of the window, in dripping capitals: THEY HATE US.

5.

Pig Question

The next day was Monday. After a meeting of the Russian Club Vecherinka Banquet Celebration Planning Committee, I walked outside and passed Khadijah, who was leaning against a tree with a black paperback in her lap. I slumped against the bark, beside her. The title of her book was written in white, stencil-style capitals: *The Anarchist's Handbook*.

"Do you want to blow people up and be lesbian, like Emma Goldman?" I asked. Last year, I had read half of *Ragtime,* by E. L. Doctorow. I knew what anarchists did.

"Pig question," she said.

I must have looked confused. She referred me to page four. "A pig question," she read aloud, "is a question that might be asked with ill intent by someone from outside the movement who pretends to be interested in joining the movement."

"Are you attempting to overthrow the government?"

"Pig question."

"Are you willing to kill for your cause?"

"Pig question."

"Are you a lesbian?"

"Almost a pig question. No."

I noticed something. "Is that nail polish?"

The question was rhetorical. Khadijah Silverglate-Dunn, in defiance of the subcultural rules observed by girls who carried apple green pens and got A's, had painted her fingernails black. She wore a pair of the imposter Doc Martens sold at Payless, jeans, and a thick gray sweatshirt. Her hair was down and uncombed. Khadijah, I now understood, was wearing an anarchist outfit.

"Yeah," she said. "It's nail polish." She reached into her purse and withdrew a large stone, flat and smooth. An *A* inside a circle was drawn on it in Sharpie, the horizontal shaft stretching beyond the ring. It was a symbol I'd seen on the prows of skateboards, and on a Dumpster behind the Wattsbury College Cinema Theater.

"I'm going to throw it through the window of that Bank of Boston on South Pleasant," she said, "once it gets dark tomorrow night."

I couldn't tell whether this was something that Khadijah would actually do. Khadijah and I were kids who didn't throw things. But given that my father and her mother were not who they seemed, maybe Khadijah and I were not who we seemed either. Maybe if I threw something, too, I would become more my true self than I was now. There was also this: If Khadijah and I threw rocks at a bank and were caught, the Dads would be distressed, and it would be a punishment for what they had done. Or if they weren't distressed, then they would be revealed to be bad parents, unparent-like parents. There were not many ways to find out who one's parents really were, but this was one of them. And if we could find out who the Dads were, throwing that rock, we could know better who we, their children, were. Besides, maybe throwing rocks at banks was a virtuous act, if Khadijah, a top student, thought it was.

"It would be safer if I came with you," I said. "You can throw it, and I can be lookout."

She weighed the stone in her hand. "Good plan," she said.

Six-thirty the next evening, we met again at Classé Café. We shared a single cup of coffee and a single monster cookie (M&M's, chocolate chips, larger than the plate on which it was served). I wanted our fingers to touch as we ate it down to the center, but Khadijah left me the core. She withdrew the stone, with its black insignia, from her bag, placed it on the table, and made a "let's go" gesture with her eyes, a dart to the side.

We were both in loose clothing, for freedom of movement. She wore a Smith College sweatshirt and I wore a sweatshirt with a flaming yin-and-yang sign. The important difference was in our shorts: Hers were khakis, from JCPenney or L.L.Bean. Mine were from the Army-Navy store by the Dead Mall, and had elaborate pockets.

"I bet your mom went to Smith, right?" I said.

"Yeah, why?"

I shook my head to show it was nothing. "Are you sure you want to do this?"

"Absolutely." She crossed her arms over the sweatshirt as we left the café and walked down the sidewalk toward the bank.

"Let me carry the stone," I whispered. "I have deeper pockets. It'll be hidden, but with easy access." I held open the flap of a cargo pocket, revealing an abyss.

She looked doubtful but finally shrugged. "I guess that's useful." She took the flap of my pocket between her fingers and dropped in the stone.

We crossed downtown to the common and sat on the cold grass waiting for the sky to go black. Across the street, a spray of birds dispersed over Bank of Boston. The bank was an old brick house, unobtrusively converted. High, arched windows offered honey-light views of an empty marble room, a stable of fuzzy-walled cubicles. It was pristine, untouched by the passage of goods, clean because it was touched only by money. It was, I had to admit, asking to be smashed.

"Fuck it," said Khadijah. She stood.

It was a shade too early in the dusk to be throwing things. A shade too bright. Black birds stood sharp against the graying blue.

"Give me the stone," she said. She stared at me as if the hesitation on my face was a symptom of an interesting pathology.

I could feel the onrush of danger as a physical ache now. But I knew I couldn't hold off Khadijah forever. I took the stone as slowly as I could from my cargo pocket and placed it on her palm. Her fingers closed.

"I'm sure for an anarchist from New York," she said, "this shit would just be nothing." She crossed the street, walking toward the bank.

I shadowed her. I swiveled my head to the left and right, and didn't see anyone coming from either direction. She stood with her nose close to the glass, like a child before an animatronic window display at Yankee Candle. She cranked back her arm.

At this moment I came to terms with what was happening, and grunted for her to stop. But it was too late. The stone jumped from her hand and hit the window hard at close range. It fell to the sidewalk and rolled. The glass was uncracked.

A suggestion of motion in the bushes solidified into shapes: more birds, rising from within the leaves. Khadijah bent to chase the stone, but it bumped the toe of my boot and I picked it up.

"You can't throw it again," I said. "We have to leave." I ran, the stone clutched in my right hand, and after a moment's hesitation she followed.

"An alarm thing must be going off somewhere," I panted as the dusk blurred around us. "Let's go to the Thing in the Woods."

As the dark became absolute, we tore through the common, the cobblestones of Market Square, the Wattsbury College football field, the soccer field of Wattsbury High, to the clearing where the groundskeeper's wheel stood in its ring of mashed filters. We sat for a moment side by side on the wheel. Ten seconds passed. In unison, strangers to exercise, we slid off, exhausted, and lay flat on the grass.

Then, the revolution: She climbed on top of me.

"Thank you for not letting me throw it again," she said.

Her breath was dark, warm on my neck. I could smell the murk of her sweat through her sweatshirt and on her wrist, which she pressed against my forehead. She took a fist of my terrible, diseased-looking hair in her hand. She hooked her other hand into mine and spoke toward the grass.

"I like being constantly checked out by you," she said.

"I know I'm gross," I said quickly. "I understand if you don't want to hook up with me."

"The only gross thing about you is you think you're gross."

I laughed at this kindness.

"I'm being serious," she said. "Look at my face."

"How do you feel about me?" I asked, looking at the sky. I didn't stop to wonder whether she would be honest; the question was a prayer for a clue to my life. "Do you like me?"

She pressed a finger to her mouth and stared at me hard. "With you and me, there are no pig questions." She reestablished her grip on my hand and lowered her face toward mine. Our eyes were as close as they'd been under the table in Gaia. She was right, I was not the person I had thought I was. I knew, suddenly, that I was someone else, with more elements. It surprised me that the touching of hands could do that: reveal to you a new piece of who you were. I dropped the stone in the grass and placed my free palm on her cheek.

That's when the cops showed. Flashlight beams crossed over the rusted wheel like spotlights over Hollywood, and patrolmen rode bicycles out of the darkness. Khadijah rolled off me and sat upright. She waved to the two men.

"Here," she said, and held out the stone.

They did not go hard on us. They walked us and their bicycles down the street, to the new station on North Pleasant, a postmodern, turreted castle of brick and limestone. The Bank of Boston branch president, Brian Stapleton, was waiting in the lobby. He wiped his wire-rim spectacles against the belt of his trench coat. They sat us before him in a second-story conference room and told us they were letting him make the call regarding consequences.

Once we were settled, Brian Stapleton squinted at us. "*That* Khadijah? Khadijah Silverglate-Dunn?" he asked the officers. They nodded. "My son Scotty still talks about the platypus this girl made for Darwin Day, in sixth grade at the Common School."

He turned to Khadijah, abashed. "Did you really throw a stone at the window?" He cleaned his glasses again, as if to dispel an optical illusion. "Or was it this gentleman?" He pointed in my direction. There might have been comfort, for Brian, in my troubled hair, my flaming yin-yang.

"It was me," said Khadijah. "He was just along for the ride."

"I carried the stone," I said. I intended to tell the story, but Brian Stapleton only wanted to know my parents' names. He asked Khadijah for her phone number. After he dialed on the conference room phone, he handed her the receiver.

Khadijah told Nancy what we'd done, but anarchism was never mentioned. "*Why,* Mom?" she said, toward the end of the conversation. "You're asking why I did it? That's a socioeconomic question, Mom. Yes, it is the reason I don't eat meat anymore."

Fifteen minutes later, Nancy walked in. She pulled a gray shawl tight around her shoulders and placed one hand on the table, to steady herself as she confronted her daughter. Khadijah's father was nowhere in sight. This did not surprise me; Nancy had always struck me as a first-into-the-fray type. What surprised me was the entrance of my own father, close behind.

"Who told you about this?" I demanded.

"You little aristocrat." He put his hands on his head. Nancy glared at Khadijah as he spoke, to extend the purview of his judgment to her daughter. "Do you realize," he continued, "how bourgeois it is to force a hardworking man"—he pointed to Brian Stapleton, who did not react to this appellation one way or the other—"to come here at dinnertime to find out who threw a rock at his place of business? To make somebody else pay for an expensive pane of glass?"

Nancy paid rapt attention to this speech. "It was my child who was the ringleader, Linus. The ringleader of this petty rebellion."

Khadijah had remained quiet as my father spoke. Now she pushed back her chair and stood. I could see the spirit of a grownup possess her; the look in her eyes was identical to Nancy's, *originally* Nancy's, presumably. This did not blunt its capacity as a weapon.

"Petty rebellion?" snapped Khadijah. *"Petty rebellion?"*

Nancy was calm. "Sit down," she said.

Khadijah ignored her. Looking at Nancy's face—there was real fear just dawning in it now—I thought of Victor Frankenstein, Henry Higgins, blitzed by their own creations.

"Speaking of petty rebellion," said Khadijah, her eyes oscillating between Nancy and my father. She spoke very slowly now. "*Gee,* I *wonder* why you guys just *happened* to be *hanging out* when I called." She looked at me pointedly before she turned back to the parents. "Speaking of *petty rebellion,*" she continued, "you two are obviously sleeping together."

"That's ridiculous," said Nancy. "We work at the same college. They called me out of the meeting and told me you were in the custody of the police."

"I found your time line," said Khadijah.

"I found your ring," I blurted at my father. When I said *ring* I made quotation marks with my hands.

Things went silent for what seemed like quite a long time. Brian tucked his head into his overcoat like a turtle, slapped his business card on the table, and left the room. "I'm fine," he called behind him, as he turned in to the hallway, whisking his scarf from his chair. "You'll get a call from our insurers. Thanks, everyone." The bicycle patrolmen looked at each other and followed him out.

Nancy and my father stood with their hands on their chins. *It's really happening,* I thought. Dad's intent was to use a cock ring on Khadijah's mom.

My father dropped into a chair. He let his head thump on the table, once, twice, three times. It was not the same as if Khadijah had presented his dick to my mother on a sword, but it was close.

With my father publicly humiliated, my world—consisting at the moment of the conference room—was new. His beard was not a revolutionary beard anymore. The revolution now belonged to somebody else. Khadijah sat, her eyes demure, picking at her cuticles as she had the day in Gaia Foods. She had cracked things.

So this was love. Here was our rite of spring.

6.

Almost More Like Poems

Rachel raised her hand as soon as we were assembled at the kitchen table for the family meeting. "Divorce," she said. My parents stared at her and I knew she was right.

"An experiment," my mother said.

"That's just about right, trying something new," my father corrected. "An experiment in living separately." He cleared his throat, switching to lighter news. "I'm moving to New York. On some weekends I'll come here and stay at an apartment I'm going to rent, and on some you'll come down on the train."

I thought, *Good.* Since Gaia Foods, it had been difficult to watch my parents speak to each other, so I was glad they'd live far apart. The euphoria that had accompanied the revelation that my father slept with Nancy was gone. What remained was the knowledge that for a long time—I didn't know how long—my parents' marriage had been a carcass walking upright. Now they were talking and listening with no expression on their faces, upright carcasses themselves.

He still doesn't know we saw him kissing Nancy in Gaia, I thought. *He thinks he got away with it for a long time.* I looked at Rachel and my mother. Did they know what I had seen in the police station last night? Did anyone know that Khadijah and I had been on the verge of a kiss?

"Josh, your father and I have talked about what happened at the station," my mother said, her voice drained of character.

"We'd appreciate it if you'd not discuss it right now." With her eyes, she indicated Rachel.

Rachel came to understand that she was being left out of something secret and horrible. She began to cry. "What is she talking about?" she asked my father. "Why do you want to move to New York?"

"I'm still going to see you every weekend, sweetie. But I've never been fully at home in the ecosystem of a political science professor. I wish I could give you a better explanation, because I love you so much, but please understand, I'm a different person than the one I've been acting like I am." His voice went high. "I'm going to try to make some connections down there, my love. I want to find some people I can talk to about the kinds of essays I want to write, essays that are almost more like poems than essays. I'll try to publish in some respected quarterlies, for starters. Since I'll be consulting for nonprofits on a freelance basis, it'll be easier to keep that work coming if I'm able to be in the belly of the beast, so to speak. So it's practical, sweetie, try to see that. Your daddy wants to make you proud."

He sounded near tears himself. I didn't understand what he was saying. I looked at the brown rug. My mother stared straight ahead, doll-faced. I felt sad for her, but I could also feel an unmistakable surge of revulsion, now that she'd been discarded by my father, and this surge in my stomach made me hate myself. The intensity of this new sensation—self-loathing—surprised me. I had seen my mother kick a potty at him across the room, heard her scream at him to leave the house. When these things happened, I knew they were technically bad. But I'd respected her. I'd been moved by her. Now that she was being Adult in the face of outrage, I wanted to run. It was like ten cups of English Breakfast, panic and inspiration all at once, a need to leap out of the skin.

"Can we go now?" I asked.

After my parents retreated to the study to compose an agreement on the sharing of resources, my little sister and I stayed on the sun-drenched first floor of the white Cape Cod. It was three-thirty on a Wednesday. We had too many empty hours in which to consider what had just happened, so we invented a game a fifteen-year-old and a twelve-year-old should not have been playing, called Googy. I was a retarded baby—Googy was my name—and Rachel was my mother. I ran to open the front door and escape into the woods by ramming my head against the door repeatedly, and she came up behind me and dragged me from the vestibule, shouting, "Googy, you'll only make your brain even worse by doing that." I gurgled and moaned, and rolled around on the floor, gripping my head in my hands—retardation and epilepsy were not yet rigorously differentiated for Rachel and me. I tried to learn to crawl and collapsed repeatedly, finally curling into a fetal position and pretending to puke on the floor.

I lay for a while in a sunbeam, like a dog. I ignored my sister's demands that I rise, until she went upstairs to her room and I looked out the window and saw ashes falling from the sky. My parents were in the study, writing their agreement, and would not have been able to see. I thought of telling them about the evidence of fire, but in the end I walked up to Rachel's room to see for myself what she was doing.

I knocked on the door. "It's me," I said. "Mom and Dad are in the study." There was no answer, so I went in.

She knelt by her open window with a sheaf of papers held together by a paper clip, with the economy-size box of kitchen matches beside her on the sill. She used a match to light a piece of paper and threw the match in a plastic cup of water, in which four other matches lay floating. She dropped the flaming page out the window.

"They're letters to my future husband," she explained. "I wrote them when I was eight."

I watched her do this for another thirty seconds. Unable to say anything about it, I went to my room, and the object that didn't feel tainted by my ownership of it was the acoustic guitar an aunt had lent me six months ago. I'd only learned six chords. But now I put it down only when my fingertips were in too much pain to touch anything, at which point I plugged in my headphones and worked methodically backward and forward through my booklet of CDs, listening in my desk chair, until I could handle strings again.

By the following evening, each of the fingertips on my left hand had grown a cloud: calluses. From that point forward, I put down the guitar only to eat dinner and to walk to a licentious Cumberland Farms, where I bought and experimented with cigarettes. Nobody asked me where I was going.

Around ten o'clock that night, my father knocked on the door. "I've come to have a little talk with you," he said. "Nancy, Khadijah, your behavior, my behavior."

He sat in my rolling desk chair. I put down my aunt's guitar and sat on the floor with my legs tucked close to my chest, tapping an imaginary drumbeat against my knees in order to be musicianly. I waited. He opened his mouth several times and closed it again, like a goldfish.

"Do you know any songs?" he asked. "I can hear you a little from downstairs. It sounds like you're playing a lot."

I looked at the guitar. The truth was I was having a hard time with chords. I was also having a hard time with playing anything and singing at the same time. The one song I could pull off, sort of—it was actually easier than "Psycho Killer"—was "Heartbreak Hotel." You could play "Heartbreak Hotel" as a bass line on the low E. And you barely had to sing and play at the same time. The singing was the call, the bass line the response.

"Sure," I said. I picked up the guitar. I couldn't sing very well. But the vocal was basically talking: "Since my baby left me (guitar: BUM BUM) / I found a new place to dwell (BUM BUM)."

My father spread his legs and clasped his hands in the space between them as I played and sang. He reached out and put his left hand on my right hand, which was still holding a tortoiseshell pick, hovering by the strings. Did he hear Nancy's voice when he heard music, like I heard Khadijah's?

"Not bad, Son," he said. He held my hand, for three seconds, or four, and then he stood and left.

7.

You've Got to Stay
Inside the Napkin

At seven the next morning, my father was perched on the edge of my bed, shaking me awake.

"How about you take the day off from school and come on a little trip to the dacha with me?" he proposed. "I tacked up a sign on a bulletin board downtown, and these people called. People who talk like gentle rednecks. We're going to move our shit out so some nice rednecks with a truck can move their shit in. I've never met these people, but they say they'll help us get our furniture in some mammoth pickup they've got and help us load it into storage. Would you care to participate?"

In the agreement he and my mother had composed in the study, he explained, it was written that my mother would keep the house and he would keep our cabin in the Berkshires, the dacha to which he referred. His plan was to rent it to the rednecks for a year and ease our new state of scarcity. It was not clear to me how he was going to fund both new residences: the New York apartment and the Wattsbury apartment, in which Rachel and I would see him on weekends.

I was tired of my room by that time, and it was almost spring. I said yes. Leaving what was now my mother's house at 7:30 in his green Subaru, we went west toward the hills.

"What have you been doing with yourself besides playing guitar, Joshy?" he asked as he drove. "These past four days have been no good fun for anyone, I know."

"I'm also listening to music." I was glad to have an unimpeachably cool response.

He stroked his beard for a while. "You want an electric?"

"Yes."

"You need an amp?"

"Yes. And two effect pedals, and three patch cords."

"How much you think that's going to set back your old man?"

I had walked to WATTSbury Music the previous afternoon, to ogle, and while there had calculated the answer to this very question. "Six hundred fifty bucks."

He drummed his fingers on the wheel. "Money is weird right now."

I was silent. I knew I was owed.

"Cost be damned," he said. "I'll have the cash tomorrow."

"Thanks, man." I felt that, because of his fallen state and his congeniality, we were rockers together now, and *man* was a fit term of endearment. "That's the shit."

His eyes grew moist. "There's a Richard Thompson show at Smith next week. I was thinking of going myself, but I'll get you a ticket. You should watch some up-close finger action, right?"

"That would be really helpful. Thank you."

"Resolved." He thumped the wheel with his fist. "I hate to lose the cabin, but I'm going to use that money to be a father," he said as he pushed the Subaru's 4WD into gear. "To pay for a Wattsbury apartment, be here for you and your sister." The Subaru growled earnestly. "I'm going to be riding the train or taking a plane just about every weekend. Essentially, I'm hocking the dacha to buy us some familial glue."

Despite his loss of moral authority, these words excited me. So he was imperfect, as a husband. Were we not both rebels, in our way, nonconformists? I hoped we would go on long walks and talk about which drugs I should try, what I should say to women, whether I should hang a certain poster on my wall. I'd been thinking about the poster, ever since Khadijah and I had gotten in trouble. It was on display in the back room of a head shop in Northampton: a black-and-white photograph of a young Parisian in a long wool coat, a radical of '68, his arm cranked back to throw a rock. On the cobblestones, his shadow was watery and vast.

"What do you want to write essays about?" I asked. "Or, like, poem-essays?"

"The first one I've conceptualized is called 'How Do We Make a Kid?' The idea is that when we, members of my generation, were young, the iconography was all war versus children. The posters that said 'War Is Bad for Children and Other Living Things,' 'Teach Your Children Well,' imagery from Joni Mitchell songs, like 'Ladies of the Canyon,' say, where you've got these nurturing, peaceful women with children at their feet, flower children, the key motif being children . . . The idea was that war was destructive, and having babies, raising a brood, was a generative, positive act. I remember looking at your mother, thinking, We will be virtuous people, with our children and our garden. I mean, *War and Peace*, it's an old dichotomy, isn't it? But pretty shortly after we had children evidence began to accumulate that suggested having kids and raising them as comfortable Westerners was—is—an act of violence, consuming more of our limited natural resources than anyone should be allowed, and now . . . I'm curious, what is your sense of global warming? You've heard of it?"

I had, so I nodded. But I didn't know what it was.

"Ah well," he said. "Scientists have been sure for a long time, but no one's hardly ever a hundred percent on anything in science, so journalists ask if they're sure, and the scientists say, well, pretty sure, so journalists say it's not sure. Anyway, we're making the climatic conditions under which civilization has been constructed permanently defunct, by building houses and driving cars and having children who will do the same. If my ancestors had stayed in Ireland, with luck we'd all be living in a farmhouse and dying young and lamenting our wasted promise over glasses of whiskey, and thereby living less destructively, better preserving the planet, contributing less to drought and starvation. Creating drought and starvation is what we're doing, you know, right now. It might as well be the blood of third-world children powering this Subaru, which is designed for the portage of first-world children. I mean, I'm just saying. It's not your fault. What do we do when the way we always thought we were building a peaceful future turns out to be another kind of killing?"

I tried to think of a countercultural response. What was the radical thing to say? "We have to compensate for existing, basically," I said.

He wrinkled his nose, as if I had mentioned a vulgar activity, such as Jet Skiing, or skiing. "Nah. Too Protestant."

We were silent again, for a quarter of an hour. The strangeness of the silence grew and grew, until finally he punched me in the arm, experimentally, a comradely gesture he'd never tried before.

"You know me and Nancy are in love with each other, don't you? We wouldn't do this, make all these changes happen, if we weren't in love. But I suspect we're the love of each other's lives."

"I understand." I apologized to my mother in my head as I said it.

"Sometimes things just become very clear, and there's not much you can do about it when it happens to you. God kind of taps you on the shoulder and says, 'Sorry, buddy, your life isn't over there, where you've been headed, it's over *here,* you have to change, or you won't be fully awake anymore.'"

"Are you and Nancy going to live together?"

He shook his head. "Nancy and Khadijah are moving to Cambridge." He spoke slowly and precisely. "Nancy's been courted pretty avidly by a couple schools around Boston for years. It's late in the hiring season, so she's taking meetings next week."

"But what about Khadijah? There's two more months of school."

"She's going to do her last quarter at Cambridge Rindge and Latin. Nancy's going to commute to Wattsbury. Those two can't be running into each other at the grocery store, Nancy and Arty.

Things in that family aren't as polite as they are in this one, right now. Fact is, things have been hard between Nancy and Arty for some time. She said it'd be better if he and I didn't wind up in the same room. But you and Khadijah should stay in touch."

"Oh, we will."

He looked at me. "I don't know if I'd talk about it to your mother too much, if you two actually get to be close friends or something. Might be weird. On the other hand, your mother's kept her cool." His eyes went shiny again. "She's really been quite cool."

Now, with the sun high in the pines, we turned right onto the long gravel driveway, and the cabin bumped into view. My father had built it ten years ago, with bearded friends. A Monopoly house, a perfect cube, unpainted sides, pine green roof. Outside, a circular clearing in miles of woods. Within, a potbellied woodstove, a loft with foam mattresses, a steel ladder in lieu of stairs.

A man and a woman waited at the end of the driveway, leaning on the hood of a red Toyota pickup.

"We can't call it the dacha anymore today," my father said. "If we do, these people will think we're assholes."

He killed the engine, jangled the keys. "Shit, I was promised a big truck. That pickup is supposed to take all our furniture to the storage space in Stockbridge. If that dinky-ass motherfucker is supposed to be the Big Truck, I will shit my brain."

He flicked off his sunglasses and waved to the couple. They waved back, struggled into motion. The man was fat and slow, the woman thin and slower. With every step, she dumped her weight on her left leg, forcing it to drag her right. Her lame right foot scraped the ground at a diagonal, like a peeler skinning a potato.

"Look at them move, Son. These people are poor. The businessman in me says, Don't touch this shit. But I'm an old lefty. I think you give people a chance."

We got out of the car, made introductions. The renters were named Steven and Alexis.

"Listen, friends," my father said. "With all due respect. This is not the truck that is going to haul my furniture."

Steven made a face that said *I am a beacon of positivity.* "One and the same," he chimed, as if to confirm good news.

My father looked at the truck, acclimating. "May I have the deposit, then, please?"

Steven took a pale blue document from his pocket and presented it to my father. My father examined it.

"I stated explicitly: a certified check."

"That's the closest we could do." Steven wedged his thumbs through the belt loops of his soft, strained jeans.

"You guys don't have a bank?"

Alexis shook her head. She drew close, her foot scraping the earth. "If you don't like it, that's fine. We can call this whole thing off."

"Oh God," said my father. "Fuck me, man."

"If you don't want to take it," said Steven, "we can go our separate ways right now."

My father closed his eyes. It occurred to me he might need money, more urgently than I'd realized. He was going to New York City, not just to write essays but to do something called consulting. What did this mean?

"No, no, it's fine," he said, twisting the hairs of one sideburn between his fingers. "It's cool." He took the money order—I could see that was what it was—folded it, and slid it into the pocket of his checked blue shirt.

The four of us emptied the cabin, to make way for the couple's things. We carried out our two couches, our dining room table, our foam mattresses, a record player, Candy Land, Chinese checkers. Framed posters from political theory conferences my father had organized when I was a small boy: Helsinki, Stockholm, Budapest. We unhooked the pans from the wall and threw them in a garbage bag. After we packed the fans, we learned each other's scents. The weather had turned suddenly warm, and the windows opened only four or five inches, hinging outward on cranks. The water and electricity had been turned off for the winter, and wouldn't come back on until the lease began. We made trips to the woods and returned with our hands smelling like pee.

While Steven and my father wrestled the couches into the bed of the pickup, Alexis and I did women's work, bubble-wrapping the breakables. I dropped a framed letter, and the glass shattered. She picked up the letter to see if it was important.

"That's from the United Nations," I said casually. "Before my dad was a professor he was one of the executives in a pacifist organization. They won international praise during the Cold War."

I felt some wincing awe would have been appropriate. She only brushed the shards off the frame.

"He met Gorbachev," I said. "Pretty fucking cool."

She looked down at the letter and back up at me.

"The leader of Russia." I jabbed my forehead. "With the thing."

"You think I'm stupid," she said. "I think you should tell your dad you broke the glass. He wouldn't want this letter to get messed up."

"He won't care," I explained. "That's not the point of these things, everything being just so, or whatever." I folded a Guatemalan tapestry over the framed letter, hiding the broken glass. I put it back in the box.

Alexis carried the box of breakables to the truck and wedged it between the backs of two armchairs.

"Everything intact?" my father asked.

"Double-checked, sir." She threw me a wink.

The furniture fit in the truck bed. Steven crossed bungee cords over the dome of wood and upholstery.

"I'll be damned, partner," said my father, slapping Steven on the back. "This shit ain't going nowhere, that's for damned sure."

Steven smacked his soft red hand into my father's. "You ready to hit the road, my man?"

After the handclasp, my father glowed. "Never be a snob, Son," he said as we rolled backward down the driveway. "You'll find yourself isolated from the people in this world who will remind you what really matters. These people don't have shit, they don't know shit, but they know they don't know shit. They go about their day and they don't expect otherwise, and there's a great wisdom in that. I always planned to raise you working-class until puberty." He shook his head. "Somehow, it didn't happen. But you're a really good guy."

The sun tore a hole in a dissolving cloud. Light split on the windshield. My father spun out into the wide gravel road, and we flew down the hill. He stuck his hand out the window and thumped a four-four allegro on the door. I did the same thing on my side, but there was something disgusting about our being synchronized, and he withdrew his hand.

With his hands at 10:00 and 2:00, we gained speed. As the tree canopy fell, we could see the other hills, plush lumps against a hard blue sky.

"Did you know working-class people growing up?" I asked.

"Sure," he said. "I caddied. That was a way of creating my own diverse environment."

"Were you already a socialist back then?"

"Let me put it this way: Your grandmother's cocktail party world? I wanted to blow it up. But hold on a minute," he said, "we're losing Steven." He slowed down, waiting for the truck to catch up. "Got a little carried away here. There's a dumb-ass ecstasy in driving downhill, you know."

Steven's large, red, shaggy head popped Muppet-like from the cab. His hand made a stop sign. My father pulled the Subaru over and set the parking brake. In the rearview mirror, I could see the truck shudder to a halt, the furniture still in the bed, the bungees still in place.

Steven climbed out. My father revived his allegro on the door.

"Hola," my father said. "How's that old machine getting along?"

Steven hustled to the open window, bent, and caught his breath.

"Dude, I have got your furniture back there, and you are driving one hundred fucking miles per hour down this motherfucking hill. This may never have occurred to you, but when you've got a payload on a truck, when you're driving and carrying something, you drive a little slower than if you're in a Subaru, taking a family vacation."

My father stared straight ahead.

"Slow down," suggested Steven, his hands on his knees. "Slow . . . the . . . fuck . . . down."

Crickets. My father took the blue money order from his shirt pocket and unfolded it. In two precise and deliberate motions, he ripped it into four pieces. He threw the quadrants in Steven's face. The Subaru spit gravel through the air. My father yanked down the parking brake as Steven kicked at the rear door.

I stuck my head out the window, my hair blowing into a veil around my face. I saw Alexis slip down from the truck and scrape after us.

"Hey, buddy!" She coned her hands in front of her mouth. "We've got your furniture back here!" She toppled over to one knee, and her hand landed hard on the gravel road. Steven circled back to the place where she had fallen. The two of them shrank into action figures.

I stared at my father.

"I don't need it," he said. "Furniture's old, not worth much."

Clearly, this was a lapse in understanding. I worked up the courage to open my mouth. "They're poor people."

"If he's telling me to fuck off already, Son, that's not the beginning of a good business relationship. I'd lose money."

My father was not alive to the implications of his behavior. My duty was clear.

"We're privileged," I said. "We should lose money."

He ran a hand through his beard. "Dear Saint Josh. This is your close friend God. You don't know what the fuck you're talking about."

I made a cry of righteous anguish. "The least we can do is help them with our stuff."

"Too late now."

I listened to the wind rush through the windows. I remembered Khadijah in her anarchist ensemble and got an instant, nearly painful erection, coupled with a lovelier, heart-based

yearning, thinking of her chipped black nail polish, her unpo-
nytailed hair thick against the back of her gray sweatshirt, and
immediately knew what I would do. I would continue to trans-
gress as she had shown me how. I would be worthy of her, so that
someday we would have sex many times, married in our apartment with cacti in the windows near downtown Northampton.
"Let me out," I said.

"You going *Dances with Wolves* on me, Son?"

"I'm utterly serious."

He thumped the wheel with the palm of his hand. "Right
away, young massah." The brakes squealed. He jerked the wheel
to the right and the car slid halfway onto the blowing grass. We
didn't look at each other.

"Another thing," he said. "You think working-class kids like
people who say 'fuck' to their fathers?"

"As far as you know," I said, performing for my memory of
Khadijah, as if she were sitting in the backseat, listening, "maybe
they do." I got out of the car and slammed the door.

I started up the hill. The engine growled. I turned and watched
the Subaru sink away. When it finally slipped out of sight, I chased
it. I swam with my arms, lifted my knees high. An insect flew into
my mouth, and I ran even as I coughed and wiped my tongue. I
wanted to throw my arms around my father's neck and smell the
sweat on him, fall asleep in the passenger seat as a crackly oldies
station read the weather. I went full-sprint downhill. Soon I dou-
bled over in pain. As mosquitoes swarmed, I paced on the grass.

I renewed my resolve to fight my father by summoning
Khadijah to mind again. Khadijah would have been able to see
the truth: My father, an unfeeling person, had made a handi-
capped woman drag herself after his car. He had made her plant
her hand in the road. He had left her with an important piece of
paper torn in four, and a truckload of hippie furniture.

On the other hand, could I expect to find Steven and Alexis
in the spot where we'd left them, meditating on their circumstances, waiting for my help? If we did cross paths, what would
happen? I imagined Steven's red truck bearing down on me, Ste-

ven leaping from the driver's seat and chasing me into the woods. Was it possible he might carry a rifle in his truck, like the rednecks who took out Peter Fonda at the end of *Easy Rider*? There was nothing to do but make for the dacha. My father would have to look for me there, eventually. I began to walk uphill.

Soon, I passed the spot where we'd left Steven and Alexis. I could make out the loop where they'd turned around. In another half hour, I reached our driveway, and found the cabin half obscured by a Berkshire of furniture. Our couches and chairs had been dumped off the truck, onto the grass. The big red couch and the blue love seat with the polka dots were on the bottom, supporting the chairs, which made a latticework with their legs that stretched half as high as the cabin itself. Between the chair legs, the upper reaches glinted with glass squares; the framed conference posters reflected the sun. Steven and Alexis could have dumped it all in a ditch. But they'd given it back.

I sat on the grass and waited. In ten minutes, the Subaru rolled up the driveway. My father slammed the door behind him and helped me up. I beamed involuntarily as I grasped his hand.

"I must say I'm relieved," he said. "I was worried you were going to return to find them burning it down."

"Where were you?" I asked, clapping him on the shoulder, to make sure he didn't leave my side.

"Got a seltzer and a coffee at a great old train-car diner down the road," he said. "*New England Monthly* used to rave about it." He put his hand on mine. "I'm glad we're doing this together, Son."

As it grew dark, we dragged the furniture inside, so it wouldn't molder in the dew and rain.

"Don't worry about making it pretty," he said. He tossed a chair bouncer-style through the door. "Your mother's never going to see the inside of this place again. And Nancy's different from her, she doesn't want me sweating the small shit while I make a life for myself as a creative person. I can't tell you how important that is to me. It feels like I have access to oxygen for the first time since I started a family. It's been a hard thing for me to be a parent, I've put so much aside, waiting for you and your sister to grow older. I've often thought that as soon as you're both in college I'm going to get on a plane to the South of France, write in a stone cottage, come back every now and again to hang out in New York, be around Jews and black people." He caught a moth in his hand and cast it out the window. "It's for the best, Son. You'll be fine seeing me on weekends for the next two years, won't you? I hate to say 'when I was your age,' but when I was your age I was in boarding school, I saw my father less than that."

"As long as I have the amp," I said, "I'm cool."

When we were done, the living room wasn't the way it'd been before. The posters were stacked in a corner, but the UN letter was restored to its place next to the photo of the shirtless Havana street trombonist.

My father stepped back and looked at the letter. "I like it battle-scarred," he said. "We're lucky glass is the only thing that got broken, buddy."

We coasted back down the hill. Salamanders fled before us, neon orange in our headlights.

"I bet you're hungry, young man."

I was. I had never labored before; I could feel an unfamiliar hardening in my shoulders.

We pulled into the lot behind the train-car diner after dinner rush. We took a booth in the back with a view of the waitress's circuit: down the counter, back up the tables along the wall.

She looked about five years older than I was, maybe a few more. The corners of moist dollar bills peeked from the pockets of her tight black jeans. Waves of dark brown hair were stuck to her cheeks with sweat. But her work was mostly over; the diner was empty. She leaned against the side of our booth as she flipped open her pad and took us in.

"Give my boy here a cheeseburger and a chocolate milk shake, please," my father said. He punched my arm and gave his head a solicitous tilt. "Am I right?"

I nodded. I blushed and tucked my smile into my neck.

The waitress laughed. "It's your lucky day, young man." She said it to me, but I knew her face was for him.

"The kid did good," my father said. "Moved the biggest pile of furniture I've ever seen."

"I bet he got some help from his pops."

"I'm used to it. For him it was a big first, doing a day's work."

"Just how big was this pile of furniture?"

"Let me see that pen for a second, will you?" She drew it slowly from the pocket of her apron and held it out like she was going to knight him with it. "Thank you," he said, "you're a peach."

She pressed her lower lip against the edge of her teeth. He took a napkin from the dispenser and drew an Egyptian pyramid. He drew a tiny stick figure next to it. "For a sense of the size of this thing," he said.

She looked around. "Let me see that." She slid onto the vinyl seat beside him. "That's a pretty significant pile of furniture, but I'd say the pile of dishes I brought out to people here about an hour ago was like this." She snatched the napkin from him and drew a second pyramid, twice as large as his.

"Now that I consider it, I forgot just how big that pile of furniture was," he said. He drew the bottom of a pyramid so enormous only the corner of it fit on the napkin.

"No fair." She slapped at his hand. "Respect the rules, you've got to stay inside the napkin, man."

Their shoulders were touching. Arm slipped against arm. I saw two children pulling a blanket over their heads, making a fortress of darkness. They were hiding in a place where everything was believed. The warmth of it was something I could feel from the other side of the table. I knew I couldn't make them come out, no matter what I said.

Sick of watching them, I took off my sneakers and rubbed my bare feet together. I stared out the window. There was a rattling outside, barely audible. A red pickup bumped around the corner.

As soon as the truck reached the black asphalt of the parking lot, it slowed to a crawl. There were familiar auras of rust around the wheels. I could make out Steven alone in the cab. He turned into the space next to the Subaru as a tall man in a hairnet and a cook's apron walked out the back door of the train car. Steven jumped down from the cab and gave the cook a high five. Wild blond curls snuck out from under the hairnet, white in the evening sunlight. With the cook looking around to see if anyone was in the parking lot, Steven knelt beside the Subaru's tires, out of sight.

"Dad," I said. I pointed. We could see the cook, and Steven's truck. Steven stood, brushed dust off his jeans.

My father cursed. The waitress slid out of the booth and went behind the counter.

My father pushed down on my shoulders. "You do not move," he said.

He jogged out the door, down the three concrete steps to the parking lot. He could have stayed inside, I thought, and called the police. That's what Mom would have done. But he believed in giving these people a chance to hurt him. The way he went through war books—that was part of it.

The door sighed shut behind him. The waitress and I were alone inside, watching. My father and Steven shouted a little while, before they reached for each other. Later, for professional reasons, I would spend a lot of time in bars, and realize in retrospect that this verbose buildup to fighting meant that both my father and Steven were inept brawlers. If one of them had been any good, he would have tried to be the first to pop the other in the face, no prelude. That or tackled the other guy, straddled him, punched his head. There would have been no throat clearing. But at the time I thought they were talking and shoving because conversation was a necessary part of the process, that they were working themselves into a godlike furor. My father twisted Steven's shirt and yelled in his face undaunted. But the cook walked around my father and took one of his arms in both of his hands. Steven did the same with the other arm. They leaned him against the back of the Subaru, gripping him by the elbow and the shoulder on each side. My father writhed against the hood; they labored to hold him down, two hands on each of his arms.

The waitress touched my elbow and pointed outside with her chin. I looked around to see what I could use. I took a serrated steak knife off a dirty plate on the counter. It looked funny in my hand; it made my wrist look even thinner than it was. She hoisted a coffeepot off the Bunn Pour-O-Matic. It was the decaf pot, with a smudged orange lip.

"Take this." She pushed it toward me across the counter. "It'll hurt. It hurts my fingers all the time."

I put down the knife and picked up the coffeepot. My father didn't want my help, but he was going to get it. As soon as I had the pot in my hand, I became aware that my body was carrying a white energy that purled in my lungs and brain and turned from fear to determination to fear and back and forth, like a kid was playing with a light switch. My arm trembled. The coffee sloshed as I walked out of the train car into the parking lot, not too fast, careful not to let any of the coffee spill over the lip and burn my fingers. Approaching these men at a steady pace with the coffeepot stable in my hand, I felt uncomfortably like a waitress.

Steven and the cook let my dad go and backed away when they saw me coming with something in my hand. When Steven took in that it was a pot of decaf, he sneered with relief.

"I'll burn you," I said.

"What are you going to do?" my father called to Steven. "Beat a kid?"

"I'm going to take that from you," Steven said to me, "unless you pour it out."

"I'm not doing that."

Steven stepped forward, and reached for the pot. I walked backward, and drew the pot close to me, like a football, but Steven got both his hands on it, and we were twisting together, and then my hands were empty and Steven was emptying the pot onto the ground, calmly, as if pouring water on a rosebush.

Three men had come out of the diner, and the one in front, who was shouting obscenities, looked like he might be the manager, a tan and wiry man in metallic math-nerd glasses. I could tell the dishwashers were dishwashers because they were only barely older than I was, one of them in a Guns N' Roses *Use Your Illusion* T-shirt, the other in a Celtics jersey.

The manager was still shouting something. There was Steven—he was jumping in his truck. He revved the engine. I scrambled to get out of his way, and then he was spitting gravel through the parking lot, spinning out onto the road.

I looked down at myself to find I had some coffee splashed on my shirt. It didn't seem like it was melting my skin. Apparently, a hot plate with an openmouthed pot didn't maintain coffee at lethal temperatures, like the metal tanks at McDonald's. I had envisioned the weapon in my hand as boiling pitch, like what you'd pour on a screaming Hun.

Still: I had been in a fight. *Khadijah,* I thought, *my love, my fellow soldier. See what have I become?* I felt that Khadijah, if she had seen me, might have been overwhelmed by a desire to kiss me, because the smell of my sweat was mingled with Old Spice, and even without the Old Spice the smell was better than how it had been before—the sweat was earned.

As we waited for the police, I leaned protectively against my father's Subaru, which was immobilized, its rear tires slashed. My shirt clung to my chest. My triceps, which ached from wrestling with Steven for the pot, looked a little more like real triceps, distinguishable from the rest of my arms.

I have been to war, my love. I mouthed the words as I watched the sunset spill red on the diner's chrome. Maybe I only needed Khadijah to watch how I was changing, how I was becoming a man, for our bond to be sealed.

The police station in Worthington was not like Wattsbury's. The room where my father was invited to make a phone call was never referred to as a conference room, and our exchange with the officers couldn't have been termed a conference. But a progressive, Wattsburian spirit prevailed. The police told us that they would keep Steven off our property as long as we didn't insist on lodging a criminal complaint; they felt pretty sure they could talk him out of lodging a complaint against us. It was true that my father had torn up his money order, and that I would have inflicted very mild burns upon him if he hadn't seized the pot, but a young waitress had confessed that she was the one who had armed me, a minor, with coffee. (She was fired immediately.) It was Steven who had slashed our tires and instigated the conflict. As far as the town of Worthington was concerned, we only had to find a ride back to Wattsbury and call Triple A about the Subaru in the morning.

At the little metal table where the white office phone waited for us, my father backed his metal chair against the wall. He leaned his head against a bulletin board and dialed a number from memory.

"Give me a little space, all right?" His eyes softened. "Won't you, Son?"

I left the room and wandered down the hallway, to the holding cell. I took the bars in my hands. While my father murmured into the phone, I studied the metal bench that ran alongside the wall, the chrome toilet. These were the state's tools for accommodating citizens who were helpless against themselves. A cage was not a place you would ever put my father, a great cat.

After about five minutes, he came out to the lobby. "It'll be two hours," he said to the officers. "A friend of mine is on her way."

We had long exhausted the game of Twenty Questions by the time Nancy arrived. I had seen my father kiss her, but now, for the first time, I saw the two of them embrace. He collected her in his big arms, her small, rigid body much the same as Khadijah's, her avian eyes and nose Khadijah's too, and soon they were sitting at the table near the phone, his head on her shoulder. These cheating old people had what Khadijah and I rightfully deserved.

"Poor baby," Nancy said. She kissed my father's hair. "My poor churl."

"I don't have any money," he said as she ran a hand down his sideburn through his beard. When she was with him, holding him, he was unashamed to say it. "What am I going to do?"

"We'll figure something out, dummy." She made a dismissive motion with one hand while she continued to pet him with the other, a coordinated movement I thought of as maternal.

"You just had a run-in with some bad people, that's all." *Bad people.* The clarity with which a neocon could navigate the world! My mother would never have said "bad people." She never would have allowed herself the certainty that the people were bad. Nancy's face, as she cooed the words into his ear, was self-assured. My father closed his eyes.

The Dads left the station with their arms around each other's shoulders, a battered pair of defectors. I followed, hoping that Khadijah waited for me in Nancy's car, although I knew it was unlikely. Before we reached the parking lot, the Dads stopped on the paved walk and allowed themselves a luxurious kiss. They performed it in part for me, I think, and for any officers watching from inside. They were having a rite of their own.

April was all but upon us. A lukewarm wind shook pine needles onto the windshields of the cruisers. I could hear them skitter on metal and asphalt, scouring away at winter.

"You didn't bring Khadijah, by any chance, did you, Nancy?" I asked. It was the first substantial sentence that had ever passed between us.

"You think she's hiding under the car, Josh?" She laughed. "Khadijah is studying, dear. Or at least she'd better be. She and I will have a dire conversation if I return to find her final Wattsbury French paper unfinished. She lobbied quite hard to come with me, actually. But I would have been a lax mother to say yes, I'm afraid."

"*Elle ne vient pas, c'est ça?*" my father asked. "*L'histoire de la débâcle âllemande?*" He was cheering up.

"*Non, c'est Wattsbury Regional, mon frère, Afrique du nord. L'histoire du colonialisme et du racisme.*"

They kissed again, in the parking lot, the gorgon of money vanquished by culture. I knew they were healing each other by speaking French, reminding each other of what they had and who they were. They were going to build a life on their romance. I thought of Nancy barring Khadijah from the car, Khadijah, who'd only wanted to hang out with me after I'd been in a fight, and I despised the Dads. Perhaps that was the useful trick I learned from what happened with Khadijah: the ability to despise them.

I reflected on the deafening musical equipment I was going to spend my father's money on. Someday, I thought, I will live in a tour bus, with only my girlfriend. I will walk and talk and dress differently from my father. I will walk and talk and dress in such a way that, as with Kurt Cobain, you take a look at me and think, orphan.

And the girl in the tour bus was the girl who'd torn off her scrunchie, who'd cast her burgundy-trimmed Esprits to the wind. Who sat beneath an oak with a manual for politically moti-vated crime. She'll be an activist, I thought, but sometimes she'll take time off and come with me, and distribute political flyers to the people who come to my shows, bring them into a movement.

But an older, drier voice told me, *Whatever sprout you've grown with Khadijah, it's going to wither and die.* No one had e-mail. To keep in touch with a girl who lived two hours away, you had to talk to her, while attempting to avoid your mother, on a beige phone whose base was nailed to the kitchen wall. That or write her letters. I knew that even if I could summon the courage to do these things, they wouldn't carry Khadijah and me through months and years. We'd never had much time together, had never done anything considered something.

If Khadijah had stayed at my school, anything could have hap-pened. But she became a story of what might have been and so became, over the years, a personal celebrity, a cherished memory I felt I knew so well that, when I reminded myself I didn't actu-ally know her anymore, it felt unfair, an oversimplification. When I needed resolve in times of difficulty, I thought of her walking the March streets of Wattsbury, back straight, sneakers squeaking on the wet pavement, the sleeve of her mother's sweatshirt nearly concealing the stone in her small, sure hand.

1995–2006

1.

I Trust Myself to Do It
Because I'm Strong

"The thing about Nancy was that it was hard to be with Nancy and have a job at the same time," my father explained. He was walking with Rachel and me from his new apartment on Sullivan Street down hot little lanes that cut Greenwich Village into triangles, formed *A*s and circles, anarchy signs. It was fifteen months after the Family Meeting of Separation and the Incident with the Cabin. Rachel and I hated the weekends we spent at his sparsely furnished condo in Wattsbury, but we loved weekends like these, weekends we camped in his tiny, entirely nonfurnished one-bedroom in Manhattan, in which white paint peeled from the heating pipe. There was a window that looked out on a brick wall five feet away—I could think of few things more exhilaratingly, masochistically urbane.

"I was consulting instead of holding down a steady gig, all to have a schedule free enough to see Nancy in Boston when I wasn't with you guys in Wattsbury. What with child support, and the two apartments, I had to commit fully to my new life."

"What does it mean to commit fully to your new life?" Rachel asked.

"As soon as you children split for college, I'm going to stay here in New York every weekend and write essays in the style of Montaigne. That's what I'll do when I'm finally unencumbered. I'll write through the lens of my own experiences. I marched against McNamara when he came to speak at Harvard. I met Gorbachev. I knew Al Gore, before he was vice president."

"So the book is, you're Forrest Gump," Rachel said.

"Dad," I interjected, "did Nancy ever say anything about Khadijah, before you broke up? Like what she's up to?"

"Thriving, she gave me to understand. Really taken to art history, apparently; a chip off the old block. Oh, and she's going to spend next year in France. That's Arty's thing, he's the one who pushed that, or so Nancy feels. If he can't have her, neither can Nancy, it seems. Khadijah's an only child, you know. They fight over her. Why don't you write her a letter and ask her?"

What would I say? Don't go to France? Consider ditching your mom and Cambridge for your dad and Wattsbury? But there was another reason why not: I wrote her letters constantly in my head. In these, I could tell her anything I wanted, speak with grace and candor. Whenever something momentous happened, I dashed off a mental note to Khadijah. *I played guitar for three hours and listened to records for four hours today. I feel my destiny is to be a musician.* Or *I'm getting a C+ in math, so I'm not going to Harvard, but fuck conformity, right?* Or, *I'm in a band, now, although we suck.*

I was sixteen, wearing a T-shirt for my band that my father had designed. He had painted "The Rational Actors" in jagged red late-seventies punk rock letters on it, and given it to me as a surprise present. The singer and I had contemplated a series of deeply meaningful names: Exiled, Black Tambourine, Agatha's Rainstorm. But the only name my father liked, the one he decided was our real name, was our lamest, proposed by the drummer as a half joke, never seriously considered.

"The Rational Actors is good because it tacitly admits who you are," he'd said. "You're creative, you're a little rebellious, but at the same time you're responsible, you're paying attention in history class, you're good." I was the only member of the band who had the T-shirt; there was only one in existence. It was a bizarre, unforeseen token of paternal affection, but I took it. In spite of every baleful father-related event, in spite of my suspicion that the Rational Actors was an unsuitable name for any self-respecting institution, it was the first shirt I wore whenever I did a wash, even though I didn't know the world would soon sprout nine hundred bands with AP-student names—the Decembrists, DeVotchKa, Les Sans Culottes, Franz Ferdinand. I didn't know that studiousness, then a liability in rock and roll, would become an asset, a genre.

We were on our way to meet my father's girlfriend of nearly a year, a native New Yorker. I knew that this New York girlfriend was a sign my father had established himself in the city, but I was confused about another thing.

"So do you have a job here now?" I asked.

"Here's Allison," he said. "With her new dog. Let's all be endearing." We knew from the way he said this that Allison was rich. He winked at us, and we became a team, the three of us, earning something together.

A woman closer to my age than his waved from the far side of the street, holding a leash. At the other end of it was a beatific little object, the business end of a toilet brush, snow white with pitch eyes. She stood with the puppy in front of a restaurant called Elephant & Castle, where we were going to eat our introductory lunch. She held the door open with her back, gripping the leash with one hand and shaking our hands with the other as we walked in.

Her eyes were as dark and friendly as the mop's, and she was almost a foot shorter than my father, five-four to his six-two. She was the same height as Khadijah, and had the same color eyes, and this made me both envious of my father and disinclined to hate him. I could tell Allison's body was meant to be zaftig, maternal, but she had enslaved it to what must have been a Khadijahan will, exercised herself thin. We ate blood sausage, and when she tore it diagonally with her knife, so did we, and when she then established a pattern of devouring these bites completely before she issued some satisfied commentary, like *pretty intensely good,* Rachel and I did that too. This was our way of showing that we wanted to continue to share with her, to be a pack of canines gorging on the same kill. Because the Elephant & Castle, as an English restaurant, allowed small dogs, the recent acquisition, whose name was Miles, stared plaintively from beneath the table, joining his solicitude with ours, begging for scraps, but subtly, lying still, only showing his desire to partake with his ears and his eyes.

Allison was earning something too. She asked me careful, indepth questions about the Rational Actors, with the attentive, empathetic, respectful expression of an MTV News reporter. How did I play guitar and sing at the same time? It seemed totally inconceivable, to Allison, that anyone could do that and remember the words *and* keep in sync with a band. I waited for my father to note that, throughout the second half of the twentieth century, some people had managed this feat on a number of well-documented occasions, but instead he looked at her as she interviewed me with a lost, dreamy expression on his face, his arm slung around her. When I explained that keeping all the chords in your head wasn't that hard because there usually weren't many of them, and Allison said, "Well, I find it really goddamn impressive," he nodded in agreement.

Allison turned her light upon Rachel. What was *The Devil's Arithmetic* about? Was it true that she had already read two non-young-adult AIDS memoirs, for a history paper that had received a special Diversity Award from the principal, and the paper had been reprinted in an alternative weekly in Northampton? Was it true that two different boys had asked to have coffee with her, and one of them had asked her out to a marionette production of *Phaedra*?

We basked in Allison's attention, Rachel and I, surprised that someone so pretty and sophisticated, someone who had obviously been a superpopular girl in high school just twelve years ago, seemed obsessed with us. And we basked in the presence of our father. I still despised him, in theory, but he was the one who provided access to New York City, the one who could reach into the crowds of Manhattan and draw out an Allison. And I still loved him. I loved the way his mouth twisted to one side and his eyes darted from table to table, exchanging glances with waitresses. I loved how he dabbed his beard with his napkin vigorously when he was enjoying himself. A new economy had developed, in the year since the separation was declared: My mother was abundant, my father was rare. He was a newly scarce commodity and his value was up. I schemed after his attention. I flirted with him.

"You were a good girl when you were a teenager, weren't you?" my father asked Allison. "Like Rachel? You must have been, to get into Brown."

"I was a good girl like Rachel until I was Josh's age," Allison said. "Then I was bad, for about a year."

"Why did you start being bad?" Rachel asked her.

"Bad school, out in Pueblo, Colorado. I lived there with my mom, who had just gotten, she thought, enlightened. My dad was here, far away, had a new wife who didn't like me. I didn't see him. He had lost track of me, so I fucked up until he started paying attention. I skipped school and smoked cigarettes under the bleachers and cried on the phone a couple times, and finally they sent me to live with him in New York senior year. Which was a major improvement over my mom's condo, let me tell you." She stared at the wall. She was with people who weren't in the room.

So: Allison was a child who knew what it was to court an elusive Dad. Emerging from the fugue state in which she'd delivered the speech, Allison looked at me and Rachel to see if she had weirded us out. I wanted to show her that I liked her story, so I nodded and said, "Fuck yeah," which baffled everyone into silence.

"This is good," said my father. "This is a good place to bring a dog and kids."

After lunch, my father said that it was time for me and Rachel to meet Allison's "family"—he raised his eyebrows as he said the word, to suggest it didn't quite apply. This was the Muellers: Allison's father, Bruce; his second wife, Laura; and their two children. We were going to visit them on their island. My sister and I rode in the backseat of Allison's black Saab east through Brooklyn, Long Island bound. Allison was the driver; my father was the talker. He waved at the public housing projects, explained the mind-set of the social engineers who created them. In the beige-yellow industrial palimpsest of outer Queens, he pointed his thumb to the south and reminded Allison that her father, Bruce, had once owned a textile factory "out there on Mount Purgatory." At the mention of her father's name, Allison became focused on the gearshift.

She flew the Saab through openings in traffic I couldn't see, and soon we found ourselves on a tine of the North Fork. We coasted at twenty miles per hour down suburban avenues where the air was scoured clean by the ocean; Miles was permitted to thrust his upper body through the window, his tongue absorbing information. We stopped at a place where the side streets curled into a semicircle of grass and kelp-covered rock, and the sun fell on scale-shaped waves: Long Island Sound.

Allison punched a code into a chrome keyboard embedded in the stone. A square of solid rock revealed itself as a garage door, and she parked the car in a fluorescent cave. She muttered into a phone attached to an interior wall, and servants came out in a boat to conduct us across the water.

Things! Objects were shocking me with their capacity for meaning. In my mind, I spoke to Khadijah, and I explained to her what I was seeing. We were reunited, somehow; she had come back to Wattsbury for her senior year, I was telling her about rich people. *They hide,* I said to her, *and they hide the signs of who they are. They keep cars behind rocks by the seashore. They go to islands nobody can find. That's why you never see them.*

"Look at this," my father said to me conspiratorially, on the boat, as Allison murmured to somebody on her cell phone. (An exotic accessory—I had never known anyone who had one.) "Bruce, he's probably worth about what, fifty million? But he's bought an island and bleached an old Tudor house." He gestured toward a blinding colossus that tottered on a green tumescence, our destination. "Not what I would do with my money, I'll tell you that much." So my father was nervous too. More than nervous; his eyes were actually frightened.

At some point on the drive to Long Island, my father had begun to address Miles as "son." "Careful now, Son," he said as we brushed against the dock. But Miles bounded off the boat as soon as the servants unfroze themselves from their nautical postures and tied the ropes. From a distance, we saw the island dogs gallop up to meet us.

"See, that's Brenda and Gopher," said Allison to Miles, pointing to the dogs. "New friends, big guy."

On the grass, Miles and the island dogs circled each other strategically, Brenda old and spry, Gopher bounding and inelegant. The islanders were both mutts, part standard poodle, part miscellany. Brenda's underbite reminded me of a terrier, and Gopher had the grimace of an angry thirteen-year-old boy.

Miles fishtailed between his hosts and finally splayed on the grass before Brenda. Gopher sauntered up behind Miles, planted one paw on his side, and humped the air above him with martial determination.

"I don't like this," mused my father, watching the dogs, stroking his beard. "Gopher's already exploiting Miles's innocence," he said, descending on the dogs as Miles rolled away. "Gopher's like the old convict checking on the new guy in prison. He says, 'You're cute, c'mere.'"

Allison stared at my father neutrally for a moment, and then the man who must have been her own father appeared, dark haired, stocky, stubble cheeked, loose armed, loping down the impeccably contoured landscape in stained khaki shorts and a black Miles Davis T-shirt. My father boomed out his name— Bruce!—sidestepping to swipe Gopher away from Miles with one hand as he presented the other to Gopher's owner.

There was still a coat of orange on the waves when Bruce's second wife, Laura, the age of Allison plus the age of Rachel, excused herself from our five-way game of catch. (We threw an Aerobie, a red, soft-edged torus not unlike a giant, flattened cock ring.) She returned thirty seconds later to beckon us inside with both her slender arms. A former teacher of special-needs children (it was in this profession that she had discovered how easy an Aerobie was to catch) her movements were lumbering and joyful, the movements of one accustomed to chasing and gathering up. Her hair, a mix of blond and gray, fell between her shoulders; her face was scrunched and kind; her smock a diaphanous tribute to the Russian villagers of *Fiddler on the Roof;* her butt, in her crimson, one-piece bathing suit, jutting and hard like the golden rocks. She led us to the kitchen, which at first looked ordinary. Only string beans and scalloped potatoes somehow hissed on two skillets, and firm flanks of white fish somehow steamed on a metal sheet. The servants had vanished after they had finished their work, so that it was as if we had cooked for ourselves and suffered a loss of memory. Ordinary: We piled our plates with food and took them to a table on a screened-in porch. Ordinary: We praised the meal as if one of our party had prepared it. Our performance was spontaneous, heartfelt, if unnatural; it had the feeling of the first practice of a rock band.

Rachel and I were seated kitty-corner at the far end of the table from Bruce and Laura. Our vantage was ideal for watching the theater of the dogs. Miles mopped at Gopher's legs with his head; Gopher leapt over Miles and whirled to charge Brenda, who tried to capture Miles's attention by running around him in a circle.

"Do you think I should go out and guard Miles?" I whispered to Rachel. "Dad has to stay at the table and be social."

Rachel assessed the dogs. Her face was diagnostic and calm the way it'd been a year ago, when she'd looked at our parents arranged in the stations of a family meeting and said *divorce.* There was an instinct for nature in her, a certainty. "Neither of those dogs," she whispered, "wants to do to Miles what Dad thinks they want to do."

Laura tinked her fork against her glass of water and said *ahem.* "Hear ye hear ye," she said. "The Annual Mueller Swim Race to the Shore commences tomorrow morning at nine o'clock sharp. Raise your hand if you're in."

Everyone except Rachel and me raised their hands.

"You're too young, Rachel," said Laura. "It's almost a mile. But why not you, Josh?" I knew, from experience with teachers, how relentless this kind of grown-up concern for my emotional development could be. I was being Challenged to step outside my Safety Zone.

"Oh no," I said, "I'm no swimmer."

"I bet you're pretty strong," said Laura, kindly and absurdly. "You impressed us all with that Aerobie out there."

Allison laid down her knife. "No one cares, Josh. If you don't feel like it, you don't need to do it."

I blushed. I had brought these two women into conflict simply by provoking incompatible forms of generosity. Allison, I thought, wants to be a mother.

After dinner, Laura brought in bowls and a pan of warm apple cobbler that must have materialized in the kitchen. She placed a hand on my father's shoulder and tucked an envelope beneath his cobbler bowl.

"Ooh, a present! Open it!" I cried, shocking everyone with my sudden volume and enthusiasm. I hoped that this was the kind of spiritedly ironical tone rich people found endearing and natural.

My father's eyebrows jumped. "All right, since my teenager is so breathlessly invested." He pushed open a hole with his thumb and teased out the contents.

For a moment, every face at the table went blank—everyone had seen that one of the pieces of paper in my father's hand was a check.

My father's face was full of death. "Thank you very much, Bruce," he got out. "Incredibly generous." He began to hum, staring into space. I didn't recognize the tune, but it was wide-ranging, fast, meandering.

Bruce stirred crust and ice cream with his fork. "It's my pleasure."

"Starting a business, or a nonprofit, sorry, you need a little help in the beginning, Linus, that's all," said Laura, nurturing, hungry to show herself a nurturer—a teacher.

Then there was an eruption of barking, a three-way debate. My father stopped humming and looked out the enormous windows, transfixed. I tried to parse what he was looking at. Paws

and tails entangled, dancing, the hard wind off the sound comb-
ing the lawn.

"Excuse me," said my father, folding the check and putting it
in his pocket. "I'll be only a moment." He dropped his napkin on
his chair, slid open a glass door, and slipped outside. We watched
as he made his way to Miles and Gopher.

We heard him shouting: "No, Gopher, no."

We watched through the glass as he threw his body between
the two dogs, issuing prohibitions. "Stay away from Miles," he
grunted to Gopher. "Don't even come close. That's my son
there, buddy."

"I just don't think," said Laura, finally, to the table, "that
Gopher would do something like that. Linus keeps bringing it
up. I mean the idea he would rape another dog. A male dog rap-
ing another male dog."

Bruce wiped his mouth with his napkin and stretched in his
chair. He glanced at the torn envelope beside my father's cobbler
bowl. His mouth bent upward, perhaps to form a discreet smile.
Who could tell? It might have been a suppressed belch.

2.

Smile, Lads

M ost of my friends from high school wound up in either Boston or Brooklyn, depending on whether their salient ambition was to be smart or to be cool. I was the only Wattsbury Regional student from the Class of '96 who went to Los Angeles. I wish I could say that I chose L.A. out of a devotion to coolness or an indifference to smartness unmatched within either contingent. But how I came to L.A. was this.

At New York University, still bashful, still a virgin, I made a life philosophy of loneliness. I perused the thrift stores of Queens for silent hours. I spent afternoons before the mirror, trying to replicate outfits I'd seen on members of Elephant 6 bands, on Beck, on Jonathan Fire★Eater, the Yummy Fur, Smog. In these outfits, I played guitar and sang to myself, in dorm rooms only blocks from the Tribeca loft my father now shared with Allison.

I ate dinner with my father and Allison every couple of months. They gave me macrobiotic takeout and sushi and were kind to me, helped me phrase the occasional thank-you note to Bruce and Laura, who were paying my tuition. But I avoided them, insofar as politeness allowed, because they asked me who my friends were, and I had none.

My roommates went to places where they spoke with other people. They watched Knicks games at brew pubs, went dancing at Coney Island High. One was in the Muslim student organization, the other played racquetball and went to the computer lab. I was different.

In Wattsbury, where the only kids available to hang out with were Wattsburians, halfway mired in childhood, still trying to make positive impressions on teachers, still attending yoga classes with their mothers, I had no trouble cultivating a few friends among the others who played guitar and drums. First we formed inadvertently folkish ensembles that practiced in the conservatories of Victorian houses, one boy on the family piano, a girl from the school chorus singing, a boy on clarinet, myself, dressed in black Dockers and a mock turtleneck from JCPenney, with a red electric guitar in my lap. By senior year we were real bands, commandeering basements, rattling floorboards with trap kits and microphones. After practice we'd drink Coke and root beer on screened-in porches, and the singers, educated by Pearl Jam, would write lyrics from the perspectives of suicidal heroin-addicted grown-ups, homicidal sexually abused teenagers, and sad old people whose lives had passed them by.

But in New York, to make friends like the ones I'd had in Wattsbury seemed an excruciating waste. Somewhere in this city, there were people my age who had a better idea of how to be artists than I did. Somewhere in Manhattan or Brooklyn a future Patti Smith and a future Patti Smith Group were meeting in a bar or at an unsanitary party or in the apartment of a rich, pervy benefactor. My mission was to find them and make them accept me. I wanted to find and join the people who had a talent for disobedience. Disobedience was the core of songs and paintings and books, it was brushing aside the story you'd been given and telling an honest one. Was this not what Khadijah had started to accomplish when she'd called that first day after the Day of the Dads and asked to meet and talk? What were Jerry Lee Lewis or the Clash but Khadijah at the police station, beautifully clearing the air? I had nothing against my classmates or my roommates, but I knew that any big city had Khadijahs in it, and I hunted the Khadijahs of New York.

On Friday and Saturday nights, after elaborate preparations, I ventured out alone, to shows at the Cooler, Galapagos, shows at apartments advertised on flyers left at the L Cafe. I listened to the bands, and I sat on a stool with a seltzer and watched people talking. New York was a place to acquire a surface so rich with sophistication that the nutrients in my topsoil would leach down to my core and make me a real rock musician, and if that didn't work, I hoped I could at least construct a shell so complex and subtle and bewitching that people more sure of themselves, people who had the right exterior *and* the right interior, would mistake me as one of their own and take me in, showing me by example how to be like them. In a dusty bookstore that smelled like fried fish and mold, I read a quotation in the front of a paperback: "Fame is the mask that eats the face." A good deal, I thought, if you get the mask right.

Some days, I tired of this creed. I wanted friends and a girlfriend. But it was hard to descend at will from snobbery into the social life of the university. The students I detained after philosophy and art history classes sensed my affectation, my pettiness, my need. I went out to coffee with two of them, and both times, suddenly, in the middle of the conversation, I began to speak about bands or clothing and my voice became louder, lower, more impassioned than when I was speaking about anything else, because these were the subjects that had occupied my thoughts for many months. My mind would go into a palace I had built of loneliness, and no one could follow me in. I would monologue about the way reverb functioned in an Olivia Tremor Control song, or about the varieties of Sonic Youth T-shirts designed in North Carolina by Tannis Root, and when I came out from under my own spell, I could tell from their faces they thought I was a shallow and annoying person.

For hours at a time, I managed to be a shallow person. But in the hours I craved companionship, I could feel that I was softer, younger than I wanted to be. I would have preferred to be shallow. What frightened me most, in these hours, was how much I thought about Khadijah. I hadn't seen or exchanged a word with her in four years. I didn't know where she was. But the fact that I still remembered her, still turned over our moments together and studied them, still summoned to mind her great acts like verses from gospel, made me feel like an inmate clutching a battered photograph. To soothe myself I would put on CDs and look at myself in the mirror until I was distracted by my face, my hair, my body. Master the way you look and speak, I would tell myself, and Khadijah's substitute will find you in the end. Get it right, and you will discover the friends with whom you will form a band.

Of course there were kids who shared my obsessions with music and clothing, slumped in the library, roaming Greenwich Village and Williamsburg. But I was too afraid of saying something wrong during my brief interactions with these strangers, smoking outside of Mondo Kim's, sharing a small, round table at a show, to initiate an ongoing acquaintance. We would look at each other's shoes and T-shirts, comment on the band, and turn away, each of us ashamed of being alone. I was blondish, boyish, striving to dress correctly, too anxious to find the right crowd to leap at the lower rungs, and therefore as common as grass—I saw my replica everywhere.

Winter break of my junior year, I took the F to a show at d.u.m.b.A, an artists' collective in a postindustrial cave with one giant hall painted toothpaste white and closet-like bedrooms with bunk beds off to one side. It was tucked under the Manhattan Bridge, across a lightless, cobblestoned street from a men's shelter. Out on the metal porch I leaned against the wall and smoked Camels in my rehearsed way, without inhaling, until three boys in their early twenties, skinny, long-haired, tramp-like, moving in unison, as if for body heat and safety, shuffled over and begged me for cigarettes. They were three quarters of a band called Shapeshifter, from Los Angeles, touring the Northeast to general indifference in a caravan of two station wagons. They bemoaned the imminent loss of their bass player, Gordon, whom they described as an energetic cigarette bummer and drink-ticket negotiator, and who had given notice that at tour's end he was quitting music to start a CalArts master's program in animation. Nobody asked me a question until Gordon himself strode over, shook my hand, and said, "You aren't a bass player, are you? You have a kind of bass-player look about you. I hope you don't find that insulting."

I was mostly a guitarist then, but I'd picked up bass, when nobody else would, in a high school band that played covers for *Pulp Fiction*–obsessed theater kids to ironically twist to at cast parties. (The cast parties were where I'd gleaned a rudimentary understanding of flirting and, senior year, had my first kisses, first with a superaggressive boy I never saw again, second with a super-drunk, ordinarily supershy girl, who sat in my lap and rested her head on my shoulder until I worked up my nerve and lifted her chin the way I'd seen my father do with Nancy in Gaia Foods.) Something about Gordon, his extensive mustache, his pudginess, his eagerness, his ruddiness, his grin, the way he cocked his head to one side and touched his bald spot, made me want to make him happy. Besides, I was lonely and wanted a band. "Actually, yeah," I said. "I am a bass player, ha."

As the opening act interminably delayed sound check, Gordon led me by the elbow to d.u.m.b.A's nonelevated performance area (d.u.m.b.A had a governing body ambivalent toward the concept of "stage"), hefted his bass guitar from its stand, placed it in my hands, and switched on the amplifier. The waiting audience, a roomful of bespectacled poker faces, turned to face me. The amp warmed up and began to buzz.

I looked at the four thick strings, empty-headed. Gordon slipped back into the crowd. In contrast to his bandmates, he was flush with vigor. I found him impressive. He looked like the alpha, the member of Shapeshifter best able to obtain sex and food, even though he was the bass player, and this represented a stunning inversion of natural law. *Don't leave me here, Gordon,* I thought. The stage felt very empty. The room went very quiet. And then I remembered my father in my room in the period of post-Khadijah, post-divorce-meeting solitude: "Heartbreak Hotel."

You could perform "Heartbreak Hotel," I recalled, with only a bass line and minimal vocal ability. Moreover, it wasn't cool. It was corny, it was old-fashioned. You shouted it. I looked out at the room of indifferent heads. *Dads = hipsters,* I thought. *Hipsters = Dads.* Here were people who, like Dads, didn't like to emote. Maybe, like Dads, they would like it if I could do some emoting for them.

I gave it my all. Halfway through the first chorus somebody turned on a microphone. I hit two wrong notes, on *dwell,* and *heartbreak,* but I had been singing and playing for myself for so long that the spectacle of a crowd unbound something in me. I didn't need to ham up my delivery, as I did in front of the mirror. There was a scratch in the way I sang that didn't need to be exaggerated or monitored. The audience didn't abandon affectation and tap its feet in unison and sing along, as might have happened in a movie, or in a location not New York City. I saw no actual smiling. But some of the kids uncrossed their arms. Some jiggled their left legs, Chihuahua-like.

When I struck the last note, the Dumbans were quiet. A flake of toothpaste white paint drifted down through the bright light. At once, they lifted their chins and clapped. After I put Gordon's bass back on its stand, I made my way off the unstage and lit a cigarette as I weaved through the crowd, and this time I really inhaled, and the nicotine was like little sewing machines under my skin.

Shapeshifter greeted me in its dark corner with four boyish grins. Gordon applauded with real force, real happiness, cleared of guilt. "See?" he said, to the rest of his band. "You're lucky I'm quitting." They closed their mouths and looked at me shyly, the three lanky, slouching Californians. I slouched shyly back. Gordon placed one hand on the back of my neck, set me between singer and drummer, and found a disposable camera in his bag.

"Smile, lads," he said. "Say 'new bass player.'"

It was a story everybody liked. Gordon liked it, I liked it, my new bandmates liked it. That was why it happened: for the story. Granted, I listened to Shapeshifter's demo on a Walkman that night. Granted, I watched Shapeshifter's set. If they had been bad, I wouldn't have packed the next morning. If I had played "Heartbreak Hotel" badly, or tried to play a cool song and been met with derision by the Dumbans, who would have rejected anybody trying too obviously to be cool, Gordon wouldn't have pressed me on his band, and they wouldn't have accepted me. But I didn't pick Shapeshifter out of a hundred bands because I thought their music of all music was the music for me. Shapeshifter didn't pick me out of a hundred bass players because of how I played. I was in the backseat of the rear station wagon, its crevices lined with Camel ash and Subway crumbs, the very next afternoon because we all liked the story of the boy who took the stage and had no fear and got in a car and drove off to California.

I liked how whorish it was, how fast. And when I arrived in Los Angeles, driving the lead wagon west, sun-dazzled, sweating in Gordon's Cat Power T-shirt, the city lived up to a shocking number of clichés regarding whorishness and speed and commerce and art, because so many people, like me, had just arrived and were determined to make it live up to those clichés. I liked how Shapeshifter gave me an instant brotherhood. How, because of the fairy-tale circumstance in which we united, our brotherhood felt fated to be. But most of all, I liked the story because it was non-Dad.

To be specific, regarding its non-Dadness: I was not studying political science for ten years, organizing, parenting, and teaching for another fifteen, only to walk out on my family, in the name of a forsaken creative endeavor, at age forty-five. I was doing what my father should have done when he'd had the chance. I was going to settle myself in the right career path, and secure a wife I could stay married to before I had kids.

And, in L.A., the right career path seemed ready and willing to be claimed. If you're somebody who spent much of your senior year of high school losing your voice trying to make yourself heard above a drummer in a basement, the moment you finally step into an acoustically perfect studio, sit on a hideous leather couch with the ink on a record contract drying in your messenger bag, and listen to an engineer adjust the timbre of your voice as it delivers a harmony line you wrote yourself, through evil-looking black speakers that hang from the ceiling and cost hundreds of thousands of dollars, you are a lucky person. This happened to me at twenty-six, five years into my stay in L.A., when Capitol, flush with Coldplay money, offered us a deal. It was what happened afterward, the moment when the claiming of the career path was supposed to translate into actual cash, that proved problematic.

If advertisers had immediately licensed "This Is Just Wrong," a vaguely suicidal dance anthem on Shapeshifter's 2005 self-titled debut, our label would have kept faith, given us an advance to cut a second record. We would have kept faith in ourselves, and stuck together. But the consultants who advised the major advertising agencies on indie pop discovered us a year later, and by that time we were all sick of near homelessness and malnutrition and not having a job and not being students in order to be available for touring, and our drummer moved to Tucson for divinity school, and Deke, who had always been the heart of the band, our lead singer and our most graceful player, returned to being David, and rediscovered the ashram in Oakland where he'd been raised and taught to sing and play. I was the only one who chose to stay in Los Angeles, unless you counted Gordon, who hadn't had anything to do with us for over five years and was now head animator on a long-running prime-time cartoon. There was no going back for me. I would find some other way to live in the corner of the country opposite Wattsbury, Massachusetts. Spiritually, geographically, non-Dadness, above all, had to prevail.

In 2006 Pepsi's ad agency licensed "This Is Just Wrong" for a foreign-market TV commercial wherein ethnically indeterminate soccer players dribbled in an alley. The chorus went "We're going down, down," but everyone thought we were singing, "We're going downtown," and for over a year, this misconception provided all former members of Shapeshifter with a subsistence living. I paid off my debts with the first payment and used the credential to find work scoring a cable drama pilot called *The Spirits of New Orleans,* in which a white woman stopped a gang war by channeling the ghosts of the gang members whose deaths were being pointlessly avenged. Manufacturing limpid music with acquaintances for television was not as fun as manufacturing undistinguished music with friends whose every rhythmic tic I'd come to know and anticipate. But it was good enough for me. It was sufficiently non-Dad.

I wondered, on Shapeshifter's frigid zigzags through the prairie, odorous homecomings in orange desert light, and later, hunched over a mixing board in Universal City, blades of sun cutting through venetian blinds, what kind of person Khadijah had become. But I never indulged in a Google search. I was determined not to be a sentimental fool. And if I was right about the degree of influence Nancy exerted over her daughter, it was unlikely indeed that Khadijah Silverglate-Dunn lived in Los Angeles.

It seemed almost not to matter, sometimes, because the Khadijah in my imagination remained my confidante and adviser. For all my whorishness in the realm of work, I was puritanical in matters of love and sex. I kept the vow Khadijah and I had signed against the rusting wheel; I never cheated on anyone. All of my six and a half years in Shapeshifter, I moved from one steady girlfriend to another, each relationship lasting three to nine months. I was on tour, for much of this time, sleeping on couches, and when I wasn't, I shared a tiny room with Deke in Koreatown. Because I could have no sustained domestic life with anyone who wasn't a dude in Shapeshifter, my dating pattern was a lush four-week romance followed by a gradual onset of frost once I boarded the two-station-wagon caravan for a slog across North America. If I had cheated, it would have surprised no one. But the bag of cookies bursting from the pocket of my father's quilted barn jacket—the memory was a whip my sense of loyalty wielded to subjugate my disloyal imagination. Whenever I was in danger with a woman not my girlfriend, once in the silver, Bacardi-sponsored tour van of a more famous band, once late at night in the Oregon summer house of a friend who'd just told me about a fight with her mother, the crumbs in the corduroy always saved me, tamed my desire. That and the shock audible in Khadijah's breathing beneath the table in Gaia Foods. And a little Khadijah I kept in my head, asking: Who are you, in the end, anyway? Will you grow into a man? Or ferment into a Dad?

3.

Again, Acceptable

I met Julie Oenervian on a blind date, insofar as it's possible to go on a blind date with a person you've watched on TV at the Laundromat explaining to a wildlife biologist why she should be allowed to craft a Komodo dragon into a hat. For Julie the date really was blind. If she'd had the inclination to Google Shapeshifter, to see what I looked like, she hadn't had the time. I could see her eyes pass over me as they scanned the bistro, in which an angry, talkative couple and a masticating, living-dead couple sat parallel in black wooden booths in the back, and a waiter in an apron stood by a Swiss resort poster from the twenties swaddling silverware in napkins. I was surprised at how tall Julie was, because I'd thought people who worked on camera were short. I stood and introduced myself.

Julie teased off thin green gloves. She looked at our fingers as we shook, avoiding my eyes. I sensed trepidation. I'd been drinking a glass of wine at the bar because I thought this was what people always did when they were waiting at restaurants. She would tell me later that something about my posture as I held the glass to my lips, slumped forward on the barstool, made me look old and bedraggled. It wasn't until we faced each other across the dark, shiny table, with a dim beam of light falling between us, that she found out I had only a year on her. I was twenty-seven then. She was twenty-six. She'd been the host of an animal show on cable television for about six months.

"So you play music? When Gordon was like, 'I have a guy for

you,' which is such a Gordon way of saying it, I was like, 'As long as he's not just someone you think I should date because we're both darkish people.' He said you were a white guy who played white music."

I quaffed the rest of my wine, hoping it made me look haunted. "My band's barely functional anymore. We're just going to be playing in the background of junk food ads from now on, if we're lucky. Fostering childhood obesity is our legacy."

"Well, Gordon says you're indie rock. You should know: I'm not into that. Everybody's like, 'Neutral Milk Hotel. Fuckin' Wilco.' Ich. I like Jennifer Lopez and Destiny's Child." She lowered her chin, issuing this challenge, as if she might head-butt me.

"Which Destiny's Child album do you like the best?"

She hesitated. "I couldn't tell you which one. But in general, I'm more, grab your girls and get out on the dance floor. Hoist a feminine-coded drink. Say 'woo.' Pop R and B is my favorite genre."

"What pop R and B albums do you like?"

She was silent. It occurred to me she didn't actually know any. She was putting on a show to amuse me and/or herself.

Her short, rounded fingers played with each other around the base of her wineglass. "You're laughing at me," she said.

"I was laughing at myself for thinking something dumb," I muttered, shaking my head. Saying it aloud would have been a questionable dating tack. But I couldn't think of anything else to say, so I decided to be honest. "I was thinking, you look like a moon goddess in that silvery dress." I sensed, from the way a muscle in her neck twitched, that I was becoming, to Julie, a person who was too nauseously cheesy to be in the same room with again. I repeated the words, "You look like a moon goddess in that silvery dress" in a bovine, phony-artiste voice. In this way, each playing a caricature of the person we feared the other would view us as, we became slightly vulnerable to each other.

Julie's professional innovation was to be the TV safari guide who responded to animals with comic detachment, rather than the infantile enthusiasm of the industry leader, Steve Irwin. The *Times* had called her "a real former wildlife biology grad student who occasionally speaks like Jon Stewart on the savannah," and the analogy was apt. Julie was nowhere near as famous as Jon Stewart—*Julie vs. Animals* appeared on a science channel—but there was Stewart/Colbert in the gaze she trained on the natural world. ("This tree sloth hasn't moved from his branch for forty-eight hours, and it's like in college, when I dated theater majors who struggled with depression: You can hit him with a frying pan and you still won't be able to make him get up and fight with you.") *Julie vs. Animals* had begun as a serious, if youth-targeted, wildlife program, but since securing her place as a reasonably popular host, Julie had worked in more and more jokes, as if her ambition all along had been to transcend the demimonde of nature shows. This much the Internet had taught me.

"Do you want kids?" she asked. This was fifteen minutes later, as her fork approached the escargot. The snails bubbled in a metal plate that resembled a painter's palette, each creature a pigment in a hole. "I want an infinite number of girls," she continued, "and for them all to stay in my house when they grow up and spend my money."

"I want to adopt two Ethiopians or something," I improvised. I hadn't really thought about it.

We ate steaks and sorbet and drained the bottle, and I paid, pretending I could afford to, and we strolled a block from Vermont Avenue to Hillhurst. She paused before a boutique.

The boutiques here in Los Feliz, east of Hollywood, weren't like the designer-brand flagships on the west side. There, an air of secrecy prevailed, with chrome racks dispersed across concrete floors. The clerks nodded gravely at you, like you were a CIA agent summoned to their hangar to train with new weaponry. This was just a crowded storefront with white wooden floors, and the dress in the window was no extravaganza of Parisian silk. It was high-waisted, white, with red tulips climbing from the hem, hanging close beside a bare-breasted mannequin in a blue and green hippie skirt.

"What do you think of these?" Julie asked. "This is a test. You'll find I'm very into tests."

I was so pleased she'd implied there was a future between us that I was able to persuade myself I had a substantive comment to make.

"I'm absolutely pro this dress," I said. "The tulips say, 'If you water and nurture me, I'll be bright and sweet-smelling.'"

"Acceptable answer. How about the one on the right?"

"It's a little Pre-Raphaelite," I said, digging in my past for a critical vocabulary. "It's, 'I'm that girl on the cover of *Reviving Ophelia*,' but that's cool."

"Again, acceptable."

On the next block of Hillhurst, we passed another midpriced boutique. "How about this one?" she asked.

It was a cerulean dress I intuited you could call a jumper if you wanted to, though I had only a foggy notion of what a jumper was. "It's good," I said. "It would make you look like a hot blue-bird."

She placed a hand on my shoulder, for a moment. "More acceptability! See, there aren't that many kinds of dresses I feel are better suited to my figure than the figure of a really modely girl, but this is one of those kinds. I saw this woman who played Nell in *Endgame* at this Beckett festival in London wearing a dress like this after the show, and she basically looked like a water bug, her whole torso was just a swelling at the end of a bunch of legs. I'm being mean. I'm not mean. I'm working on not talking the way I'm talking right now."

"I wasn't thinking about that," I said. "I was thinking about how you were talking about a Beckett festival."

She looked alarmed. "I was in London and I knew some actors that were in some of the productions there. I would have nor-mally been attending *Legally Blonde: The Musical*."

"You're pretending you like these things you say you like, but you couldn't name a Destiny's Child album. You know that Nell is a character in *Endgame*. I bet you couldn't sing a song from *Legally Blonde: The Musical*. Maybe you could sing a couple bars, but you wouldn't know a whole song. You play this girlie-girl person but really you're a"—I didn't know what phrase to use, and the one I went with embarrassed me—"connoisseur of the arts. I like it, but you're a total actor."

I thought she'd probably stamp her foot and say something to the effect of *What are you talking about, weirdo?* I thought she'd sustain playfulness. Instead, she became serious.

She turned from the boutique window and looked me in the eye. Instead of lowering her brow in challenge, as she had when she'd described her taste in music, she looked into the middle distance.

"I'm a Republican," she said. "I come from a Republican family."

"You voted for Bush?"

She shook her head. "I'm just really conservative in a lot of ways."

"Do you think gay people shouldn't be allowed to get married and abortion should be illegal?"

"I don't think either of those things. I've never actually *voted* for a Republican. But I think there's nothing wrong with somebody like Giuliani. And I really support the death penalty." She was standing with her legs spread slightly farther apart than usual, as if there was a crowd of people behind her she was ready to defend from me, if necessary.

"Hillary Clinton's pro death penalty," I said. "I love Hillary Clinton. She reminds me of a benign stepmom."

"I like Hillary Clinton too," she conceded. Only now did I realize that I had probably been looking as tense as she did. The words "I'm a Republican" had triggered a fight-or-flight instinct. The knowledge that somebody who was even sort of a Republican might kiss me was enchanting and noxious at the same time, cocaine-like.

I had the sense Julie might believe that if your parents were Republican you had to say you were Republican or you were a traitor. It was an ethnicity. Hence the wide-legged, defensive, samurai-like stance. This was a way of thinking easy for me to recognize, because it was my own. My blood-and-soil identity was liberal Democrat. I felt that in declaring her partisanship Julie had confessed she was a spy from a country at war with my own tiny, highly militant, perpetually threatened, essentially Israel-like, generally anti-Israel, nation-state: the Republic of Wattsbury/Cambridge/Burlington/Brooklyn/Eugene/Berkeley/Santa Cruz/Madison/Portland. I had been born one of its citizens. Thinking of myself differently because of a trifle like my views on a government policy was inconceivable. I was ready to slip behind Julie and drag her to one of my bases for questioning.

Spy vs. spy, I thought. I felt suspicion and desire flow between the Republican-not-Republican and me.

"I went to grad school in bio for a little while," said Julie. "Bio's a hippie-kid, jam-band field of inquiry. I know people from places like Wattsbury who've barely ever met anyone conservative. You need to know I'm different from you."

I put my hand in my pocket. It had been on her elbow, and then it had been hovering in the air halfway between us, after she turned to confront me, and gradually slipped back to my side. The date had been pointed kissward. But we'd had a different kind of collision, both more and less intimate than a kiss.

"Sorry." She looked at the boutique window again. "I'm being completely inappropriate. But now you know."

"I think I'm going to go to my car," I said, after a moment, because this felt like the end of the night. Not in an utterly disagreeable way. I felt that what she had said might allow us to be candid. I just couldn't think of what to say next. "I'd like to do this again," I continued. "Is it okay if I call you?"

She nodded and put a hand on her cheek. "I can't believe I gave you a speech about how I'm a Republican."

"I can't believe I gave you a speech about who your true self is, like I'd figured you out."

I put a gun to my head and exhaled as I pulled the trigger. I felt wretchedly lame as soon as I'd done it. But she did the same thing; only after she'd pulled the trigger, she tumbled the gun into a wave—good-bye.

• • •

Our second date was dessert at a bistro on Fountain lit by tiny purple lights embedded in the floor and ceiling. Because of our first date's kisslessness, the second was overwarm, do-or-die. A spotlight shone on each of us.

"Remind me," I said to Julie, when we were trying to get the conversation airborne. "What are your parents' names again?"

"My dad is Samson, my mom is Vanda. He's the Armenian, she's the Persian."

I asked her if they were still together. In Wattsbury or New York or Los Angeles this was a normal follow-up question, but I wasn't sure about Glendale.

"Yup," she said, "still married. I don't remember—are your parents?"

"Absolutely not."

"What was it like for you when they got divorced?"

The arm of a waitress, tattooed with a shy deer in a prospect of flowers, placed a scotch before me and withdrew.

"Formative. I think I'm here, who I am, a bass player, because of it. So good and bad. It was like, before the divorce, when I was fifteen, I was an overachiever, and after, I was an angry teen, musician material."

"Why were you angry?" She was, I noticed, good at questions.

"My dad was not that into me. You know that dating advice book? *He's Just Not That Into You*? It says, you need to stop coming up with reasons why the guy you went on a date with isn't calling you, you need to stop interpreting his behavior, and just accept he's not that smitten? I needed to do what that book says you need to do, just stop trying to read him and come up with elaborate explanations for his behavior, and accept that he didn't want to date me and my sister, as it were." I downed some scotch. The waitress brought us tiramisu. "But also still be able to cobble all the best parts of him together into this dad I carry around with me in mind, that I imagine saying dad-like things to me. Does that make sense?" I drank some more. "I mean, God, sorry. *My dad just wasn't that into me.*" I said it in the pretentious-guy voice that Julie and I had established between us the other night. "I'm a horrible person—I just said 'My dad just wasn't that into me' over tiramisu."

Julie put a finger to her mouth and tapped it against her lips, thinking.

When she eventually replied, she addressed not the joke at the end of my speech but the speech itself. "I don't know what that's like, having a parent who's not that into you. My parents always liked me. I was scared shitless of my mom, but I think it was in a good way. She was this presence that was like a god until I was eighteen. Then I got into Pomona and we became friends."

Her face became solemn, lending both poignancy and absurdity to the cheerfulness of her outfit: a black cardigan with a silver thread, a T-shirt with columns of silver clamshells. "I didn't think about what would go down if I didn't obey her," she continued. "I just knew that I didn't ever want to displease her."

After the tiramisu, I proposed another walk. We went two abreast down the side streets south of Santa Monica Boulevard. In her heels, she was almost my height. Her body was a field-hockey player's, broad-shouldered, for a girl. But she'd been a science nerd, inept at soccer, she said, with a thatch of hair she hadn't yet learned to verticalize. It now fell Pocahontas-like down her back.

"My band was more familial than my biological family," I said. "In a family-family, the parents can get divorced, everyone can stop caring overly much about everyone else, it can go . . ." I made my hands into birds, fluttering away from each other and floating on different sides of my head. "But in a band, you're all each other's livelihood. You have to have your drummer. You have to have your singer. It's like medieval Greenland or something, where if you don't have the one person who herds the sheep, and the other who churns the butter, and the other who milks the oxen, the whole economic animal keels over. A band's better than a family."

"But my family's like that," she said. "Like the band, like the medieval family. My parents aren't from this country originally. They came here from really different places and met each other and had to start their careers over and they had me right away and neither of them could have survived without the other. And so much of it was, 'We can have a kid who can do good in ways she wouldn't be able to in Iran or Soviet Armenia.' They needed me to be doing well to feel good about their lives. We needed each other." The self-professed hoister of feminine-coded drinks was gone. Her family was in a keep she protected from frivolity. "I mean," she said, "also, no offense or anything, but didn't your band break up?"

"I guess it did," I said. "So that's why it's kind of a quandary, what I'm supposed to be doing now."

"That doesn't change what you were saying about families, though. That sounds bad. I'd heard stories of superwhite families being like how you just said your family was, and I didn't believe them."

I was silent for a while. I knew this silence might make it seem like I was offended, but I had been moved by what she said. I also had the sense that now was the time to kiss her. I was terrified.

My Volvo had once been half of Shapeshifter's caravan. Its guts were even leakier than they'd been eight years ago, but I kept it clean. It was parked at the corner of Romaine and Seward, nearby, and I proposed I give her a ride in it to her car. In the Volvo, I thought, with music, that's when the kiss will feel right.

The locks had stopped working two years ago, so I grabbed the passenger-side door and opened it, with great casualness, for Julie. When I saw what was inside, I shouted and leapt back.

Sprawled across the backseat was a dozing androgyne. Usually, I found the presence of homeless drug users sad but invigorating. I fraternized with people who made their addictive behaviors look like progressive lifestyle choices, so I felt there was much to be said for people who reminded me that debauchery presaged ruin. But I was unhappy to find a cautionary tale sleeping in my vehicle. The still, lanky person, his or her face wrapped in rank blond hair, kicked to life before me.

"Hi," I said.

"Cut you," said the recumbent person.

"How are you doing tonight?"

"All my friends are coming," he/she warned. "Back up." The voice was approximately masculine now. The feet were sockless, in Brand X white canvas sneakers that could have been worn by a woman or a man.

"If you just need to sleep for a while, tell me," I said. "We'll find another way to get ourselves home—if you're in a bad situation and you need to stay here. But if you have another place to stay, maybe you should stay there instead."

"My car now." The guest snuffled contentedly. The voice was even lower, more mannish.

There was a tap on my shoulder. "Excuse me," said Julie. She cleared her throat behind me. I moved aside.

She popped her telegenic head into the threshold of the passenger seat. Her face was only a few feet from the slothful animal. "You can't stay here," she said. "You have to move."

There was a pause. "Who is this?" the person replied. I was less inclined to believe it was a man now; the needle ticked back toward genderlessness.

"My name is Julie. This isn't your car. If you don't get out of it, then we have to call the police to get you out. That means it's not safe for you to be in here, because if the cops put you in jail, you might not be safe."

"That is another way of looking at it." The voice was awake now, and verging into feminine territory.

"You need a hand?" Julie asked the person. "We're going to open the door."

"No trouble" went the more or less ladylike reply. The lanky body flipped over. The door opened, and it climbed out, never looking at us, never showing its face. It wrapped its arms over its chest and stalked off into the dark. In the glow of the generators, I could just discern the outlines of the thick blond hair, weighted with sweat and grime but abundant, an asset, hair meant to be viewed under lights.

In the recaptured Volvo, I drove Julie to her car. We were quiet. I thought I could detect the smell of my gym clothes wafting from my South By Southwest tote bag in the backseat. But it might have been a trace of the androgyne's sweat.

"You handled that well," I said, calming down. My tone was flat, because I wasn't saying what I meant. What I meant was: I know I was a pushover, please forgive me, I'll be more assertive next time. I had passed the window-shopping tests, but this test I had failed.

"No," she said, with equal flatness. "You handled it beautifully."

Shaky ground for kissing. Next time, I thought. But I was losing her; I could see life drain from her face.

I asked if I could call her again.

"Sure," she said. "Good night." She got out of the decrepit station wagon and slid into her white Volkswagen. As I pulled away, her large, beautiful head was lit by the candle-size glow of her phone.

I waited until I was on the side streets of Echo Park, my neighborhood, no longer a threat to other freeway drivers, to call Gordon and disclose my error.

"I fucked up, dude," I said.

"How so?" He sounded unsurprised.

"I should have been bringing things to a warm, fun place. But then I started making her talk about her family. And I wouldn't throw this homeless guy, or woman, out of my car. It was like, That one guy, the one you had a satisfactory first date with? Turns out, that guy was your school psychologist, disguised as a bass player."

"Hang up," said Gordon.

"I'm pissing you off too? I'm just an offensive person. Like, to everyone. I'm getting really depressed."

"Hang up and wait twenty seconds."

I hung up. I parked. I paced my hillside street. The room I rented was in a slowly imploding yellow house on a summit in the Echo Park hills, an old structure, for L.A., built in the twenties. It was owned and occupied by a semideaf hippie aunt of Deke's. I had access to the piano in the living room, and could play guitar as loud as I wanted, which, admittedly, was not very loud. The views of Chavez Ravine from the back porch were magnificent; on winter days, distant palms were green puffs suspended in a milk shake sky, their trunks sequestered by fog. Sometimes the prospect of going into my room and looking at this view consoled me, but just now my room humiliated me with its cheapness.

"One forwarded voice mail from Gordon," the screen of my cell phone read.

"Gordon, you walleyed cunt, pick up your phone." It was Julie's voice. "Do you think I have time for you to be setting me up on dates with fucking faggots? He didn't kiss me. He had me walk with him eight miles in the cold in my heels and then I threw this homeless guy out of his car and he stopped even looking at me like he was thinking about kissing me. He didn't kiss me. It was date number two, and nothing. You think I want to have a nice chat with a gay man on my Thursday night? Am I a sexual being to you anymore, now that I'm no longer twenty-three and asking you for advice about agents? Call me back."

I had a text from Gordon. "Her address is 257 glynnis off labrea."

I pulled a 180 in the Volvo, gunning back to the 101, brakes squealing, right-rear wheel clipping a neighbor's lawn.

Before I could change my mind, I strode up the walk of 257 Glynnis, noting the small snail problem at my feet. A white Spanish fountain burbled softly at my right. I registered the unassuming stucco niceness of the extensive one-story house, and rang the bell.

Peeking through one of the long, thin rectangular windows bracketing the front door, I saw a succession of lights come on, starting in a far-off hallway and moving through a living room toward the foyer. I pulled away from the window and stood directly in front of the door.

Julie opened the door three inches. Her hair, eyes, and nose peeked from behind. She took me in and finally threw the door open wide, blinking rapidly.

"I'm sorry," I said. "I wanted to kiss you, but I got nervous."

She was wearing a Wilco T-shirt and red pajama pants with candy canes on them.

"That thing I said about white families," she said. "It was offensive."

I shook my head. "It's just true."

I kissed her. We stood with the door open, in the threshold. We patted each other's hair. I felt that there was a similar power growing in each of us; we had each demonstrated an ability to calm the other's fear.

"You look like the shy deer from the waitress's tattoo," she said, when we ended the kiss.

Shy deer. This was the name we used for each other, in the years that followed, when one of us was nervous about a performance of some kind, or paranoid about a person we thought hated us, or felt an everyday dread of being sweaty and eager, being seen as a person who drinks too much wine and pushes jokes.

"Come inside," she said.

We kissed frenetically on the couch and talked about the androgyne. "You were so much cooler than me about it," she said. "I was a douche bag and you were a lady. You were like Mother Teresa."

"I was a pussy and you were the firm but reasonable one," I said. "You were Atticus Finch."

The sun went down over the fountain, whose splashing was barely audible from the bedroom, and sounded like rain. The security system issued a copacetic beep.

"Opposites attract," she murmured.

"I like your house," I told her. I was half lying down, half seated, propped on one of the couch's four throw cushions. She was curled in my arms. She pinched my ear as I took in the living room. A chrome and glass coffee table with Swedish modern lines shimmered on a faded crimson rug. A grandfather clock ticked beside a chart of Darwin's voyages. On a dark bureau stood six photographs of parents and extended family. In the dim light, I could see only the glint of Oenervian smiles and irises.

"It feels like a home," I said.

2007

1.

Tom, Myra, Julie 2

One night Julie and I got smashed at Authentic Korean and told Gordon and his wife, Cora, we were engaged. We'd made the decision a week ago. We were going to test marriage, Julie explained to them, like a new pharmaceutical, for side effects like weight gain and sexual dysfunction, and if everything was under control after three or four years, we were going to have three children. We'd been dating nineteen months.

We made a disclosure that both shamed and delighted us: For the past six of those months, we'd been speculating about what our children would be like. We'd invented elaborate personalities for all three, given them names. As we described them, Gordon produced a black pen from the pouch of his yellow hoodie. "You guys are awesome," he said, and began to draw, dedicating one paper napkin to each child. An animator, he knew what he was doing, and it was hard not to believe in what he drew. It might have been the first grave error of the evening, letting Gordon draw our kids. It's a principle from Islam, and Protestantism: There are some beings you just don't make images of.

There was Tom, our eldest, whom we imagined Julie birthing in 2011. He looked ten. He stood beside a chemistry set consisting of a Bunsen burner and a single flaming tube. His sweater was V-necked, his mouth a small, vaguely anus-like vertical line. The second napkin was devoted to Myra, our middle child. She wore a leotard and held a parasol. In lieu of a burner, she came with a swan. On the third napkin was Julie 2, named for her mother, but a musician, like me. She sat in a cubical playpen, playing the cello.

With real children, once they're born, you love them even if they were a bad idea. With these children, it was like that too; we couldn't help but love them once they'd been permitted to exist. I pounded Gordon on the shoulder. Julie yanked off his baseball cap and threw it at his head. These were gestures of gratitude. We stood behind him, looking at our offspring spread on the table by the empty glasses. Julie folded them and slipped them in her purple bag.

An hour later, we stood side by side in our bedroom and taped the triptych to the pale green wall. It would have been embarrassing to tape the napkins to the fridge, as if we were showing off, but we decided we liked them here, where no one could look at them but us. Beneath the three new members of our family, we kissed.

Then we did something strange: We linked hands and speed-walked to the bathroom. We'd never had sex in the bathroom before. But we both knew that we didn't want to do it in front of the kids, where the eyes on the napkins could see us. It was shocking to me, and I think to Julie too, how real to us the children were.

Over the course of a year and a half, Julie and I had kept performing for each other, but the performances had become play. Being onstage or on camera, making strangers like watching us better than they liked watching other people, this was the joy we'd spent much of life pursuing. But now we could perform for each other without worrying if the performance was original or distinguished. A day came on which I realized, and confirmed, and reconfirmed, that my moments of greatest happiness in the past twelve hours had been: when we'd mixed a whey shake in the early morning before going to the gym and spat it into the kitchen sink, pretending to vomit; and after dinner, when she'd let me smell a minor dreadlock that had formed unbidden in her hair.

One weekend not much later, at a farm stand in Oxnard, a stiff Pacific wind had lifted her hair into a bower over her head, and she'd talked about how badly she wanted to be a different kind of celebrity from the kind she was. She wanted to be somebody who said things that were made up, to leave behind the guile-less world of animal documentarians, and debut in the shrewder society of scripted entertainment. Steve Irwin had been killed by a stingray, but she didn't want his throne. The comic remove from which she approached nature was all part of a five-year plan: build a following, build ratings; be credited with the cross-over appeal of *Julie vs. Animals;* quietly go on auditions; wait for the right offer; leave *Animals* for a drama series. I could hear both the exhilaration and the fear of failure in her voice, above the wind.

I liked her ambition. But I didn't want to be taken care of by a rich person. It was the confession itself that crowned the romance for me, the dropping of her guard. A week later, I woke her up in the middle of the night and proposed, and she cried, and then she wore a ring I'd borrowed money to buy.

After we had sex on the bathroom floor, Julie removed the nap-kins from the bedroom wall, so that, in the future, we would be able to have sex in bed, and placed them high on the bathroom mirror, reinforcing the new arrangement with extra tape. Then we had to get ready to go to a party. The party was being hosted by the new owner of the science channel that broadcast *Julie vs. Animals.*

Ratings had lately been adequate but unspectacular. The very notion of *Julie vs. Animals* being canceled, after two seasons, was too dark for us to discuss. Julie had been making payments on this house for only twenty months, and I still hadn't managed to find a steady, non-Shapeshifter source of income. It came down to this: Our mission, for the evening, was to charm Jeremy, the science channel's new owner.

We were still drunk from Authentic Korean, but we tried to refresh ourselves by splashing cold water on our faces. We flicked water at each other, Julie starting it, I retaliating, to prove, I think, that we were fun people, that despite the weirdness of our recent behavior, we were not becoming one of those cute but disconcerting couples that live, like schizophrenic individuals, in their own tiny worlds with their own points of reference, loyal to their own inscrutable codes. That we were not only the awkward, self-conscious, overly performative ex-dweebs we knew ourselves to be, but also enchanters.

The master bathroom of Julie's house—I still thought of it as Julie's house—had two sinks, side by side. We could wash our faces and brush our teeth at the same time and console each other about how we looked. We called the sinks the battle stations, because of the *Star Trek/Battlestar Galactica* feeling we derived from speaking to each other while standing parallel. And tonight's party would be a scene of battle. In addition to the new owner, there would be people who, in the darkest sanctums of our souls, we considered cool. These people could not be allowed to suspect we thought about them in bathrooms.

In the wide mirror, beneath our imaginary kids, I could see excitement and dread in our reflections. I saw a twenty-eight-year-old and a twenty-nine-year-old assessing the persistence of youth's afterglow in their faces. I saw a couple calculating its worth in the eyes of the world.

I could not say this, so I said: "My cheeks look fat tonight. I feel like when God designed me, he was like, 'I'll concentrate fat in his face.' I feel like that's what He does with Jews in general, to make them look like giant babies, so you don't want to kill them."

"You look skinny," said Julie. "If you have cheeks it means you won't look like a skull person when you're old." She tamped her lipstick on a yellow Post-it that bore her notes from an interview with a game warden.

"And it's not just Jews people hate," she continued. "One of my great-great-uncles was slaughtered by the Turks. We're a two-genocide couple."

"Your boobs look really beautiful," I said.

"Really?"

"They're like these magical glowing orbs."

"You know what's magic?" She sat on the toilet and lifted her silver smock above her belly. "My fat can sing Louis Armstrong songs." She squeezed two folds of stomach fat into a mouth and made it move while she sang "What a Wonderful World."

"I can do that too," I said.

"That's absurd." She shook her head. "Your fat can't sing Armstrong."

"No, but it can sing James Taylor." If her stomach fat, dark, hairless, was Louis Armstrong's mouth when squeezed into motion, my stomach fat, pale, covered in short black hairs, was James Taylor's mouth. I made my fat sing "Carolina in My Mind."

Julie reached for her laptop, which sat on the floor by the toilet. Googling each other before we went out was one of our gearing-up-for-battle rituals. If people were going to look us up when they got home, we wanted to know what they'd see. We wanted to know who, outside our two-person world, we actually were.

Julie typed and waited for the screen to load. "I'm sorry, sweetie. That fucktard article about you is still at the top." She spoke mournfully, pronouncing *fucktard* with gentleness, as if mindful of the French suffix.

The feature on the decline and breakup of Shapeshifter, published last week on the most respectable music-review site in America, in which I said things that made me sound like a commerce-minded, maniacal whore, which, compared to my former bandmates, I was, had become a widely read, blogged-about fable. The story it told was that even though Shapeshifter had possessed the winning combination of a cynical, hit-obsessed bass player (myself); a pure-hearted singer with a choirboy voice; and a surefire, radio-friendly anthem written chiefly by the singer but partly by the avaricious bassist, we had been indifferently marketed, and our sales had been derailed by shifting radio-promotion laws and the growth of online piracy. It concluded we were victims of the industry.

It was nice of the reporter not to mention that we were also victims of being kind of shitty. Critics didn't so much hate us as find themselves incapable of caring about us enough to experience an invigorating hatred. We were, we gradually learned, 6.6 out of 10, *hooky new-wave, post-Arcade-Fire decency with a vein of California somnolence, passable post-punk-post-dance with a beat you can nod to, not unhappily.*

"Does mine still start with the Peabodys video?" Julie passed me the laptop.

The Peabody Awards ceremony footage in which she tripped on the hem of her scarlet gown and toppled into a nest of gift bags—this video, after twenty-nine *Julie vs. Animals* episodes, remained at the top of the screen. I nodded and stroked her head.

We were quiet for a moment as she smoothed her hair. I peed. "We're both horse-fucked," I sang in James Taylor's voice. She extended the melody in Louis Armstrong's: "Horse-fucked to death."

Side by side, we washed our hands. "You're perfect," she said. "You're all I want."

"You're my dream-girl princess," I said. Julie touched the napkins on the way out of the bathroom. I did this too. We were like teenage football players thwacking the insignia of a school, painted on a wall, on the way out of the locker room and onto the field. We went out, to charm the new owner of the science channel for the sake of our future children, to fight for something greater than ourselves.

2.

I Try Not to Think of Anyone in Terms of Categories Like That

To get to the party, Julie and I had to walk through a decorative, glowing white tube set up on a lawn. I decided the tube was not intentionally designed to evoke the white tunnel people see when they're close to death. Piped-in contemporary R & B, with its throbbing, celebratory, watery message of *enter me,* suggested the tube was intended to be more like a ghostly vagina. But the tube was everything you'd expect from a passage to the afterlife. It led to a glowing place just out of sight, and was sewn of fabric that vibrated dreamily as you walked, translucent enough that if you stared through it hard you could see the contours of the hills rendered off-white on white.

The party was in a hillside subdivision near Laurel Canyon called Mt. Olympus. The houses here had porches with Ionic columns and triangular pediments. Being almost broke, I felt out of place in a setting so explicitly divine, but, then, I found many things unsettling that other people didn't. I'd spent almost seven years in a band; I heard things through a veil. Tinnitus was like the fabric of the white death tube, a translucent material that made everything softer and eerier than it actually was.

We emerged from the tube into the glare of a spotlight erected beside the house, and when our eyes adjusted we found ourselves observed by a tiger. It paced a black cage set on the illuminated grass. A tiger attendant nodded to us as we passed, his hands clasped in front of his belly. He was a tall, strong-looking man who might have been an effective bouncer with humans, but it was unclear what powers he might exercise upon his charge. He told Julie how brave she was on television, approaching wild animals that were *un*caged, and studied my face to see if he recognized me. The predator rose on its haunches, as if it was going to apply its jaws to the bars, and ultimately to us. But it lay back down and licked its white forelegs instead.

We passed into the house itself, its dimmered kitchen, where we saw the mark: Jeremy, the science channel's owner. Julie caught him by the arm, and he planted a kiss on her cheek, delighted, before he remembered himself and composed a smile of steely command. A forty-year-old Silicon Valley eminence, Jeremy had purchased the channel four months ago, changed its name from The Zoo Channel to Tusk, shifted his primary residence from Palo Alto to the Holmby Hills, and explained in the trade papers that he hoped to improve the science literacy of the average American young person. He wore a somber, plum-colored suit; it was late October. As Julie and Jeremy lay hands on each other's shoulders, Julie glanced out the window toward four nearly nude women, who floated like corpses in a man-made cove. Above them, heat lamps glowed like magic toadstools. I added up the tiger and the unseasonably bathing-suited women and understood: Jeremy wanted the world to know he was no longer a computer person but a Los Angeles person. Julie was betting that zoological programming could be a springboard to Hollywood-Hollywood; so, I decided, was Jeremy.

"Did you hire whores?" Julie asked him. She pointed a thumb at the floating women. "Seriously, is that what they are?"

With artisanal care, Jeremy pushed back his long chestnut tresses, unveiling his ears. "I try not to think of anyone in terms of categories like that," he said.

Julie took me by the hand and led me outside to the main corpus of the party. In the center of the lawn, the guests spoke with their faces close together, but in their cove the prostitutes floated in isolation, avoiding each other's eyes. I felt a warm beam of empathy connect me to them. You are my sisters, I thought. I am an escort, like you, something trucked in here for the fun of bringing the outside (the world of vulgarity and failure) into the inside (this party) like a Christmas tree. The tiger stared at the translucent death vagina. Nobody appeared to be interested in feeding the big cat, or giving it water. We must have made it hungry, we slow-moving, unarmed meals.

After Julie was ensconced in a conversation with people I didn't know, I sat on a white rhombus and thought about fetching the tiger an hors d'oeuvre, tossing it through the bars. Something with ham in it, or fish. But the tiger guard was still there, and preventing people from feeding or freeing his prisoner was his only conceivable job.

I was midsulk when Gordon and I discovered each other. He waved to me from the bar and floated out of the crowd, bearing down on me with two large drinks.

"You guys didn't tell me you were coming here," he chided. "But it's a sweet coincidence. Now, don't get mad at me for saying this: I brought Todd Rosenberg as my date, because Cora's too pregnant-sick to go to a party, and, look, I'm sorry, but it turns out Todd Rosenberg hates you."

I gulped my drink, which was reddish, a pomegranate-infused vodka. There was a potential reason, I reflected: Todd Rosenberg might have been the one person at the party who had less money than I did. Todd made music in which microphones were dragged slowly through sand. What could he live on?

"Todd Rosenberg's prestigious." I chewed an ice cube. "I feel like prestigious people always hate me. But how would you actually know he hates me?"

"He pointed at you and said, 'Don't you hate Josh Paquette?'"

"He asked us to contribute a track to a compilation that was going to use all its proceeds to stop some intertribal war over water," I explained to Gordon, "and we forgot to get back to him. Is that was this is about?"

I spied Todd now, communing with the tiger from the edge of the throng. I took in his soft, white, high-reaching hair, his height—he must have been six three—his wrinkled black suit, his tan, his predatory dark eyes. He turned and stared at Gordon and me. We smiled and waved. His face registered surprise for a moment before he smiled and waved back.

"It sounded to me," said Gordon, stroking his mustache, touching his bald spot, "like pure jealousy. He told me he saw his fiancée reading that article about Shapeshifter. Apparently, she said she used to know you in high school."

Todd approached. He flicked the red contents of his drink—it looked like the same brand-sponsored pomegranate vodka we were drinking—on the grass as he approached.

"Hey, dudes," he said, with hatred. "Do you *like* these drinks?"

"Yes," I said, and drained the last of mine.

Gordon looked back and forth between me and Todd. After an infinitesimal hesitation, he finished his pomegranate vodka too.

"It's fucked up what they did to that tiger," said Todd.

I had an interesting desire to make him hit me. If he despised me, I wanted him to be demonstrative. "But admit it," I said. "Also awesome."

Julie joined us then, trailed by a man so clearly European I tried to think of nonstupid things to talk about in front of him. He wore sky blue overalls, an orange scarf, and a green cap with its brim flipped up.

"This guy's from Italy," Julie whispered in my ear, "and dressed almost exactly like Super Luigi."

"Where are you from?" he called after Julie, pursuing her into our midst.

"Here," she said. "Or, Glendale."

"But what is your ancestry?"

"A mix," said Julie. "Mystery meat."

"You look like one of these beautiful Jewish girls from Los Angeles," he said. "I like Jewish girls."

Julie wasn't Jewish, of course. I watched her react; she placed her hands on her hips, as if confronting a gorilla. Especially when she straightened herself to her full height, her eyes often appeared angry at first glance, allowing for a dramatic softening interesting to behold on screen. I watched them undergo this transformation now. She could forgive this sorry creature. She didn't demand any kind of response from me, and there was no practical need to defend anyone. The Italian was very drunk, and pretty small. But I felt it would be an embarrassment to all of us if I didn't comment.

"That's enough, okay?" I said to the Italian. I didn't want to hurt him; the eagerness of his face, the terrible hope in his white teeth, almost made me want to protect him.

He nodded sadly to Julie. "Your Jewish boy."

"Hey, man," said Todd, my erstwhile nemesis, to the Italian. "Are you saying some shit about Jewish people?" Todd's hands hung loose at his sides. "Because that isn't funny."

The single most common subject of jokes between myself and my friends, I couldn't help but remember, was our shared Jewishness and half-Jewishness. But I had to escalate hostilities against the Italian as quickly as Todd, or Todd would look like he was braver than I was.

"Listen to me," I said to the Italian, careful to speak exactly as loudly as Todd had. We were operating on the assumption that a language barrier could be transcended through ferocity of inflection. "Why would you want to start talking about Jews? I don't approve of that." I had never accused anyone of anti-Semitism before. It turned out to be exciting.

"I'm not prejudiced," moaned our enemy, a final *cri de guerre*. He threw up his hands, twisting back into the crowd.

"Together, you defeated that small, childlike man," said Julie. "Nice teamwork, guys."

I felt bad for the Italian. But it turned out that a shared experience of ethnic persecution was a way to bond with somebody who hated you. Todd Rosenberg and I got to talking. We did share experiences we could plausibly link to Jewishness. We'd both taken Russian in high school; we both had mothers who'd persuaded us as teenagers that we had visceral and neurological disorders it later became clear we did not have. He told me he'd resorted to writing reviews for alternative weeklies in order to fund his semiambient music without working full-time in a savory pie shop, and we wandered the house, complaining about the lot of musicians and leaving Julie and Gordon to discuss gentile matters. After we had recited Russian poetry to each other on the balcony, drinking the scarlet vodka, I felt great closeness pulse between us.

"I'm like the whores, and you're like the tiger," I explained to Todd. "That's why we were effective back there. Good cop, bad cop. I was like, Relax, we're trying to talk to you, and then you surged out of the darkness, and you were, *roar,* we hate you, you sick fuck."

He snorted and looked to the side. "A tiger," he said.

"But you are. Even like what just happened now. I was kind of kissing your ass. Like a whore. And you were like, I care not for your flattery. Fucking tiger."

He bent to one side and tagged my shoulder with a soft punch. "You used to hang out in Brooklyn, way back, right?"

"I went to your show at that loft on North Tenth and Kent with that furnace that if the duct tape came off would have killed everyone."

"Nineteen ninety-eight," he said. "I was nineteen years old."

"Me too. Good times, right?" That in these times we had both been wearing overly elaborate outfits, that we had both failed, in the intervening years, to worm into the historically significant Williamsburg cliques organized around the Yeah Yeah Yeahs, DFA, TV on the Radio, the Secret Machines, this we did not say. We swished the slush that remained of the ice in our glasses. "Speaking of being a teenager," I said, "who are you engaged to who knew me in high school?" I belched, to show I didn't care he'd said he hated me. "I didn't even know anyone from Wattsbury was out here."

He gazed at the stars, down the slopes of canyons, south into the city. "We're doing long-distance," he said. "When I moved out here, getting engaged was part of the deal. Showing we were serious. And I am serious. I fucking love her, man." He looked at me searchingly, for extra confirmation we were cool with each other. "Did you know a white Khadijah in Wattsbury?"

I hadn't had a cigarette all night, but I lit one now. Nausea flailed through my stomach on the fourth drag. With my hand on my chin, I joined Todd in looking at the stars, and the much brighter windows across the canyon.

"She said you guys had a 'weird friendship.'"

It would have been helpful to have a sharp instrument at hand, with which to discreetly stab my own leg, and thereby prevent myself from sighing. "'Weird friendship' doesn't entail boning," I said. And then: "You have nothing to worry about. I'm engaged too. Julie and I are getting married in June."

The way my eyes watered and I was suddenly cold, this was the past tormenting me. These were symptoms you ignored. Being engaged granted you freedom to ignore them.

"Hey," said Todd, pointing to the front lawn, where a rectangle of the grass lay flat. "The tiger's gone." His tone took on drunken mournfulness. "Why'd they take the tiger away?"

"Maybe they're giving him a break to take a dump, man."

"They'd better be. And a drink of water. I never saw them give that tiger one drink of water. Maybe they don't want it pissing in their little gilded cage, the fucktards." It was the second time in the course of the evening that somebody had said *fucktard*. I thought of how beautifully the word had formed in Julie's mouth. Where was she? My wistful reaction to the name of an old crush from high school made me feel I had betrayed Julie, in a small way. I wanted to be near her. I needed an excuse to end the male bonding and track her down.

"I have to take a dump myself," I said to Todd. He thumped me on the back, our bond solidified, and I went in search of my fiancée.

I meandered through the house, dark save for the spotlight, which cast white domes on the walls. Soon I was in a neo-Victorian living room. Realistic paintings of rappers hung from the walls, lit from below. There was elaborate lace on the arms of a purple and green sofa. I heard a woman's voice, from behind a closed door. It was Julie, speaking loudly enough for me to hear, but not loudly enough for me to make out her words.

There was something about the conversational music I didn't like. Julie was speaking in a low, deliberate tone, blending restraint with amusement, coy. Whomever she flirted with remained inaudible.

This is my fiancée, I thought. I'm entitled to come in. I knocked softly, three times. Julie continued speaking. The nice thing to do, I supposed, was to knock louder. I turned the knob and, in what I hoped was a casual, unhurried manner, pushed on the door.

The first thing I saw was the source of Julie's voice: a flat-screen television, fixed to a wall, turned up loud. It was tuned to Tusk, a *Julie vs. Animals* episode about crows, originally aired last year. The second thing I saw was Jeremy, Tusk's new Silicon Valley–bred owner, kneeling on a queen-size bed, his plum-colored suit discarded, his stallion hair wild. He straddled a woman who was not one of the women who had been floating in the pool; there were two piles of clothes on the floor, one the plum-colored suit, the other what appeared to be gray pants and a jacket, meaning she had discarded a complete outfit rather than a bathing suit. They were in missionary position, her back arched, his back hunched. His belly hung, her toes curled. He was struggling to force his hesitant penis into a condom, but it was soft. The third thing I saw was the tiger, still crammed in a cage. It was tucked into a corner of the room on the far side of the television. It stared into space with Olympian indifference. It was as if the humans on the bed weren't even there.

"Oh my lord," yelled Jeremy, so shocked at my appearance, I surmised, that he forgot to talk like the Hollywood-executive characters in movies and use profanity. It had been only a second I'd been tarrying in the doorway, but he might have thought I'd been watching for minutes. He put his fist in his mouth. The woman screamed and sat up.

I apologized. As I shut the door, I said, "I was just looking for the bathroom, so."

In the Victorian living room, I spun 180 degrees. I walked very fast. Out of the house, down the lawn, from one circle of conversations to another, never speaking. Finally, I made for the hedge and, hiding my face from the partygoers, threw up. I wiped the vomit from my face and wandered. I didn't see Julie anywhere.

I hadn't been able to see Jeremy's face well, because of his hair. But I understood the drama he was staging: Look, woman, upon this cable channel that is mine. He'd put his star on the TV and had the tiger brought in to show what he could have done. He'd told a story about who he was. The story was not really for the woman (she was part of the story) but for himself. And the self responded. The soft dick was the self saying, I don't believe you.

I want to see my wife, I thought, and corrected myself: fiancée. Instead I saw Todd, squinting at me from the bar. He homed in on me and took hold of my arm.

"What's wrong?" he asked. "You look like a ghoul."

I plopped down on the grass. I told him what I'd seen, and he put a hand to his brow, and said, "Oh fuck," and gave me cinnamon gum for my breath.

"That's a pig," observed Todd. He took a pen from his jeans, and a white notebook from his jacket.

"True."

"This is an article." Todd paced, never touching pen to notebook. "Industry people abusing animals the way they abuse interns. What you just gave me is all I need. That plus some background quotes, some animal rights people, an anonymous animal handler who's seen some shit. It's a potential *feature*. I mean, somebody had to finagle the tiger to the bedroom, right? Who's the tiger finagler? We're going to do to that douche bag what he did to the tiger. I mean, it might be illegal. Can you put an animal-show pig in jail for abusing an animal? Maybe you potentially can."

I saw Julie. A young red-haired woman from Tusk's sustainability division was walking her out of the garden, speaking rapidly. People grew manic around Julie sometimes, kept her in conversations. Julie was rubbing her arms. A native Southern Californian, she became cold when it became "cold." I wanted to tell her what I'd seen while we ate crackers in our warm bed.

To the tiger, I envisioned myself saying to Julie, once we were back at our battle stations, washing our faces, they would have looked like a two-headed monster. They would look to the tiger like this creature with two enraged faces, four active arms, the bottom face upside down.

I realized, as I watched Julie among her colleagues, that if Todd wrote an article in which Jeremy was described using the tiger as a captive audience, Jeremy would know I'd divulged what I'd seen. Jeremy knew I was Julie's fiancé; Jeremy would not like Julie, would regard her as an enemy and a threat. Even if the article was never published, even if it was never written, even if all that happened was that Todd called him and asked him to confirm or deny what his anonymous source had said.

Our job here was to secure the future of *Julie vs. Animals,* to endear ourselves to Jeremy. Not to fuck with him.

"Leave Jeremy alone," I said to Todd. "You can't write it."

"You'll be completely left out of it. You can blame it on me." Todd pressed his notebook to his heart with his fingers spread. "I'll tell him I promised you not to utter a word to anyone and I just broke my promise. I'll be the asshole."

"If you do it," I said, "I'll burn your house down." I looked at him until I felt sure he'd understood. We knew the same collection of people who ran independent labels and studios out of homes and low-end real estate in the Valley, and conducted business with them, such as it was. If Todd wrote the article, no matter how worthy, I would tell them he was a thief and a liar.

Todd closed his eyes. He picked up a beer can that was lying on the ground and threw it at the house. It tapped the wall and fell to the grass. He needs the money, I thought. I knew what it was like, how it made you perform your brokenness by throwing things.

But what could I do? Being in love, I thought, is being half a two-headed monster. There's a reason a creature with two heads is horrifying. You can take Big Bird, and give Big Bird two heads, and Big Bird's a raptor from the abyss, a nightmare. It's not pretty, two brains fused into one thing. Sometimes you get to be the self you've always been, but to be loyal to someone you must be willing to stop being the rebel you used to be. You give up being always the truth teller, smashing windows.

That was the difference between being in love and being young together, the way Khadijah and I had been young together, thirteen years ago. I'd thought maybe the recent change in my life was that I was with someone people recognized from TV, but now I knew it was that I had never been in love before, in this way. It was clear to me now that I could see the ugly side of it.

Todd sat down beside me on the grass again. "I'm engaged too," he said. "I would be the same way in your position."

I tried to wave to Julie, but she was mired in a dialogue with two gray-haired men in blinding white blazers. Todd threw an arm around my shoulder.

"Have dinner with us," he said. "You and Julie, me and Khadijah. Deej'll be here the weekend after next. If you and Julie could come, she'd be tripping out. One blast from the past, one person from TV."

I had doubts, grave ones, about arranging a reunion between Khadijah and myself. I looked Todd squarely in the eye and told him I would be stoked for it.

He asked me if "Deej" and I had stayed in touch.

"My dad cheated with her mom. Did she tell you that?"

He shook his head.

"Her parents split up, and so did mine. She moved with her mom to Cambridge, I stayed in Wattsbury. We didn't have any reason to see each other except that my dad had done it with her mom. I couldn't just be like, Bye, Mom, I'm going to see Dad's ho's daughter."

Todd was looking at me carefully. He sensed, I could tell, that there were many things I was leaving out. Perhaps he had already come to regret the dinner invitation. I wanted to let him know he could withdraw it, but I didn't know how.

3.

I Have to Remind Myself
of That

On the way home, I told Julie about Jeremy. She rocked in her seat and cursed. She put her hands behind her head, somewhere in the depths of her hair, which appeared to calm her down. "It's not the worst thing in the world," she said. "What's he going to do? Fire me and wait to see if the tiger-observing-sex thing gets on Gawker? You might have just done the show a favor, honestly."

I told her about Todd and Khadijah, the dinner invitation. She remained unfazed. There would be some awkwardness, we agreed, a ghost from the past floating in the air above our food, at dinner. But nothing worse than that.

"You told me about that vow on our third date, and I was like, I owe her," said Julie. "I need to send that girl a thank-you note and some scones."

"It doesn't freak you out?"

"I'd be jealous of an attractive awning, if you stood under it, but relative to other people, no. I'm not jealous of Khadijah. I mean, tell me if I should be. But it was thirteen years ago."

I was taking downhill curves in her white Volkswagen, a light and obedient car. I was the one who liked to drive.

"Khadijah's the last person you would ever need to be jealous of," I said. An exaggeration, but one meant to convey affection. I was bleary from the pomegranate vodka, and from puking, so we bought coffee with cinnamon from a taco truck on La Cienega. That was all I needed to steer us home through the flats. Back at Julie's house, in Miracle Mile, we fell to our battle stations, brushed our teeth, and had drunken sex. We lay under her down comforter, patterned with green birds, safe, nesting.

The hungover morning passed quickly. I sat on the study floor, my guitar in my lap, a Beatle in India. No "Dear Prudence" descended. I talked myself into falling in love with a meaningless chord progression, a limp melody, until I took a break to smoke a cigarette and walk to Miracle Mile's Gaia Foods. By the time I let myself back in and turned off the alarm and put down my grocery bags on the kitchen island and put the groceries in the fridge and took two Advil, I'd forgotten the song.

That evening, Julie came home from work at 11:00 p.m., which was normal, and bore down on the single bottle of wine we kept in the kitchen, beside the cartons of organic soup, which was unusual. Neither of us ever drank at home. We drank at parties, where we got drunk.

"Would you open this for me, please?" she asked.

Sitting with the bottle wedged between my stocking feet, I went to work with the corkscrew. She watched me.

"How was your day?" She clamped two wineglasses on the counter.

"Besides the songwriting failures, kind of awesome." I grunted, and the cork popped out. "The mail came, and I got this weird 'This Is Just Wrong' check from the Kingdom of Saudi Arabia. It was taxed as a performance royalty, so I guess they played it at a kingdom event? The first Bank of America I went to, the teller was a dick about the foreign currency thing, but at the second one I found this teller who was nice."

"How are your eyes?" she asked. "Did you ever get new contacts?"

"Last week I went to this optician in Little Ethiopia that has everything cheaper. They had these new disposables, with this weird generic packaging with stains on it, like when you get illegal batteries from China? The world looks, not bad, or even blurry—I wouldn't want to place a value judgment on it—just a little shimmery. The big thing is that they never slide up my eyeballs, like the old ones did, so that's good." I poured her a glass.

As I gave it to her, I was surprised to see tears glide down her cheeks. I asked her what was wrong. She shook her head and smiled. I wrapped an arm around her; she kissed me and slipped away, holding her wine close to her body with both hands, and crossed to the other side of the cavernous kitchen.

"It's nothing," she said. "I'm just being a stressed-out weirdo. I didn't get to really have dinner."

"Did something happen?"

"Everybody can eat a bowl of dicks."

I waited.

"Fiancé," she sang. "Come watch TV with me." She took my hand and led me to the living room.

"What happened?"

She placed her glass on the coffee table, appropriating a *Gladiator*-themed bar mitzvah invitation as a coaster in order to pick up both remotes at once.

"It's really nothing. The Silicon Valley guys that came in with Jeremy can just be supershallow. I don't need to want to marry them, they're just my co-workers, and it's not even all of them. There are just a few of them that are douches, and I get mad."

"What did they say?"

"Not important." The TV flashed on and flashed off. A fleeting glimpse of jocular heroin dealers.

"Tell me."

She shook her head.

I stood in front of the television. "Was it about me? I just want to know. I don't care what they said about me, if it was about me."

She shook her head emphatically.

"Who cares? I only care if you feel like I'm so fragile you have to keep a secret from me. That's more insulting than anything they could say."

"I never want to hurt you," she said, and I was frightened. She let herself slump into the couch.

I squared my shoulders. "You're not going to hurt me. I promise."

"Today I met with Jeremy and his guys, and Jeremy and I were being super buddy-buddy because we both knew what you saw last night and we wanted to show things were cool. So I tried to be so gentle. I was like, 'Good cuff links. Did you burn all your fleece when you left Palo Alto?' and he was like, 'Yeah,' and I was like, 'Nice, I'm new money too.' And he was like, 'Is anybody old money anymore?' and I was like, 'Josh's family acts that way,' and he was like, 'Josh acts poor.' And he said that thing you said at the cookout about your disposable contact lenses, how you made them last a year instead of a month. And it just turned into this thing. This science guy was like, 'Julie's man's so poor he goes fishing in Venice for catfish,' and then the Stanford Business School guy was like, 'Julie's man's so poor he's got a chicken coop in her garage,' and then the PR guy was like, 'Julie's man sells ices on Temple.'" She walked back to the kitchen as she spoke, and ripped a paper towel off the roll that stood on the island to blow her nose. "But I don't give a shit. I don't care what they think."

"Of course Jeremy's being mean. I'd be mean about a man who'd seen me lose a boner," I said. "Besides, they're clearly resentful because I'm a rock musician. All men secretly wish they were rock musicians. Sometimes when shit like this happens I have to remind myself of that."

"These men don't secretly wish they were rock musicians. These men are nerds from Northern California. They secretly wish there was a Pixar movie of Norse folklore. They secretly wish they had wineries. They secretly wish I would quit so they could hire a twenty-two-year-old with wet-looking blond hair who looks like a barbarian queen; that's what it's actually about, probably."

"It's just disbelief. You're this . . ." I arranged my arms into a cradle. "This *goddess* carrying around a baby retard."

"Did you just compare yourself to a baby retard?" She looked me over carefully as she opened a box of sea salt caramels.

"I did," I said, with righteousness.

She put a piece in her mouth, chewed it thoughtfully, like a baseball player with tobacco, sprinkled Comet on the remainder of the caramels in the box, and threw the box in the trash. "Don't talk about yourself like that. If people at work are telling me I'm supposed to be ashamed of you, and you're agreeing that I'm supposed to be ashamed of you, what am I supposed to do with that?"

She pulled her laptop from the cloth tangerine-colored case with zebra stickers that a fan in Singapore had made her and took it to the living room. Finally she said: "I can't believe I'm affected by this. They're idiots. I can't believe I'm affected by this. Fuck *me,* if I'm *that* girl, who actually cares about this."

"I wasn't supposed to turn out this way," I said, still sitting in the kitchen. We were descending into something, unable to stop. I pictured two ants swirling down a drain. "I wasn't supposed to turn out this way at all. I was going to be a classics major. Do these guys at work even care what the Athenians would have thought of them? Because in Athens, they would have been condemned. I wrote a paper about the *Symposium* before I dropped out of NYU, and when the TA gave it back to me, he looked at me, and he said, 'Your reading of Plato is terminal.' That was the word he used. He was amazed by me."

I was scratching my scalp, and I was ashamed that I was doing this, and I was ashamed of my thoughts and the words that were jumping out of my mouth, so I didn't let Julie see me. I sat on the far kitchen counter, concealed from the living room, by myself. I heard her turn on the television. Baltimore detectives conducted surveillance on a mafia brothel.

I found the most prestigious object in the house, Robert Bresson's *Notes on Cinematography,* under the master bed, brushed a dead spider off it, and pretended to read, within view of the couch where Julie had settled, to make her feel bad about watching *The Wire* to avoid conflict and, by extension, about flourishing in television, and being a happy, prosperous person. Julie kept her eyes on the flat screen. It had the word ELITE printed across the bottom in golden capitals and was connected through the walls to an R2-D2-like tower of electronics in a closet off the guest room, so that the consoles by which it functioned would not mar the living room's design. This "smart house" arrangement seemed tremendously, importantly dishonest to me right now. Neither of us spoke.

When, after ten minutes, she went to the bathroom, I crept to the couch and awoke her laptop. One window was open on NYTimes. com. The other was open on the official website of Marc Jacobs. Sweatshirts floated across a Marc Jacobsness–infused winter wonderland, in which swans pulled sleighs whisking naughty-faced maidens in white Zorro masks through exuberantly billowing snow.

Sitting on the couch, I peeled a cobweb off the spine of the Bresson. The cobweb adhered to my fingers. My hand looked to me like the hand of an undead, reaching up through the soil and grass to pull a living victim down into my earthen lair. This was, in retrospect, a clear signal that the odds of carrying on a productive, healing conversation were, for the evening, small. But hoping that Julie and I could have the kind of fight that led to cathartic sex, and believing that if we could fuck with abandon tonight it would prove that the mockery at Tusk had not gotten to our heads, had not successfully shamed us, had not victimized us, I hurried to the bathroom to engage her in another round of fighting.

I found her applying toner to her face with a cotton ball.

"Did you find a Marc Jacobs sweater you wanted to buy yourself?" I asked.

"I didn't see anything so awesome I should spend the money." She finished her forehead. "Did you look at my laptop?"

"The website was just, like, on there. Do you wish I could buy you sweaters from Marc Jacobs? Is that rough for you, that I can't?"

She shoved the plastic CVS bag of cotton balls back in its place beneath the sinks. "No, baby, I don't care. One of the makeup women today told me to look at a Marc Jacobs ad she worked on. I hope you can come home from work with a Marc T-shirt for me someday. But I'm okay with the bridge line. I'm okay with a fake from Vietnam."

"How do you imagine that I'll ever be in a situation where I come home from work? How do you think it would ever happen? What is the path that will take me from here to having a job where I come home from work every day, sometimes with a Marc T-shirt?"

She planted her hands on the sink. "Uh, I don't know, Josh, isn't that kind of what you're supposed to figure out for yourself?"

Once I had brought up my own future, I was in real danger. Palpitations began, and a moment later, it felt as if the palpitations were everywhere, up to my ears. Of course I had a plan for making money. Julie and I had agreed that her income would dwarf mine during this *time of transition,* the post-Shapeshifter years. Eventually, our positions would reverse themselves; she would retire from television by fifty, if not by forty-five; I would become a producer and sound-track composer in demand, a fixture. My job was to patiently stalk clients, build a reliable revenue stream, before we had children. But it was a spiderweb, like most show business plans, intricate, pretty, built out of a thin, bright hope you could see only from the correct angle. There was no quantifiable reason I would ever attract more bands and TV shows than anyone else, no superior business model, no diploma. If I allowed myself to look at it skeptically, it was no kind of plan at all. I felt incapable of having sex, let alone persuading Julie to have sex with me. But if I terminated the conversation now, everything would still be okay; I would be able to get to sleep tonight, I would wake up tomorrow morning ready to face the dawn. I decided to put myself to bed. I didn't speak. I turned on the water in my sink, and squirted face wash into my hand.

"Jesus," she said, looking at me closely. "Don't freak out. I don't want us to ever be affected by this. Those guys are fucking stupid."

"And yet you are," I said. "Say to me you're not affected."

"I don't want to be affected. But now you're affected, so even if I was only slightly barely affected before, now I am affected."

It was when I looked in the mirror, to apply the wash, that I came face-to-face with terror: Tom, Myra, Julie 2, staring at me from their perch. I took in the hopeful little dots of their eyes, and the evidence of their talents: Bunsen burner, leotard, cello. I had always known my plans for the future were wisps. But the prospect of taking care of a child with a wisp had not felt as absurd, as obscene, as it felt now, beneath the doll-like figures on the napkins.

"How am I supposed to be a father to our children?" I demanded of Julie. "I actually just want to know how I'm going to be providing in five years. I can't see it."

"When we have kids, you can't make that face in front of them."

Indeed, the expression on my face reminded me of the face in an anti-meth ad, only with face wash on it. "How did I get to this point where I promised something I can't deliver? How can I give you this? Draw me a diagram." I sat on the floor, the face wash still foaming on my cheeks. "How am I supposed to do this?" I pointed at the children.

If I continued on my present course, the children on the napkins would be raised by a resentful, embittered, flight-obsessed father, a man ashamed of joblessness, a man who half-believed he should have found another band and lived on the road, a man who considered his life the wrong life, a man with one eye ever on the door: a Dad. In running from my father's professional compromises, I had failed to give adequate consideration to conventional success. I had spent my postvow life running from my father only to inscribe a circle in the ground, so that now, staring in the battle station mirror, I stood mere inches from a familiar pair of restless, Dadsian eyes.

"I wish I could go back in time," I said. "Start over from high school."

"Thanks, Josh," said Julie. "Meeting your high school sweetheart is going to be really fun." She got into bed, and turned out the light.

The future-kids looked at me.

4.

I Feel Like I'm Looking at Two of You

Halfway through the night, I woke up calm and sorry. Julie was half asleep, stretching her legs to full length, a hand behind her head, gripping the headboard. I put her in the crook of my arm and kissed her neck. "We're not affected by them," I said.

"Not affected," she muttered into her pillow. This was just convincing enough, just final enough, to send us both to sleep. An important function, because Julie had to catch a flight to the Everglades at 7:00 a.m.

In each of our calendar applications, on our phones, there sat a rectangle with rounded corners: a reminder of our dinner with Khadijah and Todd, the weekend after next. If the dinner had been scheduled for sooner I might have canceled, citing work, because Julie and I had been fighting, and seeing Khadijah at a vulnerable time seemed dangerous. But Julie and I had ample time to restore normalcy before we faced Khadijah. So the rectangles remained.

And it is impossible to overstate the zeal with which normalcy was courted, starting on Julie's return from Florida three days later. More important than sex were the things we said to each other immediately before sex. Julie asked me to go to a therapist, and I agreed to go as soon as I could afford nonemergency health insurance. (My current plan, Toniq, was youth-marketed.) I recited the Five-Year Plan by which I would parlay my Shapeshifter credentials into a lucrative business career, building wealthy Angelenos highly soundproofed home recording studios in their garages, guest rooms, and Joshua Tree country houses, even as I continued to pursue sound-track work in television. I wrote old acquaintances, asking if they needed a studio built or a sound track composed; I established a Web presence. It was progress toward my ultimate end: to become an adequate father. The key to not becoming my own father was to become somebody worthy of my own regard, and to thereby rid myself of the resentment and restlessness that would make me want to run as my father had run. I restuck the future-kids to the bathroom mirror, with fresh tape.

The day of the dinner with Todd and Khadijah, I spent much of the afternoon chatting with a music supervisor about a new, haunting tack-piano interlude for *The Spirits of New Orleans*. It was late afternoon when Todd's name appeared on my phone.

"What are you doing right now?" he asked.

"Random correspondence," I said. "What's up?"

"Would you be up for rescuing Khadijah in South Central?"

My first thought was, What will be the Relationship Impact of this decision? And then an urgent countervailing thought: You're being asked to rescue a person. Julie wouldn't want you to not rescue a person.

"Wait, really?" I said. It occurred to me he might be kidding. "That sounds so Wesley Snipes movie."

"I told her not to take public transportation," he said. "But her mom is obsessed with the Watts Towers. They're both art historians, and her mom is all into outsider art and shit. Her mom told her she wanted a picture of her next to the Watts Towers, because they're apparently the Parthenon of retard civilization, and she *went*. By *subway*. The Watts Towers are in *Watts*."

"Is she okay?"

He seemed not to hear this question. "She's so Bostonian, it pisses me off. She just called me like, 'I took the bus to the Blue Line and now I'm on a Hundred and Third Street. How come there are no pedestrian walkways between here and the Watts Towers Center?' And it's like, I'm at work. Even if they let me off early, I can't get there for an hour and it's five-forty right now so we'd be screwed for seven-fifteen reservations anyway, which I can't change."

"I'm in Miracle Mile," I said. "I'll do side streets."

"Oh my god, really? Dude, you are a dude. I'm a teensy bit stressed about her being alone."

We agreed that Todd would text me Khadijah's location and I would convey her to safety. Khadijah and I would then meet him and Julie for dinner. I drove my Volvo backward down the driveway and toward the first major knot of traffic, which I knew would be La Brea and Olympic.

It was gelatinously slow. I called Julie and told her what I was doing.

"I'm really sorry," I said, "she just doesn't understand California, and it's part of our culture, not driving."

"That doesn't correspond to what I've heard," said Julie. "Your culture is: lavish birthdays during puberty, usury, providing excellent boyfriends, talking about yourself."

"I mean Wattsbury is kind of my real ethnicity."

"If you're late, and Todd and I are stuck together waiting for you guys, will he and I hit it off?"

"I will make sure that doesn't happen."

After we hung up, I got Todd's text: Watts Coffee Shop.

The Watts Coffee Shop was housed in a squat concrete building that looked like one of the community centers built just after the riots of '66. A plaque by the door confirmed that this in fact was what it had once been. You could see the anxiety in the design. It was a government saying "We are your friend, here is a place to gather," even as the government projected strength, nailing its name to a wedge of concrete with railings of rectangular metal slats, a fortress of the state. Its location was a sunny, tree-lined street of four-unit apartment buildings that also exuded governmental anxiety. They were built with what looked like an effort at cheer; they were painted the red of Arizona earth, but with peaked roofs, as if awaiting blankets of snow.

Inside, the coffee shop was decorated with memorabilia: posters of Sam Cooke and Otis Redding, Jesse Jackson. It was a place where tourists were expected. I saw Khadijah at a table by the far wall, bent over a stack of papers. I had a strange impulse to remain invisible. I murmured to the hostess that my friend was in the back and crossed the room. Finally, I planted my hand on her shoulder.

"The Anarchist," I said. She yelped.

"It's all right, it's all right," she croaked to the hostess as she ran over. Her knobby, small hand was on her heart.

Thirteen years had hardened Khadijah, distilled her. There were lines under her eyes and a wiltedness in the way the stray locks of her hair lit out from behind her ears. But so much of what's pretty about youth is the way it promises to expire. Seeing Khadijah at the end of our youth, the two of us clinging to it by our fingernails—I had an impulse to kiss her splayed fingers. I wish you well, I thought, no matter who you are now.

"If it isn't the bassist from Shapeshifter."

We didn't embrace, as would have been normal. I stood gawking. She was, for me, doubly there. A ghost from the past and a real person, one layered over the other.

"I feel like I'm looking at two of you," I said. "Old Khadijah, New Khadijah."

"Likewise," she said. "It's like double vision. Like being drunk."

I fell into a chair. "We kind of have to get going."

"It's six-fifteen." She squinted at me. "Dinner's at seven-fifteen."

I explained traffic. She gestured to a waiter, who went to the register. "The only thing is this," she said. "We have to pop by the Watts Towers and take a picture of me standing in front of them. My mom will flay me if I don't."

I thought of reminding her that the last time I'd seen her and Nancy in the same room, in the Wattsbury police station, rote obedience to Nancy's program had not been the rule. But Khadijah stared at me the way she had when she'd said *Give me the stone.* She was going to obey her mother now, and nothing I said was going to sway her.

"Sorry," she said. "Is that totally impossible? You should go. I'll catch a cab."

"A cab will cost eighty dollars," I said. "We're cool for time."

The part about the cab was true. The part about our being cool for time was not. Khadijah might have been able to tell we were late from the agressiveness with which I drove to the towers. But she only asked, "How's your dad?"

"Oh, I don't honestly know. Still remarried. Happily, maybe? We talk, but we don't talk. Things have always been"—I waggled my hand in the air—"fraught."

"Oh, it's fraught between my mom and me too. I do what she says, and then I grind my teeth." It was strange, the level of familiarity. That double vision, remembering the kid in the adult you were speaking to, it disarmed you.

I spun into a parking space, and we took in the not-that-towering towers. They were encrusted with pieces of broken glass that had been embedded in the cement coating their iron frames as it dried.

"Why is outsider art always so underwhelming?" She sighed, digging through her patchwork bag. "It's like you're supposed to react as if your kid did it."

I thought I detected an invitation to open a can of worms.

"Is your mom underwhelmed by *your* work, Deej?"

She squinted up at the towers.

"I mean," I continued, "you're both art historians, right?"

"Well," she said, "I'm not sure my mother would respond to these towers so enthusiastically, if I had built them. I'm not an outsider. My mother's not easily impressed, by me."

She waved to a man eating an enchilada off a paper plate by a taco truck and extended her iPhone with a plaintive face. She pointed to me and the towers. He took the phone and nodded.

We stood hands on hips before the towers, as if they were whales we had harpooned together. The enchilada-eating man gestured for us to squeeze into frame, and we drew closer. As our arms made contact, and then the backs of our hands, I realized that this was one of those moments in which I might have to remember the cookies falling from my father's barn jacket in order to behave like a loyal fiancé. I had to preserve the vow. But in this circumstance in which, unlike the others, the person with whom I wanted to break the vow was the person with whom I had sworn the vow, the mnemonic exercise was not as effective. I was very much awake. I was attentive. I saw wind scratch the bases of the monument with dust. I saw a burrito wrapper crawl like a crab across the shadows.

I realized that my exhilaration at Khadijah's reappearance was delusional, evil, and not unlike my father's feelings for women other than my mother, over which I had exhausted maybe 35 percent of life frothing myself into self-righteous outrage. In other words, my father's disloyalty might have felt to him the way I was feeling now. It had been an act of weakness and selfishness on his part to disregard my mother's child rearing, postponement of career goals, her sacrifice of relationships with men from whom it was a simpler matter to extract empathy than from him. But it was confusing to me, to discover, at twenty-eight, that temptation could feel not at all like temptation but like a battle cry. Go forth, temptation said. Have courage. How uncanny that out of nothing, a face from the distant past, a ghost, imagination could build a battering ram against loyalty.

"What is it with my dad and your mom?" she asked, as we smiled our death's-head smiles at the man taking a picture of us with her phone. "This underwhelmed-with-us thing they both have going?"

"To put it brutally," I said, "they were in love with each other. We were in the way."

The phone's camera began to flash. Squares of light zigzagged like Space Invaders before my eyes.

"They resented us," I continued, "because we stood between them and the person they loved. You were the one who figured that out."

The man with Khadijah's iPhone looked at the screen and shook his head at the result. He motioned for us to be patient; he'd try again.

"I've done a lot of work trying not to judge my mom," she said. "So I had kind of forgotten about . . ." With her index finger, she wrote the words "they hate us" in the air and said them, softly.

This was when our hands slipped together and our fingers linked—it was a pose, for the camera; I knew we were telling ourselves that, but after half a second we couldn't make ourselves believe anything so flimsy anymore. We weren't looking at each other. Blinding squares continued to materialize in the air. Her hand stole away from mine, and the horrifying moment ended.

"I'm sorry," she said. "That was weird. I wasn't trying to be weird." She ran over to the man and retrieved her iPhone. The pictures showed two people staring into something they didn't understand.

I drove us north through the sludge of cars. Neither of us spoke.

"That was awk ha-ha," she said.

"Yeah, it's like, of all people to have strangeness with—"

She cut me off with another burst of ha-ha-ha-ha-ha. "It's terribly nice to see you, Josh. But let's just make a few rules."

I nodded emphatically. "Let's be the good kind of friends, not the constant is-this-going-to-get-fucked-up kind of friends."

She looked out the window at the lake of chrome and rubber in which we sat. "So, yeah. First rule: No more hand stuff."

"No one-on-one dinner."

"Falafel," she said, swaying her shoulders side to side, the gesture people make to show they are easing into a groove.

"Falafel's what it's all about." I, too, swayed my shoulders.

"Have you kept the vow?" She looked me in the eye and said, "Ha, ha-ha. The Vow Never to Cheat on Anybody?"

"Yeah. It's weird, I have," I said. "I wouldn't hold it against you if you haven't. When we made it we were infants."

"I kept it. I plan to keep keeping it."

A beep let me know that Julie had sent me an urgent text. "Where are you guys am pretending to know what noise jazz is Todd is weird I'm sending this from the bathroom please tell me you are close." I cared, notionally, that we were late and that Julie was having a poor social experience. But I was high. Between Julie and me, there were miles and miles of sprawl.

5.

Their Whole Actual House

K hadijah and I were forty minutes late, in the end. Dinner might have been torture, except that Todd and Khadijah turned out to have an artful and mesmerizing couple-shtick, a routine developed unconsciously over years of get-togethers, a performance of themselves. There was a thrill in watching them coordinate comments and gestures. It was like RUN-DMC.

"We're collaborating," said Todd, "on this thing where you smash your own house."

Khadijah's turn to speak came next: "The deal is, there are these miniatures we make of people's houses—I make the miniatures and Todd is composing a score he'll play live while people smash them."

"You smash your own house," Todd repeated, "if you're one of the rich people who's hired us to do the performance."

"We come to their house and we give them the miniatures of their houses—they can put themselves in them if they want, I can make figurines if they want them—and they can—"

"They can choose how they want to destroy it," said Todd. "They can use this lighter we made." He turned to me and spoke to me particularly, to share information of significance to men: "It's shockingly easy to make a lighter, bro." He returned to addressing both Julie and me: "They burn the little houses, while Deej stands there with a fire extinguisher . . ."

"So they don't burn down their whole actual house. Or—"

"Or there's also a crowbar."

"Todd's playing the score on a guitar usually, or an organ, but he keeps a fair distance back so they can smash with abandon."

"We were going to call it Homewreckers, originally, but that was too on-the-nose. So now it's the Homelessness Initiative."

"Who's doing it?" asked Julie. "I mean, that's so amazing, it's a fucking awesome idea, but who's— Do you have customers?"

"We have five, right now," said Khadijah. "My mom has a friend who knows a lot of people who— We couldn't have found them ourselves. Three of them are out here, one's in Boston, one's in New York."

"I'm so psyched for you," I said, clawing crescent-shaped wounds in my leg. "These baguettes are choice."

"Do people want huge loud music when they smash the house?" Julie asked Todd.

"I don't care deeply about what they want, it's that *I* want to make it weird and delicate and mournful. I suspect that that's what *they,* the patrons, so to speak, really want, deep down, when they break their houses. Also, it's let's not fuck with the neighbors too hard by playing something super fucking loud. Also, Khadijah has made such beautiful houses, the music should feel sad when you see them destroyed. She's such a masterful craftsman."

"Shut up," Khadijah said. To us: "*He* made this top."

The top sported not one but three small mustard-colored owls. As the dinner wore on, with Khadijah and Todd explaining the difficulties of long distance, I felt this reunion was not enough. I wanted more one-on-one conversation with Khadijah Silverglate-Dunn after so many years of silence, with so many years more of silence to come. When everyone was drinking Thai iced coffee, the meal winding down, I found it necessary to continuously remind myself to sit up straight. To hide my grief, I went to the men's room.

The men's room was organized around a communal urinary trough. Water cascaded down the tiles into a basin of gray stones, to which stones there must have been attributed some cleansing or deodorizing or muffling effect. They coated the floor of the trough, so that you peed on them, rather than directly into the trough itself. I checked that no one was looking, and scooped up the most substantial stone I could find. I washed it in the sink with cucumber soap from the dispenser, dried it, and put it in my pocket.

I approached the host at the front. "You don't have a Sharpie or a marker around, by any chance, do you?" I asked. "Sorry to be a pain."

This wasn't breaking any of the rules Khadijah and I had just made, I reminded myself.

The host stroked his own cheek with one hand, to help himself remain calm. "No problem," he said, and pawed through a drawer in his little podium until he came up with a black Sharpie and thrust it violently into my hand.

I scrawled a circled *A* on the stone. The horizontal shaft was crooked. It looked more like a geometry proof than an anarchy sign. But Khadijah would remember the object to which it referred. We couldn't have the kinds of conversations I wanted us to have, but I could leave her with this. *I don't actually know you, but I see something in you no one else can see. You were a rebel, remember?* I squeezed the stone, to feel its hardness, and thought: You were like *this*.

Back at our table, Khadijah was debunking a celebrated whalebone sculptor, Todd and Julie listening with their hands on their chins. None of them were looking at me. As I sat down, I slipped the stone into Khadijah's apple-green-handled tote bag, which was leaning against her chair.

When the bill arrived, Todd seized the plastic folder, held it to his chest, and took his wallet from his back pocket. I put my credit card on the table. Khadijah took her tote bag from the floor and rooted for her purse. She stared into the bag, gape-mouthed. I could tell she had the stone cupped in her hand.

Todd was now flagging down the waiter, oblivious. Julie was trying to get Todd to take her credit card. They'd seen nothing.

Khadijah dropped the stone back in the bag. I could hear it whish against the cloth. She turned her face from me, to stare at the wall.

Outside, the four of us embraced and told each other we would do it again.

As I drove Julie's VW home, she pointed out a clear passage through traffic in the left lane of Olympic Boulevard. I steered sharply, and we were in it, and Koreatown moved so fast outside our window it became abstract. We floated past Authentic Korean, where the children had been drawn. The white neon Authentic Korean sign flickered spastically, a little life.

When we got home, the house was spotless. A woman came and cleaned every other Saturday. She did the laundry, full of foul gym clothes, washed the sheets and towels, polished the floors— I didn't know everything she did, and neither did Julie. We only recognized its effect. The clear surfaces, the neon smell of cleaning agents, the dustless clarity of the air. I walked in through the front door and looked through the high-raftered living room into the wide marble kitchen, and remembered the Bank of Boston, how it had asked to be smashed, that spring day in Wattsbury, with the stone. I'd been thinking Julie and I should have sex to put Khadijah behind us. But now I wanted the punch of honesty—the rock through the glass.

"I did something wrong tonight," I said.

Julie turned to face me, sucking her lips. I took a breath. I told her about the stone from the urinal trough, the Sharpie, the look on Khadijah's face as she scooped it from her bag.

Julie's neck twitched as she listened. Finally she flinched as if an insect had bitten her. She took the rose-hip soap bottle from the kitchen sink and threw it against the wall. She dropped to her knees and pulled me down to sit next to her, our backs to the island.

"From now on, she and I don't talk," I said, and she squeezed my hand like she was escorting me from a shark tank.

The security system issued a copacetic beep. I had lived in the house long enough to know that this meant Current Setting: Armed. Julie had hit the button that conveyed we were in for the night. The alarm would go off if somebody breached our invisible wall.

I harbored a family feeling toward the security system, this robot that kept us safe. Once, I had pushed the button that caused it to declare its setting aloud, its voice emanating from a small, powerful speaker, and it had spoken a little like David Byrne. I felt that even though Julie and I were the only humans in the house, we shared our home, even now, sitting on our kitchen floor on an autumn night, bare feet on cool tile, with buzzing presences: the Oenervians in the picture frames; Jeremy and his cohort; the children on the mirror; the ambitions that hovered over us like animated billboards; the shame of our little betrayals; the possible lives we'd abandoned for each other, for this.

6.

What Kind of Honesty Do You Think Is Going to Come out of Me?

Three days later, Rachel and my mother flew in for the party celebrating the third-season premiere of *Julie vs. Animals*. This was a form of tribute. They wanted to show they didn't look down on Julie for making television, although my mother hadn't said this explicitly.

"I'm curious to know what your life is like in Los Angeles, and I hope to come to appreciate it," she had said on the phone. "Even though it's probably my idea of hell, over there."

My mother had asked my sister to join her pilgrimage, and Rachel had said yes. They'd both met Julie several times, but in Wattsbury, down in the snow and the smell of soba noodles, my mother's turf. Rachel would be nice to Julie without being cowed by Julie in Julie's own fiefdom. Rachel would be Virgil to my mother's Dante, in Probably-Hell. In the thirteen years since the divorce, Rachel had filled the spousal role in my mother's life, the role of protector, of Dad.

I picked them up at LAX while Julie spent the morning with her parents. The two families planned to converge on the Grove for lunch, but my mother's plane was on time, traffic from the airport nil, and we arrived forty-five minutes early. Rachel and my mother squinted at the Grove, with its fountain, trolley car, its Mediterranean village, its cobblestones. Its "Farmers Market," a dense village of outdoor taco places, bars, and chocolatiers.

Rachel noticed an Anthropologie across the cobblestoned boulevard from the Apple store and informed my mother she was going to buy her a dress.

"Here, Mom," she said, "is where we will maximize your chances of finding the one good man in Wattsbury."

My mother unfolded her damaged golden glasses and put them on to inspect the goods through the window. "This smacks a little bit of internalized oppression, pathetically trying to be youthful," she said. "But that might be an interesting kind of pathetic to try being."

It was in Anthropologie that we ran into the Oenervians. Both of our parties had arrived at the Grove early, and each had happened upon Anthropologie unbeknownst to the other. Julie and Vanda were browsing neo-Victorian lampshades, Samson standing apart with his arms crossed, bemused, manly.

When I saw them, my mother was already modeling an outfit for Rachel. "It's you, Mom. It's sexy." My sister's tone was diagnostic. "You have these amazing gams. You gotta show them a little."

"Gams?" My mother made one of her neutrally inquisitive therapist faces. "What are gams?"

"Legs. Your legs. Get the dress. Get the hippie top, sure, but also get the dress."

"They might be very expensive. I can't even find the price tag, can you believe how stupid I'm becoming?" I was delighted to hang out with Rachel, pleased to hang out with my mother. But part of me, slightly more powerful than the part of me happy to see them, urged me to wait a few more moments before saying hello to the Oenervians, who had not seen me yet. I had an apprehension that the Paquette/Beckermans and the Oenervians would not swoon for each other.

"I can afford it, Mom," Rachel said.

"Are you in a long-term financial position to go around buying people dresses?"

"I could not drive around L.A. gathering women and buying them dresses in Anthropologie, no. But this particular dress for you, yeah."

"How stable is your job, really?" My mother took off her glasses and looked at Rachel gimlet-eyed.

"I work for the state of Massachusetts."

It was time to face the Oenervians like a man. I swallowed and called Julie's name. My mother's face took on the same amusement and triumph it'd taken on when Khadijah had called in 1994. When I introduced her to Vanda and Samson, she and Vanda exchanged smiles that were mildly incredulous, as if they were saying "We actually birthed these people." I could feel myself floating to earth; there were stores of humility and self-lessness in our mothers' faces, a variety of feeling I had forgotten about. Much the same way I had forgotten about snow.

My sister purchased the semisexy dress for my mother, and we made our way as a group of six through the Grove.

Our destination was a restaurant on the far side of La Brea. On Rainwater's lime-colored walls there were large black-and-white photographs of monsoons in progress. A waiter sat us at a big table in the middle of the room.

"Ms. Beckerman," said Julie, "that dress looked amazing on you. Your daughter is an excellent personal shopper."

"Please, call me Virginia," said my mother. "But thank you."

"Beckerman?" Samson addressed his daughter. "I thought it was Paquette."

"We have different last names," I explained. "I got my father's and Rachel got my mother's."

"To be equitable," Virginia said, smiling at the Oenervians, who were all Oenervian. They nodded, serious, open-minded. Rachel reached out and adjusted my mother's glasses, to convey that she was being weird.

My mother still taught psychology at a small, nonselective college in the Berkshire Hills—a department at a fancier school might not have allowed her to remain openly Jungian and Buddhist. She was wearing a red wool dress with a high waist and short sleeves, and the same John Lennon spectacles she'd worn for fifteen years and repaired with an equally ancient eyeglass-repair kit she kept in the old desk given to us by my father's friend from the Lampoon. (The desk had remained with my mother in the divorce.) To be Jungian is to feel at the bottom of one's soul the permanence of problems. ("Psychology teaches us that, in a certain sense, there is nothing in the psyche that is old; nothing that can really finally die away. Even Paul was left with a thorn in the flesh." "The Stages of Life," 1930–31.) To be Buddhist is to feel the impermanence of everything else. The glasses perched on my mother's nose crookedly; there would have been a kind of futility, for my mother, in throwing them away and buying a pair that would sit, for a while, noncrookedly, before they, too, fell into disrepair. Her hazelnut curls, half gray now, exploded from behind her head, as if she were falling through life, the wind blowing her hair around her as she fell. Her face signaled bemusement at this flight, when it wasn't marred by flashes of dismay at same.

Across the table sat Vanda and Samson, engineers, Vanda of investment portfolios, Samson of medical technology. They solved things, or so I imagined. The Oenervians looked aerodynamic to me, as if they were propelled upward through life, as if air pressure smoothed their hair and clothing as they rose. Vanda's hair was a dark shell combed backward from her forehead. Samson was owlish in his round tortoiseshell glasses, his thick, side-parted black curls flat against his head, his hands folded. His eyebrows, bushy and soft, were impossibly still. (My own father's eyebrows were rarely idle; even when his mouth relaxed, his eyebrows continued insinuating.)

"My ex-husband and I agreed to the different last names before we got married," my mother continued.

"A fair contract, right at the start," said Vanda. "I applaud you."

An auspicious beginning to lunch. Julie kept her chin down, her eyes up, a dedicated psychology student at the seminar table, clinging to the professor's every word. Rachel, for her part, did not fight Julie for alpha. Lanky, like me, she assumed a laborer's slouch in her chair, legs stretched to one side, an arm slung over the back; in her jeans and plaid shirt, she was, for the moment, relatively butch, Julie's amicable foil. Her hair, which she'd recently had pixie-cut, made us look even more alike than usual. We looked like half a band. I placed my palm on the top of her head and took it off again.

"Rachel, Julie tells me you have an interesting job," said Vanda, "working on poverty."

"Oh, well," said Rachel, "I try to keep people off the streets. *Try* being the word." Everyone looked at Rachel, inviting her to continue. Rolls arrived with green flecks. "What we're working on now is, no matter what, you don't let people bum around in a shelter. It's counterintuitive, there's a part of us that wants to believe there's someplace you can always go. But we've found, that on Christmas, shelters are empty. People have some other situation they can go to temporarily. And it's far, far more expensive to put somebody in a shelter for a few nights than it is to pay somebody's rent. So we're designing a program where it's, if you have a problem paying your rent, you notify the state, we pay it."

Murmurs around the table, of "So interesting."

"Like, there's this ritual, with underclass teenage girls in Boston—when you find out you're pregnant, you go and spend the night in a shelter, so you can get Section Eight housing later on. But we don't let you get evicted, and we tear down the shelter, which is crawling with bugs and criminals anyway."

"See, I think that's genius," said Julie. "God, Rachel, you're doing something so real and important. I'm just glad there are people as smart as you figuring out new ways to take care of poor children, instead of making TV. Everything here is spit in the wind by comparison." She turned to my mother. "You must be so proud of her."

My mother was. She was blushing. "Your show isn't spit," she said. "It's educational."

"It's fascinating, this policy," said Samson. "But if you're paying people's rent, my question is, There must be a mechanism in place for preventing abuse of the system?"

"It's complicated to get into," said Rachel, batting away the question with the back of her hand. "But even if people do get some free rent they don't totally need, it's cheaper for Massachusetts than maintaining all these shelters, where you have to have security and maintenance."

For the first, time, Samson's eyebrows jumped. A twitch of skepticism. Immediately, the eyebrows fell back under his control and went still.

"The ritual of going to the shelter when you get pregnant," I observed, "is kind of like the upper-middle-class ritual of moving back in with your parents after your first internship and you can't find a job in New York, or whatever. Or it's like the ghetto version of being all but dissertation in grad school and letting your parents help with rent. It's like, Time to fall back on the Man. Just listening to Rachel talk about it, I want to go take a month off at my dad's loft."

My mother tipped back her head and released a laugh that started at a high note and swooped. "Or my mom's house," I amended. My mother smirked and patted my hand.

"Um hmm," said Rachel. "I'm not sure the analogy holds, Josh. You clearly *want* to crash at Dad's. That might be understood as 'falling back on the Man.' But I would hesitate to characterize a pregnant fifteen-year-old girl in Dorchester as *wanting* a week at a shelter."

Vanda spoke. "I think what Josh was saying," she offered, "was that they're both cultural habits. The struggle is to figure out a way to help a person break a habit, exercise will."

Rachel opened her mouth to respond to this incriminatingly Ayn Randish comment. Beneath the table, I kicked her solidly in the calf. She closed her mouth, fished the lemon wedge from her water, and bit it.

But my mother, unlike Rachel, could not be prevented from saying whatever she was inclined to say. I didn't feel comfortable kicking her.

"I respect that, Vanda," my mother said. "But who do you blame, when a teenage girl from a marginalized minority group in a culturally isolated urban area plays into an economic system designed to exploit her?" My mother's voice was friendly, and I believe she wanted both to defend Rachel and to clarify Vanda's position. But Vanda's expression soured. It was the discrepancy between my mother's words and her conciliatory tone, I think, that rankled: academic condescension. Vanda studied one of the monsoon photographs.

"Of course it's very sad," said Samson. "But ultimately, there are people who make themselves something out of nothing every day in this country."

"We can't know," said Rachel, "whether it's possible for any given person." She was slightly wide-eyed. She kept her tone of voice on a very short leash.

Julie cleared her throat. "Maybe what my dad means—correct me if I'm wrong, Dad—is that his parents were Armenians living in exile. They came here when he was a teenager. English wasn't his first language. He didn't have the world served up to him. He worked hard."

Rachel smiled. "I'm looking at your father, and he seems like a smart, hardworking, really nice, cool guy, but he does appear to be a guy."

"Therefore?" asked Julie, smiling.

"Therefore he benefits, like my father, from being a guy. Just because that's how things are, not because he did anything wrong or he didn't work or something."

"How do you feel about it, Samson?" asked my mother. "Do you feel that has been your experience?"

Samson chuckled. "Oh yes," he said, "if you are a little boy, a big light comes down and shines on you." He chuckled again and looked at me, hoping for camaraderie. "What do you say, Josh?"

I returned a meek smile. I had discussed gender with my mother and sister before, and felt that, while it was possible to hold a productive conversation with one of them at a time, to speak with both about gender simultaneously was to subject yourself to a good cop/bad cop. It went like this: My mother asked you in an amused voice to describe your experience of male privilege in an uninhibited fashion; you did so; she withdrew into shadows; Rachel yelled at you in response to the feelings about male privilege you had uninhibitedly expressed.

"Well, in any case," said Julie, "I think it's awesome to keep teenage girls out of shelters."

"Thank you," said Rachel. She pushed back her chair. "I have to go to the bathroom."

"Did I say something wrong?" asked Samson, once she was out of earshot.

"Nothing," I said.

"It's probably not the conversation, Samson," my mother said. "Rachel gets terrible cramps, and then she takes aspirin for the pain, and the aspirin gives her these unimaginable stomach pains. I worry about her stomach lining." Her voice was flat. We took up our menus. My mother's was open in front of her face, with only her eyes visible. She removed her crooked glasses, to better read. Now that her eyes were finally unadorned, I could see that they were dull with indignation.

This wouldn't have happened if Julie had Wattsbury parents, like Khadijah, I reflected. Even with Nancy, it would have been fraught, but there could have been debate in a common language. The thought was so evil that I dropped it and ignored it, let it scurry like a cockroach in the dark.

After lunch, the Oenervians went to Bed Bath & Beyond, and the Paquette/Beckermans repaired to Julie's house in Miracle Mile. My mother locked herself in the guest bedroom and did her prostrations. I could tell from the soft thumps of her palms on the floor.

"It's weird you never taught us how to do those," I said, when she was done.

"You can easily find out," she said, her face flushed, her hair held back with a tortoiseshell clamp. "You'll come to Buddhism if you need it."

• • •

The third-season premiere party took place at a Japanese restaurant in Century City. As Julie received congratulations from acquaintances, I watched a man with cheek implants wander the room, looking lonely, cranially impaled.

"So unnatural, right?" said a tall, red-haired man my age, wearing a cardigan and a green tie with yellow skulls on it. "It makes the rest of us look puffy."

"If women grade our cheekbones on a curve, he fucks the curve," I agreed. We were now better able to understand, we agreed, what it meant to be female in our contemporary, media-saturated culture. His name was Simon. A producer on Julie's show who was really a writer, but for complicated guild-related reasons couldn't be described as such, he'd grown up in Maryland, outside D.C., worshiping Scream and Fugazi. He pinched the freckled bridge of his nose and drummed on it with his index finger as he spoke of Le Tigre, and Le Tigre's ruinous loss of Sadie Benning. He seemed non-evil. I reconsidered my across-the-board hatred of Julie's co-workers.

He asked me what I did.

"You were in Shapeshifter?" His mouth fell open just slightly. "I saw you guys at the Echo. You were tight. Some fat, drunk guy got onstage, and your guitarist was playing some kind of seventies synth, and he just ducked over and tackled the guy, just fucking ran him off, like it was all in a day's work, and then went right back to the synth and picked up the riff. It was fucking pro."

I thanked him. "Let me guess," I said. "You wrote that line where she says lobster is the gangsta rap of seafood, once considered low-class and disgusting, now considered festive?"

He blushed. "I originated that, yeah."

Soon, Simon and I committed to a hike in Runyon Canyon, and held our feet side by side, to confirm that we were really wearing the same Tiger sneakers with the same brown and orange color scheme. Julie disentangled herself from a news crew across the room and threw her arms around both our shoulders. "Protect me, entourage," she said. "Put your matching sneakers up that anchorwoman's ass." She tilted her head backward toward her tormentor, a brunette, angular as a microphone stand, who appeared now to be summarizing the night's footage with one hand on her hip, the other on her Channel 7 KATV microphone.

I was feeling good about the party and, by extension, the future. Julie's world was cosmopolitan and well-informed about my band, and I was a necessary part of a retinue. But we left, so that Julie wouldn't be prodded into further mandatory extemporizing for news cameras. I grabbed a half-empty bottle of gin standing on a table—when Julie was walking next to me, I'd learned long ago, this was sometimes acceptable at catered events. The four of us—Julie, Rachel, my mother, and me—piled into the Volvo, and I drove us to the Holiday Inn in Silver Lake, where Rachel and my mother were staying. There, I hoped, Julie and Rachel would have the opportunity to drink together and female-bond.

Back at the room, it quickly became clear this had been a fine idea. When my mother went into the bathroom to take out her contacts and wash her face, Julie and Rachel, without prompting, poured the gin into glasses and lay on the bed side by side to watch Rihanna videos on Rachel's laptop.

"She's grinding the hedge," observed Rachel. "I feel like not even M.I.A. would be grinding up on a hedge."

"But if you're in a video, your job is to commit frottage with any object that's placed in front of you, or behind you," said Julie. "Be it Will Smith or like an Easter Island head."

"If you're a girl, can you technically commit frottage?" Rachel wondered. "Is there a dictionary here?"

"Just Google; see 'Frottage: A method of making a design by placing a piece of paper on top of an object and then rubbing over it, as with a pencil or charcoal.' What? This dictionary is bullshit."

"But that means if you were to put a charcoal crayon in Rihanna's vagina, you could get a rendering of hedge with superincredible verisimilitude."

"Yeah, if you were like, Excuse me, I'm just going to put this piece of paper here." Julie drank her gin.

"And this charcoal up in here." Rachel sipped, keeping up.

Julie thought about it. "That would be money in the bank, charcoal-drawing plants with your vagina, if you were an artist, and you wanted a grant or something? 'I will use my female orifice not merely as inspiration for my work but as the implement itself.'"

Rachel nodded. "Cunt charcoal." On screen, Rihanna writhed obliviously. I looked at these women lying peacefully together, drinking, and felt sleepy with happiness, an overwhelming contentment with the women life had given me. The desire I'd had to add Khadijah seemed obscene, a barbaric invasion of this sweet idyll.

"Rachel, you have to do it, you're such Whitney Biennial material. Especially if you do the frottage on people live in the museum."

"I'll try it out at Art Basel. It seems more sanitary if there's just rich people around."

"I'll do Basel Miami," said Julie. "My exhibition will be called 'Eighteen Studies of Viggo Mortensen's Face,' by Julie Oenervian."

My mother emerged from the bathroom. "What are you two talking about?" she asked. She was in her askew golden spectacles again. Her hair was down, and she wore a turquoise bathrobe. "Josh, do you understand what the hell they're saying?"

"Dirty jokes, Mom."

"I don't mind dirty jokes if they're not degrading anybody. Sometimes I still like them if they're degrading the right person."

"It would take too long to explain," said Rachel. "How are you doing? Do you want us to stop being noisy, so you can go to bed?"

"No, that's fine, thanks, you two are very cute." My mother smiled. "What I would love to do is turn on the television for just a second, and check the weather. If we're going to do Joshua Tree tomorrow, Rachel, I want to make sure this rain that's supposed to start tomorrow night doesn't really get going until after we get home." She picked up the remote and studied it.

"We can look it up online," said Julie. "Believe me, we're not doing anything important."

"That'll take too long," said my mother, with an authority born of deep, generational ignorance of the Internet, and turned on the TV. As local news buzzed to life, I joined Julie and Rachel on the bed to see if we could YouTube people drawing with their genitals. We were finding them surprisingly elusive when my mother took a sharp breath.

"Look, look," she said. "It's Julie, where we just were."

"Oh my god," Julie said. "We really don't have to watch this, you guys." It was the skinny newscaster from the party, shoving her mic in Julie's face.

"What do you think you would do," the woman asked Julie, "if this turned out to be the last season, as some have speculated?" *Be funny or colorful* screamed the woman's eyes.

"You look so pretty," said Rachel. "I could never be so poised on camera."

"Oh God, please change it," said Julie. "Please." She sounded genuinely distressed.

"Well, hmmm," her television image said, stalling.

Rachel put her hand on Julie's arm. "It's cool," she said, "we can just turn it off, if you don't—"

Then something horrible happened.

"I think it could be nice to be homeless. There's this law they're going to pass in Massachusetts . . ." said the Julie on the television. The Julie in the hotel room with us covered her face with her hands as we watched the TV version of Julie describe Rachel's program.

"And it says that if you're about to be homeless you can just call the state of Massachusetts, and they'll pay your rent. Which I think is an awesome policy."

"Massachusetts, of course!" said the newscaster.

"Right? So, if we get canceled I'm going to buy six hundred Dean and Deluca to-go meals and a Netflix account, check into the Boston Ritz-Carlton, and be homeless in Massachusetts."

"Thank you for that," the newscaster said. "Julie Oenervian, informed and hilarious."

My mother clicked the remote, and the picture flickered away, just as the serene, corpse-like face of a meteorologist appeared. There followed about two seconds of silence.

"There's nothing wrong with what you said," my mother said. "It was slightly weird because you sounded so enthusiastic over dinner, so, I thought, Why watch? Who cares, is what I mean."

"I'm so ridiculous," said Julie. "Sorry, oh my god, I was just looking down at a microphone trying to think of something funny to say. Silliness came out of me. I'm so embarrassed."

"It's okay," said Rachel. "I get it. I mean I don't totally understand why you were so into it before and then . . . Or actually, I do understand, you were being nice. Which is cool."

"I meant what I said when I was being nice, it was just I had to say something spur of the moment, when the microphone was, you know, in my face."

I felt an urgent need to defend somebody. But I didn't know who I was supposed to defend.

"I am so so sorry, I suck," said Julie.

"Let's just not talk about it anymore," said Rachel. "It doesn't bear discussing, it doesn't bother me." She rose from the bed, walked to the sink with her glass, and tipped her gin into the basin.

Once Julie and I were in the car on the way home, she was the first to speak.

"I was extemporizing."

"Exactly." This wouldn't have happened with Khadijah, I thought, and dropped the thought.

"What?" She threw up her hands. "You want me to be tactful about your sister's welfare thing when I'm trying to make up a joke about what I'd do if we got canceled? I'm sorry, stuff comes out. It's part of my job."

"The truth comes out when you need to be funny."

"As I just explained fifteen minutes ago, I didn't mean it as a criticism of your sister. It was bullshit for a reporter." She clutched her seat belt with both hands, as if to brace for a crash.

"Yeah, I mean, everyone gets that, so, hey. It was just, whoops, awkward, change of tune."

"WHEN YOU MEET YOUR BOYFRIEND'S FAMILY, YOU'RE SUPPOSED TO BE SUPERNICE TO THEM. I WAS BEING NICE. And later, it was, What kind of honesty do you think is going to come out of me, after what she said about my dad? She was looking at him like she was going to bite him in the neck."

"He denied the existence of male privilege. You don't do that around Rachel."

"He downplayed its significance in his particular, very difficult life. That's different."

"It's just what every bourgeois libertarian does, discount their own particular privileges as irrelevant to their success."

"'Bourgeois libertarian.' Would that be me, for example?"

"You're a dark-skinned woman, so I never think of you that way, I just think of you as really good. You're excused."

"What does that mean?"

"I don't know," I said. "I'm sorry, it's just been a rough visit. I didn't eat enough at the premiere. I'm really hungry."

Some strangeness worse than fighting bubbled up beneath us. We rode the rest of the way home in silence.

We were back before the battle stations when we started to speak again. "You clearly don't—you don't see us, my family, very well," she said. "I don't get your mother and your sister either."

"I'll try to get your parents better," I said. "I'm just trying to be loyal. My dad picked women he loved over his family. I can't be like that."

"Do you like my parents?" she asked.

"Yeah. Yeah."

"I don't want to be your Khadijah's mom," said Julie. She slammed the door.

I flossed, alone at my battle station.

7.

The Opera

Two and a half days later, Rachel and my mother had left Los Angeles, and a cold peace prevailed in the house. But Julie and I weren't touching each other.

As dust particles swam in brutal morning sunbeams, I sat at the desk in the study and sent two e-mails to my manager: one checking on a Portuguese hedge fund that wanted to license an instrumental remix of "This Is Just Wrong" for its website, another checking on a Ukrainian cell phone commercial, which was going to play "This Is Just Wrong" as gendered cell phones freak-danced each other. Sending them made me feel that the way I supported myself shared a common ancestor with employment. I so enjoyed this sensation, the warmth of purpose, that I wrote a third business e-mail to Gordon, whom I was going to see that night; he and Cora and Julie and I had a long-standing date to see Joanna Newsom at Disney Concert Hall.

"This is a wild proposition," I wrote. "But would you ever be interested in having me build you a home studio? In that big-ass garage of yours?" This was entrepreneurial initiative. "I'd give you the bro rate."

The response was swift, festooned at beginning and end with garlands of exclamation points. "Yes," wrote Gordon. "How can we make this happen quickly? I have SO MANY SONGS IN MY HEAD AND SOON CORA IS (Cora and I are) GOING TO GENERATE A BABY."

We resolved to explore specifics at the concert. I hid my laptop and my cell phone from myself, under the covers of the bed, and took out my acoustic guitar. I was still waiting for notes on the *Spirits of New Orleans* score. It was the time of day Julie had encouraged me to set aside for songwriting. Since our evening with Khadijah a week ago, I had known—how I loathed this knowledge—whom the song must be about. TV could show us wish fulfillment, but pop songs were for longing. Replacing the woman with a song about the woman—surely, this was adulthood.

I slung the guitar strap over my shoulders and whipped around a corner and aimed the guitar like an M16 at the block of machinery in the hall closet, the brain of the smart house, with its red veins flowing to the DVR, the AC, the alarm system, the sprinklers. I charged out of the closet and down the hall in bare feet. A white swath of kitchen spread open before me.

I swung the guitar onto my back, hoisted myself up onto the kitchen island, and sat cross-legged beneath the hanging pans.

"Good evening," I said, addressing the track lighting. I strummed an open chord and waited for a song to come. I stared at the ceiling and hoped to hear a melody reverberate around the kitchen like a bird.

Instead I saw, reflected in the side of a hanging pot, the distorted bust of a twenty-eight-year-old man: the expanding forehead, the thickening neck. The person on the side of the pot could not with credibility write any song I would want to write, so I stood on the island and gingerly removed the pots, the insidious, face-fattening wok. I dismounted the island, found a photo in a bedroom drawer, the one our Australian label had taken of me three years earlier, and placed it in the island's sink. Looking at it as I played, I searched for a loop of four high minor chords, the song the boy in the picture would write about a sad-eyed girl he loved.

I shut my eyes and was in a department store covered with dust. It was a picture that came to me from the photo spreads of downtown Manhattan after the towers fell, but that didn't matter. Dust coated the shoulders of shirts on their spinal racks.

Khadijah sat on a desk beside a cash register, in a wool sweater and a wool skirt, dustless, kicking her feet to a muffled floor tom counting four—that rhythm was the first component, perhaps.

In the department store, I saw everyone I knew in high school break in, through the emergency exit, and run laughing through the room. They were still teenagers, and they ran like Vikings in a church, unopposed, rustling the rows of sleeves. Dust carpeted their faces, so that you couldn't see their eyes, and so that their hair stuck limp to their necks. They converged upon us at great speed. They were memories who wanted to be made corporeal, from my song, but Khadijah slid off the cashier's desk and said, "It's me you'll bring back." Sounds started to form discrete chords as she touched her fingers to my hand.

This was when the front door of the house opened, and there entered not a high school's worth of spectral adolescents but Julie's father, Samson.

"I was just reading about your father's country house in the paper," he called to me from the foyer, a Crate & Barrel bag full of wineglasses supported by one forearm as he locked the door behind him. Julie had warned me this morning he might be coming over to bring what he felt were necessary additions to our kitchen. "The one he converted, from a little cabin in the Berkshires."

The *Times'* Sunday Real Estate section had a piece in which my father was featured: "The Death Grip of the Summer Home." Of course Sam had read it.

My father's recent additions to the cabin had been a dramatic, autodidactic experiment in residential architecture. The Monopoly house of my childhood, the dacha, had grown three stories tall, retaining its original small, square footprint. Each floor was an undivided room strewn with beds and desks. It was an outpost where troops might be marshaled, where conquests and retributions might be planned. The roof was trimmed with a green stripe, and the stripe was full of white Celtic knots.

"Oh, that, yeah," I said.

"No, no, it's a courageous thing to design your own house," said Sam. "A brave risk." He stopped to glance at my head shot, lying in the island's sink, in which I was twenty-five, long-haired, smoking a cigarette and wearing a tincture of eyeliner. This gave me enough time to seize the Crate & Barrel bag and march with it toward the guest bedroom, leading him away, I hoped, from the head shot.

"It's good of you to carry something," he said. "In the *Times,* he says the contractors have been stringing him on, making him spend money left and right," Sam followed me through the kitchen. "It's terrible what these people do."

"His biggest mistake was granting this woman at the *Times* an interview," I said. "She's the new girlfriend of this guy he knows from college, Beanie Camden, and my father will do virtually anything for any person named Beanie Camden." I shrugged to convey insignificance. I realized that, out of great insecurity, I was bragging about my family—implying a picturesque insanity, a glorious downward mobility, *fin de race.*

Sam looked at me sadly. "Ah," he said, "old guys have their dreams, you know."

Somewhere in Massachusetts, my father, buffered by Mueller-affiliated income, was lavishing cash on improvements to the cabin, instead of writing the essays he'd moved to New York to write. I began to reinterpret his story. Perhaps the problem wasn't that he'd cheated on my mother; perhaps the problem was that he'd never gotten what he'd pursued. I could write songs about the ghost of a teenage girl and age into such a man. Or I could stop dreaming about Khadijah and get her. She'd be back in L.A. to visit Todd. Giving her the stone might not have been such an infantile performance after all. And Khadijah, whoever she might be now, would not mock a member of my family on television for liberalism.

I was able to bludgeon these thoughts into submission by the time Julie came home from work to spin into a concert-going outfit. I gave her a breezy kiss, as if affection were flowing freely between us. Samson's voice rose and expanded with joy through the guest room as he greeted his only child. I knew from the creak of bedsprings that Julie had sat on the bed to embrace him, and for a moment they became quiet and affectionate. I could just barely overhear them.

"Sleep here tonight, Dad," Julie said, "if you don't feel like dealing with the traffic on the way back to Glendale. It doesn't bother us."

"What is this music you are going to see, Jules, instead of staying here to hang out with your decrepit father?"

"It's indie-rock music, Dad; it's this horrible thing. Her name is Joanna Newsom. She's this singer with a tiny voice who plays the harp. Everybody loves her, for reasons no one can explain."

Gordon met us in the lobby of Disney Concert Hall, in a tweed suit and tie. He wore a vest, a watch chain, and a longer beard than the one he'd had three weeks ago. Cora hadn't followed him into the Edwardian; she wore a wool skirt and a pigeon gray cowl-neck that made her pregnancy more visible than usual. I'd known she was due in three months, but it wasn't until I saw the mound that I recognized the threat it posed to my career. It might give Gordon a deadline by which to record his songs, but with a house full of puling, Cora might not permit the garage to become a second source of bedlam on the property.

"What do you think of the new album?" Cora asked me. "As a musician?"

"I mean, she's fucking amazing," I said, "but I kind of miss the home-studio sound of the first record." I realized at this point that my need to make money had taken whole possession of my tongue, but there was nothing I could do to stop it. "On that album, you could feel that it was just her, in a space where she felt *at home,* and it was so *warm* for that reason. I actually think that's how a huge proportion of great albums are made. People put their studios in their guesthouses, or whatever structure is at hand."

Julie squeezed my hand and flashed me a look: Calm down. She toed Cora's leather sandals with her black flats.

"You know how to dress for the occasion," said Julie. "You look like a beautiful elf. Not Santa's workshop, Middle Earth.

You're like the best version of all these other girls here. This is Elf Night."

She had a point. Last week, Joanna Newsom had publicly renounced her medieval outfits, but this audience gave off an unmistakable vapor of Tolkien. A slender young woman quested among Gehry's escarpments in pointed boots, her hair parted down the middle, her collar up and ready for the alpine frost. Two teenage girls stood apart from their dates as one adjusted the other's tunic.

"This album has finished music for me," one of their dates explained to them, loudly. "It's complete. I'm done."

"Julie, you are so right," said Cora. She pointed her chin to something behind me. "That girl over there is a perfect little Sephardic elf-princess."

Before I turned around, I knew who it was. Of course she and Todd were here. Why hadn't I seen it? Going to Joanna Newsom Accompanied by the L.A. Philharmonic at Disney Concert Hall was like going to the opera in *Dangerous Liaisons*. It was where you looked at everybody you knew, and they looked at you.

Todd and Khadijah stared at me goggle-eyed for a moment, and we might have kept the conversation brief by unspoken consensus had not the third of their party, whom I recognized from an early mumblecore film, approached Gordon and Julie. He reminded them, in triumphant tones, that they'd hung out with him in Williamstown, three summers ago.

"Gordon, Cora," I said. "This is Khadijah. We went to high school together."

"I love that," said Cora. "I was just talking about how pretty you are."

Khadijah's thrift-store dress was hideous, and would have been merely hideous placed on any other woman in the hall. But on Khadijah it was wickedly hideous. Two strips of a thick, bright red plaid material began at a point on the small of her back and crossed in the middle of her stomach. These components were so crudely stitched together as to seem to have been sewn, as a healing activity, by the inmates of a group home. It was only because of the absurd size of Khadijah's eyes and nose in proportion to her body that the dress took on its evil prettiness. You are *so liberal,* I thought, full of longing. You believe so strongly in the contingency of your own success on factors beyond your control, you're game to dress yourself like a crafts project gone wrong. No libertarian would wear such a dress. I could feel, as an almost tactile presence, the warmth of the northeastern hearth.

This was not an easy circumstance for Julie. Because I knew her face, I could see the weight it carried. But she kept her composure. I was smashed by a wave of guilt.

"Did you guys see Andy Samberg?" asked Todd. "He was on the escalator like five minutes ago. He was wearing purple high-tops." His voice grew louder. "He and the Newsom came to an opening at our friend's gallery last night and they canoodled by the donations tube for like twenty minutes. He made so much money—everyone was going over there to look at them. They had to donate to justify being in that part of the room."

There was a strange silence. We all experienced, I think, a brief shiver of further degradation. The chill of caste. We didn't like that Todd, Todd who stood straight, possessed a noble chin, made music nobody wanted to buy, would speak of Joanna Newsom and Andy Samberg as if they were higher beings.

"It doesn't shock me at all that Andy would do that," said Julie. "I've met him a couple times. I can completely see him going apeshit for the Queen of the Elves."

"And I have no idea who he's talking about," Khadijah said to us. Everyone stared at her for a moment. "Sorry," she said. "I haven't, like, been in front of a television in, like, fifteen years."

"You can't say that in Los Angeles," said Todd, looking at everyone and smiling to show it was a joke.

"He makes funny videos," said Cora. "For *Saturday Night Live.*" She crossed her arms, stuck out her hip, and changed the subject. "I guess it must be over with Joanna and that musician dude named Smog. I feel like there were new pictures of them together on a blog last month."

"That all went down like eight months ago," said Williams-town Guy. "Maybe that's what she'll sing about."

The lights blinked. Our parties separated, and we rode the silver escalators to our seats.

"Well," said Julie, "that was the worst conversation of our lives." "There was no vibe between me and Khadijah whatsoever. Couldn't you tell?" A stone—what did it matter? It was an injoke between high school friends.

"Please try to help me believe it," she said. "I know I'm being difficult. But maybe a little harder than you're trying, please."

During the first half of the concert, Joanna Newsom played with the orchestra. For five minutes, this was dazzling. The sheer gall of her was an act in itself. Her hair was up in deep red ribbons, and her gown and heels were the same color. In front of all the professional musicians in tuxedos, she plucked her giant harp with her gawky arms. She growled out the low notes and howled out the high ones, like a horny, lonely Appalachian.

"She's sitting on some great big balls," whispered Julie in my ear. "You have to give her that. To sing like a country-ass little girl, next to pogrom survivors with violins? She's like this alien being."

But the songs she played with the orchestra were the songs from her most recent album, which were long and impersonal and complicated and very smart. They were not the songs of hers I loved. Soon I felt she was dragging the orchestra behind her, and I wanted her to shed them.

We were all growing restless. Cora tapped me on the shoulder and handed me a pair of opera glasses. They were made of brass, small and gleaming.

"Gordon found these at some vintage store in Vermont," she said. "Aren't they awesome?"

They were. I found I could sweep over the faces across the chasmic hall, and catch people I knew with their guards down. Directly across from us, a little ways down, I found a multigenerational encampment of Lampoon people. In the center there was a senior *Simpsons* writer, based in the reputedly less funny, older, more powerful *Simpsons* writers' room. He sat with his arm around his girlfriend, an arborist suffering cancer or alopecia, who wore a pink kerchief. I'd once seen her at a party, watching her three-year-old daughter from a defunct marriage admire the hair of the woman playing Legos with her, and the look on her face as she watched was one I could not decode: maybe horror, maybe delight. To their left, a row of twentysomethings, legs crossed, from the *Simpsons'* reputedly funnier younger room, one of them with a brunette who had a late-night eclectic hour at the public radio station in Santa Monica, drinking from a large, surely smuggled-in bottle of beer, shaking a pill from a red case into her hand, chasing it down, scribbling a note in pen on her white, hard palm, brow furrowed. Someone had told me once that she was so revered as a hookup that undergrads who had never met her compared reports of her behavior in the Lampoon Castle. To their right, a muscular, young graphic designer, with a scrawny, bearded animator who lived in the desert. They appeared to watch the stage with diminishing interest. This would have been my father's world, I thought, if he'd been born fifteen years later, twenty; the great error of his life was to show up at the Lampoon before it became a portal to comedy. He might have turned his will to rant into a marketable skill.

Khadijah and Todd were a few rows to their right, a little higher. I averted my gaze.

I handed Julie the glasses. "Sorry this is boring," I said, and took her hand. I felt at home, in an egg I didn't want to break.

"Look at the nosebleeds," she said, adjusting the focus. "See the guy with the shaggy gray hair and the glasses? With the Asian girlfriend? He was Cora's English professor at USC. He took her virginity when she was twenty, a month after her dad died."

I took back the opera glasses and found the couple she'd described. They were dignified, contemplative, frowning at Newsom from their inexpensive seats. His glasses were blocky and green. Hers were diamond-shaped, purple.

"He cheated on Cora with that woman," Julie whispered. "She's something called a Language poet. How humiliating, having a pretentious asshole cheat on you with a pretentious loser."

"You're being very subtle," I said. We kissed, fast but hard.

With the glasses, I gave the English professor another look. He was leaning forward now, one elbow on his knee, his hand on his mouth, as if he was deeply moved.

"There is something all of the people here have in common," said Julie. "But I can't put my finger on what it is." She rested her head on my shoulder. It was a joke between us, the size of her head; it was truly large, almost doll-like on her body. "It's on the tip of my tongue, what it is, this thing connecting everyone here," she whispered. "The name of the category."

Intermission came, and I wanted the weight to remain on my shoulder. The offense against my sister still smarted. But I wanted the place we occupied in this egg with other people we'd met at parties to remain recognizable, to our friends and to ourselves. Something of this bond was in my blood. Something in me loved this kingdom. Just as forty-five minutes earlier I had felt the warmth issuing from the hearth of the motherland, so did I now feel that the home I had found in Los Angeles with Julie was twice as warm, twice as real.

"Come with me," I said.

There were lines out the bathrooms, but I found an unmarked door a few feet left of the bar that opened on a supply closet. A bartender in a vest looked at us for a moment as if to stop us, but I thought she'd leave us alone when she saw who Julie was, and she did. There was a cinematic quality to Julie's life, in which the boring obstacles remained out of frame, because people deferred to her. It infuriated me, and made me hate the world for its submissiveness, even as I felt like I was riding in a car through the Great Plains, very fast.

I closed the door, after I'd put back the three mops I'd knocked over, and the three cardboard boxes of sponges I'd knocked over putting back the mops. I leaned against a wall and pulled her toward me. The knowledge that my behavior had endangered what we had, had hurt her, made me want to give her something.

Julie checked her watch. "If this concert wasn't so boring, I might not be this kind of girl. But oh well."

At first it was awkward. We fell back on our usual talk as we kissed and put our hands down each other's pants. The words were so familiar they were more comforting than erotic: the schools we would get our children into, Crossroads and/or Saint Ann's; the things we were going to say to each other on our wedding night in Topanga Canyon; the fact that we owned each other.

"Do I really own you?" she asked. A warmth circuited between us.

"You own my back, my labor," I said. "You and your babies own my hands." The plain fact that neither my back nor my hands had any market value was banished by our kissing, by her hands and mine. It was one of those moments in making out when dry old promises bloom unexpectedly into strange new ones. We were safe.

The mops and the boxes fell over again as we fled into the light. I thought of the bartender in the vest. She or one of the custodians would have to clean up the mess. In the orange-carpeted hallway, I felt I was rushing upward, to take my place on Olympus among the gods, and toppling downward, to some plush vermilion level of Hell reserved for jail punks and homeless people who blew teenagers in Grand Central. Both seemed tolerable. Perhaps I was a traitor to my family. But this engagement, I thought, this soon to be marriage, is my home.

We reached our row before the ushers shut the doors. Cora and Gordon looked at us with poker faces as we fell beside them. Julie sat next to Cora this time, and put her hands on Cora's belly.

"You are going to be the most cultured little baby," Julie cooed. We were both in good spirits, contented, slightly sleepy. "When I was your age, all I heard was people talking about money."

Then everybody stopped talking and clapped, because Joanna Newsom had swished back onstage, in a new dress, with new hair. There were whoops, and libidinous grunts. She had the knack for shapeshifting so prized in musicians. Her legs were exposed, and her hair fell across her shoulders. The orchestra was gone. She sat alone on a hard stool, by her towering harp, and the dress she wore was a silver that toyed with the light.

"BAREFOOT?" wrote Julie in the little red Il Bisonte notebook she kept in her bag. "ARE YOU FUCKING KIDDING

ME?" And barefoot she was, her feet gleaming in the lights. Julie laid her head back on my shoulder, and we were safe in our egg.

The stage was almost bare now. There was only the twenty-five-year-old before us, and her otherworldly harp.

"This is a new song," she said. "I don't even know what it's called yet." She reached out and hit the first strings as she sang a high, pigeonish note. The words were indecipherable. The note spilled down into a staccato flourish; it sounded like Smokey Robinson and like *The Marriage of Figaro*. Now that there was a solitary voice with one instrument, the orchestra retired to the wings, I couldn't help but remember Khadijah's voice imitating Nancy's, the high, sharp tones that rose up and filled the classroom.

"Do you think she's singing for Andy Samberg?" Julie asked me. "Or for the guy she left named Smog?" It was the question that must have been on any number of minds in this room: To whom did this music belong? The new man or the old?

"Both," I said. Her head reestablished itself on my shoulder.

The Smokey Robinson/*Marriage of Figaro* theme was only prologue to the body of the song. It was a folk song, in its essence, a lament. Technical training gave out. Newsom drew her face close to the microphone and confided.

"You've got the run of the place," she sang, "now that you're running around." And on the last syllable she drew back and rasped, her throat half closed. The pleasure of running, and the dizziness and illness of it—that was her subject. I turned to see the faces of my friends and found Cora looking up at the professor in the nosebleeds, though she had her hands on her swollen belly. I took the glasses off the arm of my seat and looked at the spot where I had not allowed myself to look before. Khadijah was a head in a honeycomb of heads, and I didn't dare linger on her. All I could read on her face was a tension, an absence of happiness.

This music was for fallen men and women, I decided, gazing into the sectioned hollows of the ceiling, though the notion was jejune. The betrayals that bound Cora to the professor and bound me to Khadijah and bound the professor to his girlfriend and the singer of the song to the men we couldn't see, they would all be forgiven. We would all be spared, because our type of behavior had its place in the world. This music could not have been written without shame.

"The phantom of love," sang Joanna Newsom, "moves among us at will." It wasn't until the song was over and applause filled the room that I missed Julie's head on my shoulder. She was sitting erect, looking at me. The opera glasses were in her hand. She'd deduced, I knew, whose face I'd been searching for and staring at. The warmth we'd earned in the closet dissolved in the air, victim to a colder, prettier truth.

After the encore, we filed down the escalator, and outside to the podiums where valets took our tickets and ran for our cars. Khadijah and Todd must have street-parked; they were nowhere to be seen.

Gordon and I embraced. It was what we had to do, after a concert like that. As two musicians, or at least an aspiring-musician-cum-animator-cum-aspiring-musician and a middling-to-failed-musician-cum-aspiring-studio-engineer, we had to acknowledge we'd witnessed a moment of brilliance. We didn't say the word, but that's what it had been. Whether Joanna Newsom would be able to sustain it on an album, she'd struck that golden bell.

"We have to get you in the garage." He whispered in my ear, so that his pregnant wife couldn't hear. "I'm going to have the talk with Cora in the morning."

We shook hands and belabored each other about the head and shoulders the way I'd seen the popular seventh-grade boys do when I was a despised pacifist in the school yard. Segueing into self-parody, we bumped chests.

"Look, Cora," said Julie. "The men are so hot from the elf queen show they have to blow off some steam."

"Didn't you guys like the concert?" I asked.

"Her persona can be a little annoying," said Cora. "But the music—"

"What's wrong with her persona?" asked Gordon, too quickly. He was smiling, but there was gravel in his voice. "Can you not be jealous of every female artist your age who gets to be the center of attention, even when she's kind of yodeling with a harp?"

"Can you not interrupt when your wife occasionally tries to say something?" Julie asked him. She placed a hand on Cora's shoulder. "I mean, if we're on the topic of wanting to be the center of attention."

This did not augur well. When Julie criticized Gordon to his face, it was often a prelude to darker observations about men in general. It was time to speed our exit. I put on my jacket, which had been draped over my arm, and detected a strange weight in the left pocket.

I shoved my hand in the pocket and closed it on a stone wrapped in a napkin. It was the same size as the one I'd plucked from the urinal trough. Khadijah must have dropped it in during intermission, when I'd left my jacket on my seat. I was aghast—it could have slipped out and tumbled onto Julie's shoe. Could Khadijah have kept it in her bag all this time, and carried it to Massachusetts and back to Los Angeles? What was the function of the napkin? Was something written on it? Could my sweat have soaked through my body into the pocket and destroyed a freshly written note, or poem? My face, probably, was not normal.

"I'm sorry, Gordon," said Julie. "That was an unfriendly thing for me to say." She put a hand to her chest. "Sometimes my mother just sort of explodes out of me. It's why I work with wild animals."

Julie's VW came and we said good-bye, each couple leaving the other to fight.

I steered through the net of traffic between the concert hall and the 110. Usually I liked to drive, and Julie liked to enjoin me to drive faster with jokes at my expense, and usually I liked these jokes. But now we were both silent.

When we were on the 110, she cleared her throat. "I'd like to advance a theory."

I waited. I took the ramp to the 10 for the short jump to Olympic.

"The theory," she said, "is called the theory of elves."

"I gave you something reasonably similar to a hand job," I said. "Why do you sound like you're going to say something divisive?"

"It almost redeemed the concert. Thank you. But what I was about to say was just that it was like being an anthropologist, watching this intriguing tribe of people who enjoy this music. And this tribe I will call the Tribe of Elves. The theory of elves states that many pretentious, young, white and whitish people want to be like the elves from The Lord of the Rings. The deal with the elves in The Lord of the Rings is that they're on their way out. They're this vanishing race of willowy, pale, scruffily elegant superpeople, and they like to be out in the woods, and they speak this soft, pretty language, and they're kind of constantly unfazed. They wear doilies on their heads, and they play the harp. They have this better land they're eventually going to go to. But they can't just get in their magic boats and disappear. No. They have to persevere, and save Middle Earth. They have to stick it out just a little longer, so they can help the humans and the dwarves and hobbits and all the shorter, stupider people fight the evil wizard and the orcs. And the elves are like, 'Take hope, Stubbier Ones, little dwarves and hobbits and shit. For we just barely remain, with our sense of noblesse oblige, to save you. And by the way, our numbers are dwindling, because we're about to sail away to our just reward. Look upon us while you can. You should be grateful for this Language poetry we're writing, and this beautiful folk music you should like, because they're our vanishing art forms, and they're how we will keep you away from television, which is the Eye of Sauron. Well, my friend, I am Gimli the Dwarf, and I am proud. I have a big head, and am thus well-suited for television. My arms couldn't reach halfway across a harp without my arm flesh swinging into the strings. I am not an ethereal girl. I appear on TV for money. And my parents actually want me to make money, because they just arrived in Middle Earth, which was what the Jews were like fifteen minutes ago. So you can jizz all over your Sephardic elf, in her raggedy clothes, and Andy Samberg can have his elf queen, and you can all go *dwindle* together. I'll go find a rich dwarf, and everybody's happy. It's like that book they talk about in *The Great Gatsby,* the book Tom likes about the passing of the great race. You're just passing from this Earth, you and your elf sisters, and I'm going to stay here, and I'll be okay. I mean, I hate Persians and Armenians too, and I forget that I am them, but at least Persians aren't like, 'Look at me, you guys, because I'm the last unicorn.'"

"I think I missed Olympic."

"That response didn't have enough words in it."

I put my hand in the pocket of my jacket.

"Why are we talking about race?" I demanded. I rubbed the napkin-wrapped stone with my thumb. "We talk about race in this country when we don't want to talk about something else, like economic equality, or global warming."

"Yeah, *those* are the topics on my mind. I was trying to tell you how I feel without being accusatory. I take back what I said about finding a rich dwarf. I am angry!"

I yanked the VW off the 10 so we could make our way west on side streets and cut over to Olympic past Koreatown.

"Baby, don't drive one-handed. This is silly."

"You're absolutely right." I extracted my hand from my jacket and put it on the wheel.

"Do you have something in your pocket?"

"Sorry, my cell phone was vibrating."

"Do I scare you? Does it scare you when your baby talks about race? You look like a tiny, frightened deer."

"Tiny, frightened deer" was a relatively recent variation on the traditional "shy deer," which we'd coined on our second date. It was what she called me when she'd asked me to try on a membranous Prada bathing suit at the outlets near Joshua Tree and we found it could hide either my butt crack or my genitals but not both, and we'd made out on the bench in the dressing room even though we knew the clerks could see our legs.

"It's all good," I said. "It's just like what do you say to assure someone you love that you're not racist?"

She took my hand in hers, which prevented two-handed driving and thereby signified that our love was more important than safety. Warmth filled the cockpit of the VW and made it a pair of battle stations.

Back in the vestibule of the house, we assumed a shoe-removal posture in which we placed our backs side by side against the wall. Once we were barefoot she threw her silver cardigan on the living room couch and I stayed in my jacket. We were quiet; Samson's Mercedes was still in the driveway, so he must have decided to stay the night in the guest bedroom.

"Are you cold?" She squinted at me. "Why do you still have your jacket on?" She whispered, although Samson might have already been wakened by the engine in the driveway, or by the three inquisitive beeps emitted by the alarm system as we opened the front door and entered the code.

"Yeah, I've got the chills for some reason." I buttoned my jacket, and crossed my arms in front of it, in order to ensure that it would not be taken from me. My hand itched to sink into the pocket and hold the stone. But I knew it was there from the way it brushed against my waist.

"Oh no," she said. "Sick boy. Lie down." She took me to the couch, made me lie on it, and crawled on top of me. "I'll keep you warm," she said. "I'm like a seal shielding its pup from the wind. In medieval Greenland." And then: "Ow. What do you have in your jacket?"

"Listen," I said. "I need to tell you something."

She could move gracefully, Julie. Maybe it had to do with having logged so many hours with lab mice in grad school. Unhurried, her hand slipped into my pocket. She drew out the stone and its napkin sheath, flipped the stone, unfolded the napkin, studied both, separated her body from mine, and rose from the couch without looking at me. She walked with the stone and the napkin through the living room.

Her chest rose and fell. I floated to her side, feeling like I was hovering over my body, a ghost in the house. I read over her shoulder.

The message was written in blue ballpoint pen on the kind of cocktail napkin that comes with the cups of seltzer you buy at intermission. I could not help but note that it broke none of the rules Khadijah and I had set for ourselves.

K HAS WRT. ON YR WALL:
GO AWAY

It was the same stone I had given Khadijah, with the crude circled A. I backed away from Julie to address her. I needed some physical distance from the stone to convince myself I was a real person in the midst of real events, to shake the feeling of unreality.

"Baby," I said, trying to conjure heat in the air.

Julie looked at me with no expression. The stone still in her hand, she cranked back her arm like a radical of '68. I wondered if she was going to throw it at my head.

I flinched, and the stone went wide. It struck the window, near the corner where the living room met the foyer, and cracked the pane. Julie had not, I realized from the crack's location, had the intention of throwing it anywhere near me.

But because the window had been struck, the banshee wail of the alarm system saturated the house. It was everywhere all at once, with no point of origin. Beneath it, the male robot began to speak. *Security breach, team mobilized, patroller now in route.*

Julie ran to the alarm box and jabbed the keys. The voice would not stop. Nor would the wail. Indeed, subtracting elements from the picture proved impossible; elements added themselves. First, Sam ran into the living room in his pajamas, his mouth moving, inaudible. Second, the security firm arrived in the form of a helicopter. The blades filled a midrange between the Talking Heads baritone of the robot administrator and the banshee wail. Then the helicopter switched on its spotlight, and the scene assumed the quality of war.

Julie didn't look angry now. I could tell she had the same vegetable taste in her mouth that I had in mine: humiliation. This only child, who had surpassed the wildest expectations of her father, had thrown a stone into a pane of glass, and it was inconceivable that the damage could ever be undone.

8.

It's the Spontaneity
That Will Make the Energy
Feel Real

The next morning, Julie had to wake up at 5:30 to spend four-teen hours in the editing room. The starfish-focused epi-sode currently in progress at *Julie vs. Animals* made no sense to anybody narratively or scientifically. "Their mating," Julie had explained to me a week ago, "is too slow, and when you watch it in fast-forward it looks like fractal art or something. We actually made two of the writers do an enactment in costumes, but that was unfunny because you felt bad for two guys who aren't actors trying to be actors." If the episode could not be edited into an acceptable state, Julie would have to put on a puppet show with two dried, store-bought starfish, and make them speak in funny voices. This was a recourse she hoped dearly to avoid.

I had no such reason to rise before dawn. But when Julie's phone sounded its alarm tone and she rolled out of bed, I fol-lowed her into the bathroom. As she showered, I closed the lid of the toilet and sat. We did not speak.

When she emerged from the steam, I moved past her into the shower. Our arms brushed, like the arms of strangers passing on a bus. She washed her face beneath the future-children as I ran cool water over my head.

"I can't morning-talk with you right now," she said. "You don't look like my husband to be, to me, in this moment. When you look halfway like that guy again, I'll talk."

When she left the house—no kiss, slammed door—I shadowed her all the way to the front door. It was strange how acutely I felt it, having to say good-bye until daybreak came and the world went dark again.

I drove to Canters, the only restaurant open at 5:55 a.m., and stewed in coffee through the dawn. I did nothing for ten minutes. Only after I had an egg sandwich in my hands did I realize what booth I was in. It was irregularly shaped, secluded, wedged in a shadowy corner. It was here that Julie and I sat whenever she'd need last-minute prep for an audition. We'd convened such sessions three times, the two of us face-to-face, she delivering her lines, I staring at her, trying to hold myself like an enigmatic director.

"I am actually saying these things in front of people in three hours," she'd said, on one of these occasions, drawing skulls on a script. "This is happening. This is happening." My main job, I had known, was to persuade her of the possibility of her non-fuckedness. "It's being relaxed that will make the spontaneity possible, and it's the spontaneity that will make the energy feel real," I said once. "It'll be more like just you talking and they've brought you in because you talking is enchanting." She called me uxorious; we held hands. Desperation, teamwork in defiance of a fast-falling night, medieval Greenland.

I will write a song about my internal torment, I thought, like Joanna Newsom's. I took the paper place mat from the seat across from me and lay it beside my own place mat. I will write lyrics about what it would be like being with Khadijah, I thought, on the left, and lyrics about what it would be like being Julie's husband on the right. But no lyrics came. Instead, to my surprise, I drew two houses.

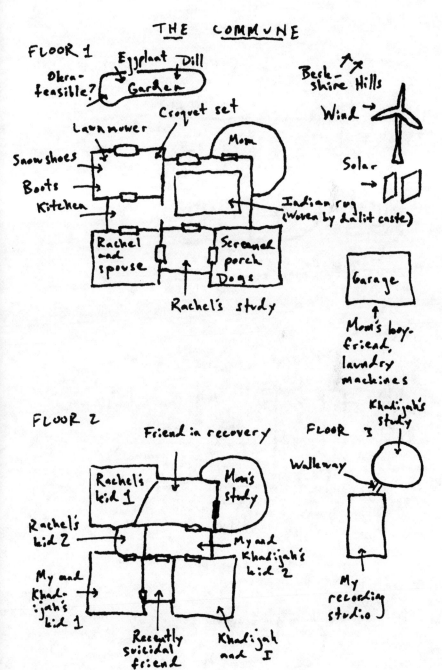

THE COMMUNE

FLOOR 1
Okra-feasible? Eggplant Dill
Garden

Berk-shire Hills
Wind →

Lawnmower
Croquet set
Mom
Snow shoes
Boots
Kitchen
Solar →
Indian rug (woven by dalit caste)

Rachel and spouse
Screened porch
Dogs

Rachel's study

Garage

Mom's boy-friend, laundry machines

FLOOR 2
Friend in recovery
FLOOR 3
Khadijah's study
Walkway

Rachel's kid 1
Mom's study

Rachel's kid 2
My and Khadijah's kid 2

My and Khadijah's kid 1
My recording studio

Recently suicidal friend
Khadijah and I

169

THE AERIE

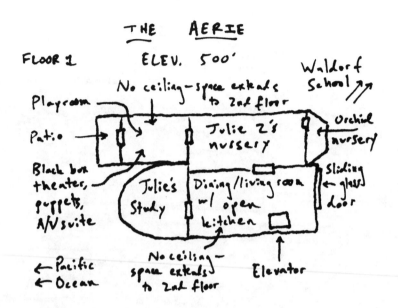

FLOOR 1 — ELEV. 500'

Playroom
Patio
Black box theater, puppets, A/V suite
No ceiling—space extends to 2nd floor
Julie 2's nursery
Julie's Study
Dining/living room w/ open kitchen
Waldorf School ↗↗
Orchid nursery
Sliding glass door
← Pacific
← Ocean
No ceiling—space extends to 2nd floor
Elevator

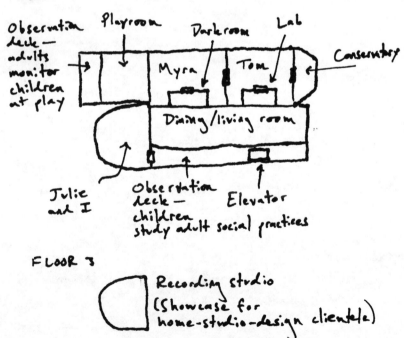

FLOOR 2

Observation deck—adults monitor children at play
Playroom
Darkroom
Lab
Myra
Tom
Conservatory
Dining/living room
Julie and I
Observation deck—children study adult social practices
Elevator

FLOOR 3

Recording studio
(Showcase for home-studio-design clientele)

When the place mats were done, I looked up. Hours had passed. Outside, rainy Fairfax was clogged with lowing rush-hour traffic. If I had written lyrics, as I'd intended, expressing the same sentiments as the drawings, I might have called it a productive morning and gone home to find some chords on the guitar. But these floor plans, and the zeal with which I had composed them, made me pause and contemplate the condition of my mind.

Cruelty manifests in confidence and clean lines, I decided. It's sanity that resists architecture. I had not been aware of how mean I had become until I found a way to express my meanness.

I had been living in the belief that I could choose between lives, and that these lives were paths with calculable ends. I bit down on the fleshy base of my thumb, moved by the hugeness of my own stupidity. I felt like I had when one day, at age eleven, I turned and knelt on the floor, pants down, before a full-length mirror, in my grandparents' basement, in order to see, for the first time, what my own bare ass looked like. That seeing-one's-own-ass-cheeks sensation of *I am as soft and absurdly constructed as everyone else.*

9.

The Cats

I t was 2:30 p.m. when, in the process of ordering business cards for my studio design venture, I received a phone call from Julie. "Where are you?" she asked. "Can you come home?" She spoke in exactly the tones I'd hoped to hear, tones of reconciliation, clemency.

I pulled into the driveway and found her sitting on the front step, her maroon flats on the walk.

I sat down beside her. "I really don't want you to break up with me," I said.

"You're not going to feel that way in two minutes." She began to cry.

A vision came to me, complete. An office, trembling. A Peabody Award trophy toppling off a windowsill.

"You cheated on me. You slept with a guy from work who made fun of me," I said. "Or you slept with Simon, because he was the one who liked me."

I waited for her to correct me. She looked at me.

I knew her well enough that I could feel her reasons for doing it, as if I were the one who had done it. She was not to be mocked by her colleagues. I was not the only one with options. She was part of a palm-shadowed world of which I knew nothing.

She shook her head. "I kissed Gordon."

"In his garage, right?" Before I knew I was moving, I was walking up and down the lawn. My hands were taking turns scratching each other, as if I had mosquito bites on my fingers. I could hear the crack of snail shells under my boots. "Where I was supposed to build his studio."

"No, we went to the Peninsula."

"Do people go to the Peninsula to make out? Is that a thing?" I'd always pictured old, rich people going to the Peninsula to get drunk and revive their marriages.

She looked at her flats. "First we went to get a drink in the middle of the day. I played hooky from starfish editing. Couldn't do it. You can understand that, after what happened. Then we were at the bar at the Peninsula, because I wanted to go someplace so stupid and fancy it was going to suck me out of my head. And then we were at the bar and it was like, People are looking at us, they'll get the wrong idea, let's get a room and eat cake there." She paused. "Then we got in the room and we started kissing. And then I freaked out and left."

"You both started kissing?" I asked. "Like a spontaneous explosion?"

Julie said nothing.

"Just two wildly successful TV people finding each other?"

I knew she would not let this go unanswered. She didn't.

"I'm sorry, baby," she said. "But there are things you don't totally understand. It's not your fault you haven't experienced them." Through my rage, I could see her trying not to be cruel.

"I'm sorry for the things I'm saying," she said, "but look, you know what you did. I just don't envision myself being treated like that. It's just not the way I pictured my life when I was fourteen: 'I'm going to have a fiancé who flirts with his high school crush and then we'll have this massive fight in front of my dad, and everyone will be embarrassed for me and I'll marry him anyway.'"

"Gordon has a wife." I half-swallowed the end of the sentence, quieting down. "She's having a baby." I recalled that I had wished Cora's pregnancy would disappear, last night, when I viewed it as an obstruction to Gordon's home studio, but now I was the baby's committed champion. "This isn't just about us."

"We can't do anything for them at this point," she said slowly. "It's just us we have to worry about."

I lay down among the snails, on my back. A crow was loping through the sky between two trees.

"You were my dream-girl princess," I said. "Remember? The night of Authentic Korean? Why did we go to Authentic Korean? Why did we let him— I should have known from the way he wanted to make your babies."

We both fell silent. I closed my eyes; there was an evil green pulse inside my brain, and I needed to make it stop. It reminded me of something: the last days of Shapeshifter, when the wheels began to separate from the chassis, when things went numb.

A band, I thought, can only play well if it's a happy family, whereas a family can soldier on as a shell of itself without anybody outside it noticing. A family doesn't perform for anybody but itself; a band performs for a crowd, and so cannot hide its unhappiness. Its unhappiness rots its music from within.

Or maybe it was a matter not of happiness versus unhappiness but of passion versus blandness. A band had to be an *impassioned* family. I never envied happy families. Instead, I looked back, with nostalgia, to the time before the divorce, when my parents drew blood from each other. There was the night I sat awake, six years old, upright in bed, as I listened to the rattling of doors in their frames, the clatter of silverware drawers overturned. My father's short, declarative sentence: *You stabbed me.* The melody in his voice. And the counterpoint in my mother's apologies, her sobs. They were a band; I didn't sleep on nights of fighting, I twisted my sheets into ropes and looked up at the glow-in-the-dark constellation stickers that still adhered to my ceiling. I was at the age where I could lie safe beneath fading green comets and yet understand and love the way my mother and father attacked each other. I loved the Band-Aid on my father's thumb at breakfast. After the divorce the essence that we lost, it wasn't happiness. What we lost was being a band.

I remembered this too: There was one night in Shapeshifter when Deke was doing yoga backstage at Mercury Lounge, and our guitarist was so angry at him for doing yoga before he went in front of our paying customers and sang about wanting to kill himself that he poured his can of beer down Deke's pants while Deke was in Downward-Facing Dog. And Deke leapt up like an eel had bitten his leg and they threw each other onto the couch and Deke's face was in the ice bucket with the beer cans in it, and we were a family, and we played like a family that night, a family that hadn't yet lost itself.

"We can just throw them out, the last three days," Julie said when she finally spoke. "We both were dumb."

I nodded. "I've been cruel."

But how can I begin to describe the feeling that came over me? I felt like a mule being harnessed to a tank and instructed to pull. A strong breeze carried a hint of sulfur from the tar pits three blocks away. I could feel that forgiveness would be like a tar pit, for both of us—a pit into which neither of us could bring ourselves to descend. Forgiveness—the word sounded lofty, but it was a willingness to be soiled. A sinking down to how things were. We could do many things, Julie and I, but accept degradation? Tear down the billboards for ourselves we carried in our heads?

"Let's walk," she said.

We rose, and moved quickly, going in no particular direction, two abreast, down the sidewalk.

The neighborhood was not West Hollywood, nor really Miracle Mile, but a no-man's-land in between. Without a car, you could still eat. By foot you could reach the Whole Foods, the tar pits, the boutiques and brunch restaurants on Third, Mäni's Café, the Farmers Market. You could walk to the Grove, the fountain that sprayed jets of water in rhythm to the Sinatra that played on hidden speakers. Fifteen minutes on foot brought you to Ukrainian delis—in an anomalous week of anorexic behavior, I'd once awoken so hungry in the middle of the night that I'd gotten in my car and driven to one that was open all night and devoured a Reuben sandwich outside on the sidewalk as homeless men and women slept in apparent tranquillity at my feet.

The neighborhood didn't have the green acidic smell of the Silver Lake hills ("Really healthy cat pee" is how Julie had described the smell of Silver Lake's highlands to me once). Nor did it have the salty ocean air of Malibu and Santa Monica. The sulfur from the tar pits was overpowering at Sixth and La Brea but died almost completely outside its ring, like a spell. There was only the late-fall bouquet of exhaust and cloud, general to the flatlands of the city. The houses were large but not grand, and the ones that were two stories tall had been converted into apartments. It was densely populated; it had been safe for at least ten years. But 1992—the flames and helicopters and transparent shields and bricks and stones in the air—it lingered like a pestilence. You could see it in the slicked face of a dead squirrel. You could imagine you tasted the smoke near colossal Samy's Camera, which had been burned, whose great, lens-like windows had been cracked.

"I'm sorry I threw something, I'm sorry I made out with Gordon," she said. "It was childish, it was fucked. But my inclination is to go utterly apeshit on you when you hide shit from me that jeopardizes my entire fucking vision of my life from this point forward, do you understand?"

"When you act violently hostile toward me, my inclination is going to be to look toward some source of familiarity and home and trustworthiness," I said. "Someone who represents where I come from, when I feel this."

"Feel what?"

"Like you're someone I love, like in the sense of I'll always want to make love to you and talk about movies with you but not in the sense, right now, of, like, you're the person I could have a marriage with and depend on to be the mother of my children."

We stood in the dry gray afternoon on one of the side streets near the Farmers Market. Lying down on the pavement, curling into a fetal position, Julie cried into her hands. It was something about her I'd always found lovable, her sense that the public space was her stage. I was filled with horror by what I'd said. I knelt beside her on the ground.

"Just go," she said.

"I had no idea that I was going to say something like that."

"That's the whole point of you, to be the man I marry and be the father of my children. That's who you are."

"The point of me?"

"Aren't I a fool? Look at me." She laughed through her tears. "It's over. Just go. It's over, okay?"

I shook my head and dabbed at my eyes. "Let's keep walking. Let's not have it be like this."

We turned right on Beverly. Just after we passed Design Within Reach, its trio of adjacent parlors lit like a circus, I noticed shapes that moved low to the pavement. I followed them down an alley to a parking lot and saw they were cats. I couldn't tell if they were a social gathering or a litter. But they were lean and small, not much bigger than rats, and they writhed like snakes by a hedge at the lot's far end.

We approached but kept our distance. "We wouldn't be able to get some cat food around here, would we?" she asked. "That's crazy, right?"

"The store on the corner of La Cienega," I said, "I'm pretty sure has tuna." We bent our steps to the mini-mart, a crowded yellow box where a man in a turban opened three cans for us behind the counter, a service he must have performed regularly for the homeless.

All we had to do was lay the cans on the asphalt near the place where the cats swirled around each other. They ran from beneath the bush, more than we had seen before, and ate.

The cats turned into piranhas, for those cans. I could see the muscles in their threadbare backs work hard as they chewed. They weren't looking at us, only the gift.

"Julie Two," she said, pointing into the mass. I didn't know which one she had in mind, so I picked one with a hooked tail.

"Tom," I said, pointing to one whose face fur went in all directions.

"Myra." She pointed to one that was pushed back from the central squall, maybe starving. We stood side by side with our arms crossed. "That's all three."

"Good-bye," she said conclusively. We embraced. The weight

of her head lay one last moment on my chest. I could hear the cats, eating. By the time she lifted her head, teeth scraped at the bottoms of cans.

I texted Khadijah when I arrived at the motel on Franklin where I'd stayed my first night in town, a new college dropout. Deke had required one more night of privacy with his girlfriend before I moved into his room.

"Engagement no more no residence. Have falafel with me?"

"Last night here," Khadijah answered. "Then I'm going back to Boston for two weeks."

"Falafel in Boston?" A pause of several minutes followed. "Ok."

Tucked in a fuzzy orange blanket, beneath a marbled mirror, I failed to sleep. I woke up early, and drove to Julie's empty house. The sun was barely up, but she'd left for work. I emptied my bureau and my bookshelf and dumped my papers in recycling bags. I snapped shut the clasps on my guitar case. I never looked up—not at the kitchen, or its island, or the bedroom, or the mirror. I slapped my key on the coffee table. In the bathroom, I took the three napkins taped to the mirror—Tom, Myra, and Julie 2—folded them sharply in four, and tucked them in my wallet.

Once I'd packed my possessions in the Volvo, I parked it on a dead-end street in Atwater Village, by the Los Angeles River. At an Armenian coffee shop on Hyperion I booked an evening flight out of Burbank. To do something, I walked beside the water. There was a concrete trench, broad as a freeway, covered in white birds, bisected by a thin mercurial stream. It trickled close along the 5, the sigh of the water amplified by man-made banks, and it was in that noisy confluence, in California's major-key morning, that I said good-bye to my discarded world.

I composed a mantra for myself: *Do not think of Julie or you will die.* I took even more comfort in this: Soon, I would have my father to distract me, to fill my head with his designs. I was going to take a little time off at the loft. It was time to fall back on the Man.

10.

It's a Good Thing,
Just Moving Through the World

The door to the loft was never locked. Allison was a Native
New Yorker and trusted the city to protect her. It was this gesture of aristocratic faith that showed the loft was truly hers and
not my father's, though they had moved here together, just after
the wedding, ten years before. Bought and furnished with Mueller money, its contents were Allison's to gamble.

Closing the noiseless door behind me, I trod lightly on the narrow green carpet, inch-deep, that extended from the door across
a hardwood vastness to the barely perceptible kitchen. I wished
I'd grown up on this enclosed prairie, where privacy was achieved
most often by placing sheer distance between yourself and others,
rather than by shutting yourself in some kind of enclosure, such
as a room. I picked up a chew toy—a disemboweled duck that
could no longer squeak, softened by spit and teeth—and lobbed it
like a Molotov cocktail through the empty space. Miles exploded
from behind a chair, barking. The quiet shattered satisfyingly, all
at once. Allison and my father looked up from their desks in the
study area, and we all joined the dog in making noise.

"So here I am, guys," I said. *Guys* was the only term of address
I'd found that could signify *Dad and Stepmom*. I dropped my lug-
gage to the floor to punctuate the announcement, the sound of
the straps sliding off my back like the hiss of a falling bomb, followed by the thud of canvas on wood.

My father put down his book—*Alpine Castles: An Illustrated Compendium*—and for a moment I could see the distress on his face, before he remembered himself and smiled.

I was not good news. There was much that was homeless about me. I had my messenger bag for my MacBook and notebooks, my guitar, and my black Eastern Mountain Sports zeppelin, full of clothes, receipts, contracts, tax documents. As soon as they were off my back I realized how burdened I'd been the whole subway ride from Kennedy, and what a burden I was. I was tired, and must have looked it. Worse, what I wanted was not quite reasonable. I wanted to claim a couch and stretch my feet— the grown son home for a visit. But I had not grown up here. And while my father lived here, in this canny real estate investment of Bruce Mueller's, it was not quite his to offer.

I had texted my father that morning and informed him I'd be paying a visit, but I hadn't brought up spending the night. If it was not a good time, I reasoned, I could always couch-surf across the ocean of musicians in Brooklyn. Now that I was here, I saw that showing up was in and of itself a major imposition, for my father and Allison. Telling me not to stay would be just as bad an experience for them as enduring my presence. It would make them feel like bad people. And to welcome me in would be to share the loft with my father's past, a memory of an old family, an old wife. I was a Catch-22. Allison and my father knew I knew this. But we went through the motions of ecstatic reunion anyway. My father placed the ice cream bowl he'd been cradling in his lap on the floor, and rose from his armchair to hug me. Allison silenced the gasping espresso machine and crossed the hardwood expanse that lay between the kitchen and the door to take my hands in hers and kiss me on both cheeks.

"What a keenly delightful surprise," my father said.

"It's such a good feeling to have you here, Josh," said Allison.

"A guest from Hollywood," my father said. They looked at each other.

"Sorry," I said. "Should I not have flung myself on you like this?"

They shook their heads. "It's just that when you said you were coming we hadn't anticipated so many bags, maybe," my father said.

I felt sorry for my father. His loyalties were so sharply divided he had to treat everyone lukewarmly. When your wife and your son have opposing needs, you chart a course between.

"I promise I won't stay here longer than pragmatically necessary," I said.

"We want this to be a home to you, Josh," said Allison. "But we're going through . . ." She put her hands on the crown of her head. "A weird time. A deeply weird time. We'll be able to explain very soon."

"Quite so," my father said. He put his hands on the crown of his head, too, making himself symmetrical with Allison. "We hate to be so enigmatic, Josher. But I guess the issue is: What, approximately, are your plans?"

"How long," asked Allison, "do you need to stay?"

"Maybe just tonight?" my father suggested. "And maybe you can articulate what it is you're doing here?"

I said that I wanted to stay one night, and visit an old friend in Boston the next day.

"That sounds just fine," my father said. "And who, pray tell, is your Boston friend?" As he formed the question, he lowered his arms and made his hands dance before Miles's face, absentmindedly mesmerizing the animal.

"Khadijah," I said. "Khadijah Silverglate-Dunn."

My father scooped up the eviscerated duck and threw it. "No mercy, Miles!" he said.

Miles fell upon his quarry, whipped it back and forth to break its neck. A family feeling mushroomed between us, one of those clouds of intimate silence. Allison must have felt her semi-outsider status, because she straightened the reading material on a coffee table: a mock-up of the article she must have been editing, called "Luxury on the Road to Marfa," and some literature that was clearly my father's, *De Gaulle* and *Amnesty International Report: Torture in the '80s.*

"I broke up with Julie," I said.

Allison hugged me. She murmured "sorry" and "oh" and "sweetie" in different combinations in my ear. I couldn't feel what I'd just said. I knew that the breakup was hovering over me, a piano hung from the ceiling by a fraying rope. It would drop soon, but it hadn't hit me yet.

"The engagement is off," I informed my father, over her shoulder. He paced, holding the book behind his back. "That's why I need to stay here tonight. Julie and I are over, so tomorrow Khadijah and I are going to have an informal meal."

Allison pulled back and stared at me.

"There's this falafel truck in Jamaica Plain," I continued, "that's actually pretty acclaimed."

My father considered the news. "Why don't the two of us road-trip?" he suggested. Allison redirected her stare, toward him. "You and Khadijah can be informal with each other, I can see an old friend who's very sick."

"Who?" Allison asked.

"A guy from college you never met, he has cancer. I want to see if he can still hold down a bottle of wine." He averted his eyes to the green carpet. "Very sad."

Allison took my father's hand and escorted him to the far side of the loft. There followed a clenched-looking discussion to which I was not privy. Here I was, an envoy from the past, and already my father was floating away with me, to the city of Nancy. The way he had paced when I'd mentioned the daughter of his former lover, like a scientist struck by a solution to a problem he'd been slaving over for thirteen years—I could only imagine the effect on my stepmother. But after they were done speaking, Allison began to wipe down the countertop, and my father warned me he expected an early start in the morning.

That night, failing to sleep on the foldout couch, I heard their fighting: harsh whispers merged in the dark. But by dawn, Allison was stoical, gym-bound, murmuring to herself as she zipped her bag, shook on her hoodie. My father made her coffee, carried it to her on a saucer; she tugged his beard. I waited, pretending to sleep, until they had said good-bye—it was the least I could do to allow them this tiny solitude. I took a shower while my father did his push-ups, his salutes to the sun. It was only 7:30 when we walked seven blocks to a garage—the car had sat in storage for fourteen years, four years longer than Allison and my father had been married. It was an MG convertible, chewing gum green. Allison had a car for daily use, and my father usually didn't believe in driving, so the MG, her spare, an old gift from Bruce and Laura, was never touched. You could tell by looking at it. It projected dormant lust, like a sleeping beauty in a tower waiting to be roused. And it gave every appearance of immortality. No rust, despite a long hibernation. No stains on the leather. Only a layer of dust so thick I was able to draw a heart on the hood.

We coasted from the garage in the Meatpacking District up the Henry Hudson into Sunday as the sky shed its pink skin and turned blue. It wasn't yet November.

"Maybe we'll have lunch in the North End. New Haven's better for pizza, but we'll be in Boston before noon at the speed we're going now."

I nodded sleepily. "The Italians aren't really about breakfast, as a culture."

"You said it." This point of accord wedged something open. I could almost hear it.

"I'm not sure whether I want more children, Joshy," he said. "Allison would like to have a pair of them, is the issue."

The oaks on either side of the highway tried to pet the car. We were on the flank of Harlem now, with the river on our left, screened by leaves.

"Your stepmother and I went for a stroll in the park a couple years ago. We got to the top of this hill, and it was raining. She said, 'You must have two children with me or you have to leave me,' and I said okay, we could have some kids. But I don't respond well to ultimatums. I might like to move to the South of France, very soon. I'm a creative animal, and I want to write a book of essays. I mean, hell, I might decide to go to Africa, write it there."

183

"Have you not been able to focus on the essays the way you'd like over the last ten years?"

"We're not all musical gentlemen like yourself." He shot me a furious look that smoldered away in two seconds. "Some of us working people, we have responsibilities that we often find prevent us from concentrating on the artistic pursuit at hand. Or romantic pursuits, I might add—Khadijah Silverglate-Dunn! A hubbub, after all these years." He grinned, involuntarily, and my happiness stunned me.

"I've worked," he continued. "I've raised children. And, now, to speak truthfully, Son, drawing up new additions for the house is a lot easier than conceptualizing some sort of lyrical screed. Allison doesn't give a shit what I do in my spare time, but she doesn't like it when I get into bed talking about my objections to rich people and excessive breeding. When I have to tell the truth, I become shitty to people, and I want to be nice. How do you think about shit honestly, and still be nice? When I actually let myself look at how shit is, I either have to forget about it and go draw some new gables on graph paper or I can stay in it, I can root in it, like a Scorsese movie, or maybe more a Van Gogh, and be fucked up in the head, and mean. I want to be nice. So how do I be an essayist?" He paused for breath. "Sorry. I'm going off in an unbecoming manner. Sorry."

He took a joint from his backpack, which I held in my lap. He pressed the joint to the dash lighter, elbows on the wheel, got it started. He offered me a drag, but I turned him down.

"I'm too self-conscious to be stoned around family," I explained.

"Oh, that's psychologically interesting." He finished an exhalation. "See, I prize my relationship with Allison. There's also the little problem of what I'd do for work without Bruce." I knew that the tiny nonprofit he'd founded after we got back from the island had continued to benefit from Allison's father's support, but I didn't know whether new donors had been found. "We're a pretty hungry animal, even though it's just me and a couple interns writing reports on Zimbabwean farming.

"I suppose," he said, and dragged again, "the idea of a couple of little girls running around me in circles shouting 'Daddy, Daddy,' that is somewhat appealing. But I'm scared beyond reason. I'm fifty-eight years old. It's the rest of my life, another kid meandering through whatever fields of bullshit he'll meander through, and finally fetching up on college after the whole thing and needing so much money, which would leave me begging Bruce for more of it." He turned over the joint in his fingers, watching it burn.

"It's a good thing, just moving through the world as a solitary grown-up," I said speculatively. "Maybe you want to chill for a while. Tell me something." I worked up my courage. "Did you like having children the first time?"

"Oh yes. We were so starry-eyed about you and your sister. The children of the future. The horrible poems I wrote about you, when you were a baby! I still have them somewhere."

"What about— Didn't you say you were going to write an essay about how destructive having children had become, or how destructive we figured out it was, after it was too late, or whatever?"

"Sure, but we didn't think about that *then*. We loved the mission of making you, so much that we couldn't see how—how jagged, shall we say, a combination we were, your mother and I. Well, your mother did see. She didn't want to get married, you know, she just wanted children, and she was thirty-one, which in those days . . . And there I was. Wait, oops. Did you know that?"

I looked at the cherry of the joint. I hadn't.

"Oh. Fuck. Sorry. Anyway, I was the one who said we had to marry. I was the one who said we had to make a life together, with our children. I saw it, it was a vision, very clear. That's probably why things didn't work. But it was just kind of dangling before me, like an icicle."

I almost reached across the seat to embrace him. I didn't know why.

"How do you envision me proceeding?" I asked, a minute later. "From this point in my life?"

"I can see you with Khadijah," he said. "But I can't be objective."

"Why not?"

He hesitated. "Have you ever read that John Donne poem about the flea? John Donne's lost his lover. They've split up but they're hanging out together, he and his lover, and he sees this flea on the table between them. And, man, does he covet the soul of that flea. Insect, he says, you're the only place our blood can mix, you who have bitten us both." He nodded. "That's you and Khadijah—the flea, in a positive sense. The last place Nancy and I are together."

It was then that the engine made a sound that communicated, to some intuitive organ in each of us capable of interpreting the protestations of machines, that it was helplessly sick, and wanted us to know it was going to die. It let out a parched screech that descended slowly, operatically, to a nauseated growl. It was the most human sound I had ever heard from an expensive car. *Brothers,* it said, *I am melting.* It faded quickly into near silence.

"This is fascinating," my father said. "I mean, we *were* supposed to put oil in the engine." The floor beneath our feet began to quake. "Allison was being a little hysterical about it. She's hysterical, as a tendency, sometimes."

I stared at him. Even stoned, he could read the question on my face: Had he cheated?

"She and I are doing fine," he said. "Being responsible to your partner comes a little easier at this age." He threw the roach into the road. "The proper course now is to reach a gas station before the *Hindenburg* here bursts into flames and the two of us burn in a German car. That'd be an ironic death for a nice Judeo-Hibernian lad like yourself."

"Is that irony?" I asked. Even under the present circumstances, it was thrilling to correct him.

"I'm not quite sure that I've retained my faculties with regard to literary distinctions right now," he said. We were moving slowly, down an exit ramp. The grass was unruly on either side. Postwar houses rose before us, uniform in shape, modest in size, painted shoot green, deep tan, every shade of decent stationery. We came to a stop at the same moment the car ceased its muttering altogether. A man sitting on his porch began to speak to us in Italian, his hands stroking his belly.

"Inglese?" my father asked.

At this, a tall, skinny man wearing glasses and overalls emerged on a porch on the other side of the street. He had gray curls, little, silvery granny glasses, and lawns of salt-and-pepper hair on his shoulders.

"This guy doesn't speak English," he called to my father. He said something dismissive to his nonanglophone neighbor in Italian. "Your car is smoking, sir?"

My father parked the convertible in front of the man's house. I grabbed the backpack and vaulted out as he idled the engine and guided the roof back into place. Once my father had turned the engine off and the smoke had stopped billowing, the man gave us lemonade in his yard while we waited for the tow.

The man's son was visiting. He was my age, short and fair with a braided ponytail, a first-year in med school. He was his father's pride—you could tell by the way the old man's gaze tracked him from his perch on the stoop, as he poured us seconds of lemonade from an orange cooler, and brought them to us with a physician's air of significance and concern. They gave no indication that they noticed my father was stoned. They seemed to see before them a mild and gentle man who thanked them profusely and remarked on the beauty of the park and the trees, who told them that this landscape was making a profound impression on him and that he was seriously considering a move from Tribeca to a neighborhood like this one, in which to raise two more children with his wife. They agreed it was a good idea.

"Excuse me, friends," he said, putting a hand on my shoulder. "I'm a proud dad and I need to brag. My son here is a musician." There was sun shining on his beard, and the wavering leaves made patterns on his forehead. "He wrote part of a song that was on a Pepsi commercial." His smile was real. "It was broadcast in Europe, Australia, and the Middle East."

The tow truck came and dragged the MG to a repair shop. We walked a half mile to one of the northernmost outposts of the 4 train, where the wooden platform was speckled with fangs of glass. My father stared down at the platform and tilted his head, like a curious boy.

"Am I just stoned?" he asked. "Or is this subway platform beautiful?"

The possibility of deflating him was too seductive. "You're stoned," I said. I immediately regretted it. His face collapsed.

"You mean it's not beautiful?" He shrugged. "Ah well. I'll stay up here and see what can be done for Allison's car. It has sentimental value for her, I believe. But don't wait for me, Son."

"I might as well hop on a train." My voice was colder than I'd intended. I was too focused on falafel in Boston to see that the convertible's death had been my opportunity to mend fences with my father. We might have fixed the natural bond between us that had begun to fray in Gaia Foods. We might have talked about the new-kids concept, had a calmer, seated discussion, over a pizza in New Haven. I could have explained the delay to Khadijah; she would have thought it was sweet of me to lend my stoned father a hand with a car. Instead I rode the 4 train back to Manhattan. I climbed the stairs at Grand Central, rode Metro-North to Stamford. Rented a squash-shaped yellow Daewoo from the Stamford Avis. Some part of me knew that the breakup with Julie was going to become real to me soon, and that if I could keep moving—keep pursuing—the moment it struck me would be delayed.

It was only outside Bridgeport that I realized I still had my father's backpack. It might have had his wallet in it, or something else, experience suggested, that was very much private property. As I drove with my left hand, I searched in it with my right, unable to stop myself. First I fished out a Ziploc bag of joints, and then a manila envelope full of something slightly heavier than paper.

Because I was running late, now, it was only when I was waiting in line at the Mass Pike toll that I opened the envelope. The

Polaroids were not of my father and a school chum; they were twelve-, thirteen-year-old pictures of my father and Nancy. Never posed together, they had taken pictures of each other rather than allow an interloper to photograph the two of them. In three shots the cabin loomed behind them. In two more the Berkshire Hills, in another the dunes of the Cape. I thought of Khadijah and me, by the Watts Towers.

Seeing a sick friend from the college days: a typical Linus Paquettian lie. But there was some Truth with a capital *T* in his story about the man on death's door. Nancy was a companion from the past who was mostly memory to him now, and she would be gone for good if he had another set of children. Like the mortally sick, she was fading. I could see my father's plan: Arrive at her office with memories in a sack; wrest her away from her new life for an afternoon; keep the central tale of his life alive another few years.

I thought of my father reaching for the icicle in front of him, and I thought of him reaching out and giving the envelope of old pictures to Nancy, and I thought of the napkins in my pocket, Tom, Myra, Julie 2. I knew this was important, somehow; but the tollbooth was upon me, and it was time to take my ticket from the machine, to make up time on the Pike. I had an appointment with a goddess from my childhood, Khadijah Silverglate-Dunn.

11.

The Mansion

I was a proud son of Massachusetts, but I'd forgotten what Cambridge was like. Packs of cars drew me in, enslaved me, husbanded me into tunnels. I pined for the straightforward hell of the freeway system, pounded the neck of the Daewoo's meek little steering wheel. After two involuntary trips down Storrow Drive, I shot past Khadijah before I spotted her, and realized that I was on Bow Street, our agreed-upon meeting place. She was able to dodge across an alley I faintly remembered for a store with hand-cranked ice cream and wave me toward a crooked little lozenge of asphalt wedged between a Harvard memorabilia shop and an institute dedicated to the prevention of nuclear war. Here, I was allowed to stop long enough for her to get in the Daewoo.

She toppled into the passenger seat dressed, I noted with joy, for something grander than food truck fare. She wore a green corduroy dress that rounded her body, and a purple cardigan that made her look plumed, a lost tropical bird.

From the beginning, our attempts to reach the falafel truck were dependent on her Bostonian's intuition for the landscape. My cell phone, which had a map feature, had run out of batteries way back on the 84.

"It's perverse I don't know how to drive through this city," she apologized. "I've never lived anywhere but Wattsbury or Boston, so I've never needed to drive."

We decided to perform a pageant for the truck's proprietor that would make our need for directions understandable.

"My husband and I," she explained into her cell phone, prim, as if to a maître d', "are from Des Moines, and we are very excited to eat your Middle Eastern food, and we are crossing some sort of bridge from Cambridge into Boston"—indeed, we were on a thoroughfare that led up to a bridge across the Charles and into a thicket of skyscrapers. "And we're having a little bit of difficulty finding you, so perhaps you could give us some instructions?" I got the sense, from the helpless sounds coming through her phone, that there were language issues. Brown leaves twisted in the air and flew up throttled roads, down the riverbanks. There was a half of my heart loyal to Julie that saw a black Lethe as I drove over the bridge. *Do not think of Julie or you will die,* spooled my mantra. *Do not think of Julie or you will die.*

Now that we were in Back Bay, Khadijah pointed us in what must have been the correct general direction and named the streets we were on as I drove. I turned over the words *Jamaica Plain* in my mind, as if to will us there. Absent a map, a higher power than human reason asserted itself. Massachusetts required faith of its returning children. We did reach the legendary truck eventually, but it was battening down the grates over its windows by the time we arrived. We sat in the car, trying to decide what to do. Now that conspicuously informal eating was no longer an option, what would our pact allow?

I reached into the backseat for the envelope and tossed the photos of my father and Nancy into Khadijah's lap.

She shuffled through them, holding them up to the streetlamp light through the window. "They're kids," she observed. "I mean compared to how they are now. Look at their faces! They don't have the faintest clue what they're getting into."

"Look," I said. "Do you want to just have dinner? There are no public places to go that aren't restaurants. I know we made a rule, but no one deserves to go hungry."

It's possible that if we had tried harder we could have found a place less violating of our agreement than the tiny Italian restaurant with checkered tablecloths that stood two blocks west of the truck. We might have found the fortitude not to order wine.

"My dad always used to take me to places like this when my mom was late at the office and she wasn't around to tell him not to spend money," she said. She encircled the base of a flaking candlestick with her index fingers.

"Did it freak you out that he treated you so much more licentiously?" I was hungry for her confessions. I wanted us to be close, and the way I knew to create closeness was to induce her to describe her own suffering.

She shrugged. "Maybe my dad is gay. Wow, that just occurred to me. Well, no, it's occurred to me before. But I don't really think he is. It's more just I think about the education he gave me, and it's essentially a fabulousness-based curriculum. After the divorce, he paid my mom to send me to Paris for two summers. The family he embedded me with had these three teenage daughters who were walking ads for France, and I was an American teenager with my backpack and my sneakers. They left me entirely to my own devices. I was incredibly depressed, but I didn't know this was what depression was, I thought this was just life, that life was this little, wet grove. I didn't have much concept of how to obtain food; I had this barely adequate allowance, and I didn't know what to eat except to go get another crêpe. I went to every museum in Paris, but I could have become a prostitute. Whereas my mother, hoo boy. She gave me a Sufi name and then raised me to be the Anti-Sufi. I mean, I was not allowed to go through a fuckup phase, ever. Maybe I'll go through a fuckup phase now."

Envy washed over me. To be overdirected by a parent, made to live according to a parent's image . . . To have one's parent expend a disturbing *excess* of money and attention to make you turn out just so. And envy and love are close cousins; I wanted to hold her. I had that familiar sensation from early childhood of loving a baby chick or a tiny dog so much that I insisted on clutching it to my chest even on the swing set, until it fell from my hands and hit the grass.

"Do you still feel depressed?" I asked. I was dimly aware of a hazardous dynamic forming, in which I was more a therapist than I usually was and she was in all likelihood more a patient than she usually was. But my appetite for her confessions had been whetted.

"I am whole," she said. "I'm just sick of being an intellectual. Is it boring to say that? Is it clichéd?"

"Not to me. I don't know any intellectuals."

"What are you actually doing? Why did you come here? This anarchy-stone thing . . . You ended things with this person I met, Julie?"

"We're done. Parents informed."

She took an absentminded gulp of her wine. "Where do you live?"

"Homeless," I said proudly. In the universe of musicians, this implied a certain sensuality of lifestyle, a seriousness with regard to one's career.

"So, what are you like?"

"Basically flexible. Shapeshifter ha ha. I was thinking of becoming a recording engineer and building people's studios. Like in Greater Boston. I'd be good at that. And I've been writing songs again. Tell me something." I, too, did some damage to my first glass. "What's it like working hard at something and having it work out? Being like, Oh, people are asking me to do this homework, guess I'll do it, and then becoming a professor? My career has been, you get a bunch of drug addicts together and put instruments in their hands, and you drag them out of bed to practice as their girlfriends throw cat toys at your head, and then you play a show and somebody puts a couple twenties in your hand and says sorry it's not what we promised, we didn't get the free case that Heineken promised us for putting the Heineken banner behind you as you played, and then you spend all your money to make a demo in a basement and then a record label is like, Here's a contract, and you make a record in a deluxe studio, and they don't do anything they said they'd do to promote it, or pay you the royalties, and then the drug addicts are demoralized and won't get out of bed anymore, and no longer even have girlfriends to throw cat toys at you, and move back to wherever they're from, and then Pepsi starts shooting money out of its ass at you. Or it seems like an ass-ton of money because you've been living on Pall Malls and Subway. So you spend a lot of it going out to eat. Then you're twenty-eight, and your hair starts to fall out." I refreshed her glass.

"Guys I've dated have had the same story without the Pepsi money or the record label. Also, that sounds vastly superior to grad school. That's all I've done. I mean I started right out of college, and now I'm an academic. Before that I was in high school. So I can't say what it's like. There's nothing to compare it to. Where we both failed," she continued, after taking another sip, "was our careers in anarchist terrorism."

We looked at each other seriously. Maybe it should have been Todd and Julie that made us feel like this, feel that we were lovable for our moments of stupidity as well as for our accomplishments. But Khadijah and I had known each other as stupid children. Todd and Julie could never look at us and see the child still in each of us as vividly as Khadijah and I could see it in each other. We didn't have to imagine those hapless kids to ignite mutual empathy. We remembered them.

Once we had polished off the wine and a substantial portion of a tilapia and a rabbit, I felt even better suited to intuitive Boston driving. Khadijah, for her part, was not alarmed by the way I guessed my way helter-skelter back to Cambridge. Rubbing the back of her head against the plastic seat, she spoke clearly and calmly.

"I can't do my job," she said. "My mom pushed me into this shit and now I can't do it."

"What do you mean?"

Central Square felt inevitable. It drew us in, a vacuum.

"When we get back to my apartment," she said, closing her eyes, "I'll show you what I mean."

When we did finally waver up the stairs of her building and through her door, she ushered me past the entrance to the bedroom and through the tiny kitchen. She sat, almost fell onto the floor of the living room, beside a bookshelf. On the other side of her, cowering in her shadow, was an exquisite little house that would have been a vulgar monstrosity at actual size. A component, no doubt, of the Homelessness Initiative.

It was a miniature version of the kind of glassy parallelogram I'd seen blocking public access routes to the beach in Malibu, but deprived of mass, waiting, by design, for its own demise. It was precious, asking to be protected. So that was what the performance was for: to show the fragility of things that otherwise appeared obnoxiously stable.

Khadijah's purple cardigan still covered her shoulders, but she'd pulled her arms from the sleeves. She took a glossy academic-press paperback from the shelf.

"Deleuze and Guattari, *Capitalism and Schizophrenia, Volume II: A Thousand Plateaus,*" she said. "I've read to about page thirty. Not the rest. Cited it any number of times." The pages made an almost excremental sound when they hit the floor, so zealously did she throw the book. She took another off the shelf. "Giorgio Agamben, *The Coming Community,* about page twenty-five." She threw. "Latour and Woolgar, *Laboratory Life,* about the first third." She threw. "Children, this is what happens when you let your mother pick out your career for you. Do you know how insane it is to have my job at twenty-nine? I can't keep up with some of the brighter undergrads. There's a *reason* people don't have my job at twenty-nine."

In music, our age was too old. In academia, apparently, it was too young.

"It's just arbitrary," I said happily. I had her confessing! "If you were a twenty-nine-year-old rock star, you'd be having to fuck up hotel rooms right now to show everybody you were still wild and young and full of cum, you know?"

"I'd fuck up a hotel room right now, to show them they made a mistake with me."

On the wall were three photographs containing bones—the use of bones by three contemporary artists was the subject of Khadijah's dissertation. One picture was a backlit sculpture of a middle-aged woman in a business suit, holding a shaman's wand decked with bird skulls. The second was a young, dark-haired woman, presumably the artist, dancing with a robot skeleton. The third was of a mobile, the kind Calder might have made, only using what appeared to be different-size femurs and fingers from various animals. Beneath the pictures there was a tiny wooden desk half-buried by dunes of paper, save for a framed shot of Todd in pajamas, tilted on a stand in one corner.

"Nobody knows this about me, Josh, just FYI. And now you are the exceptionally privileged person who gets to see someone do this for free."

She took a Taschen coffee table book of Chinese propaganda art, about the size of a lobster tank, and held it over the miniature house, so that it cast its shade like a cloud over the little office additions, the pixieish railing around the kidney pool. It was at this point that I began seriously to wonder whether my campaign to make myself Khadijah's psychoanalyst, to urge her into a state of catharsis, might not have been doing her a true favor.

"I don't know if you want to do that," I said. "You're smashed."

She let it drop. The book stove in the roof of the elaborate little manse, and its walls collapsed over its pool and its porches. A faint smell of dust and glue rose through the air.

I knelt beside her on the floor. She put her hands on my shoulders. I thought of that moment she'd thrown her arms across the table at Classé Café—*do you think I'm overdramatic?* I felt tenderness and desire—the hairs on my arms were twisting wicks.

"The vow," she said.

"We already broke it," I said. "With the stone." I took her face in my hands and kissed her.

As we listed downward, I helped ease her to the floor with one hand on her back, and ran the other up her rib cage. A door that had stood locked in the corner of our lives for thirteen years was open. I was holding her breast, her knee, that was all; but I closed my eyes and I was running out of a bright little apartment down a passage with no lights.

We held each other side by side, until with an effort she straddled me, and lay her head on my chest. A moment later, her eyes closed and her breathing filled with sleep.

I stroked her hair, the curl like loose tobacco. I wanted to touch the arcs beneath her eyes, these signs of time's passage. Her face was pressed into my chest, and it was like the teeth of the tiger, unreal.

While she snored, I composed a plan. I would work as an engineer in a studio in Brooklyn. We would begin a train circuit between Boston and New York in which we spent every weekend together, summers rent a cabin on Vinalhaven Island, Maine. Given that kissing Khadijah Silverglate-Dunn was possible, all this was possible too. Life included things I had not known it included. It was the same feeling I'd had when I discovered instruments, at age five, banging on a piano in a dying commune in the woods.

She woke suddenly, snapped back her head. I took her hand, and she pulled me onto a chair with C-shaped legs. It looked like something Nancy would have owned, sky blue, aerodynamic, modern, a pilot's seat of command. It probably *was* something Nancy had owned, back in the Age of the Dads.

And we kissed, side by side like fetal twins, in that Dadsian chair. I knew some, if not all, of the things this meant: Here we are, full circle; here we are, our parents; here we are, in rebellion against our parents, no longer obedient children; here we are, to usurp their territory. Khadijah took off her shoes and socks, and they were red socks and white sneakers but I could also see the burgundy-trimmed Esprit socks of 1994. She took off her dress and I almost saw the gray Smith College sweatshirt she'd worn when she'd thrown the stone at the window of the bank. I looked at her, both of us naked, and was ringed in old fantasies. It was as if I discovered, still in my mind but heretofore concealed, a younger version of myself. It was an ecstatic state; I was not myself.

When it was just our bodies on the chair, the two of us kissing noisily, I felt less and less like I was in my body, more and more of a spirit. I pulled her toward me, and she sat on the edge of her chair as I kissed her breasts and eventually spread her legs and tried to eat her out, before her hands cupped my chin and brought my face back up to hers. I was still soft.

Surely, this was only a temporary setback. I kissed her rib cage, her hair. I memorized the curves of her breasts, I learned the taste of her sweat, I studied the calluses on her bare feet, her interestingly smashed-together toes. My heart was full of gratitude, full of blood.

But my penis. That most beloved of organs, least obedient, Satan in *Paradise Lost*. Once frightened into self-consciousness, it would not communicate. I am, I thought, a performer! But I couldn't make it stand more than halfway.

On the floor, we still tried to get me inside her for a moment; if we could only get this far, I reasoned, everything would proceed well enough. I thought of Jeremy, my nemesis, battling his own reluctant cock, trying to get it hard enough for the condom, as the tiger looked on. I thought of all the other men before me, who had battled with their members, argued with fate. This was what defeated me for good.

"I can't," I said. "I'm sorry."

I flopped down on the floor and lay on my back. I expected to have injured Khadijah. I was ready for tears. But she slid beside me on the rug and said nothing. After a while, she spoke, not with resentment but with curiosity, with the voice of an intellectual: "I wasn't in it either."

It was a part of my soul that didn't touch my body, the part where I kept Khadijah. This cold, pretty truth I had felt floating like snow in the air in the concert hall—it sparkled, but it couldn't translate into sex. It wasn't of the flesh, what we had. Not at this point in our reacquaintance, not enough for us to jump in a chair and ravish each other. It was as if Khadijah's hands and lips and breasts were waiting for a different person, a fifteen-year-old boy who hadn't had the life I'd had, the derangement of late adolescence, the construction of a band, the collapse of a band, dawn after dawn with Julie in the egg. That child was unrecoverable, and would have had to be recovered if we were to pick up where we'd left off as children.

We didn't touch each other, lying there on the white rug. I was putting on my socks, our clothes arranged around us like sterilized instruments, when she began to speak.

"I'd like you to leave, please, Josh." She was moving things in a closet off the kitchen. She extricated a broom and a tin dustpan, with some clanging. Stumbling, slightly, from the wine, she carried them back to the living room. She looked down at the aftermath of her collaboration with Todd, the little mansion shattered by the book.

"You and my mother are so much the same," she said. "You like to have a story of how things go. My mom saw her life as featuring a certain kind of kid. You see your life as getting a girl you liked in high school. I'd prefer it if neither of you would see me as who I'd need to be to make a story happen. I wouldn't mind being that person, but I'm not."

"You led me to believe," I said. Believe what? But I couldn't say it better than that: You led me to believe. "Did you think I was going to take your little gestures lightly?"

"I liked the idea that I could just turn out to be on the wrong track for the past thirteen years and then snap back onto the one I was on before. I was into that. Is that so wrong? But I'm not going to switch lives. You're fifty percent make-believe to me, Josh. I don't actually know you all that well, can't you understand? Todd's a good man. You could be a lot of different things—how am I supposed to know? I can only live according to what's in front of me."

Well—my god.

She was doing her best to wake herself up, using the broom to try to make order of the shards. She was drunk, but she was fighting it.

Khadijah cast aside the broom. She didn't throw it; she only gave up on it, letting it fall to the ground. She went back to the closet, hauled out a black, new-looking, Earth Vac vacuum cleaner, and plugged it into a socket in the kitchen wall.

"Please go," she said. She switched on the vacuum cleaner, giving herself a force field of noise.

It was when I was back in my rental car, driving into the first blue suggestions of daylight, south of New Haven, that I was able to formulate what I had done. It had felt to me as if the person who was at the core of my life—Julie—was dispensable. And the person who had felt like the real core—Khadijah—had turned out to be someone who could only walk around the margins.

For a long time I pounded on the steering wheel and cursed. But this could last only so long; after forty-five minutes, there was an oasis. A brief moment when reflection overcame confusion and self-flagellation.

When a band is good, I thought, it doesn't sound like music somebody composed. You don't get a good band by hearing music in your head and making that music real. Maybe a good painting or a good poem can be the realized vision of an individual; Joanna Newsom's a vision made real, and she's good, but she's not a band. A good band happens because two or more people play music together and, either immediately or over time, surprise each other with a sound conceived jointly. The music is sovereign over its players. Nobody's in control, and you can hear it.

The same is true of true love. *True love* being understood here to mean sustained love. It's better if you don't place your faith in a vision of how things are going to be. The shock of what happens can be superior to any concept you had in your head at the start. But you have to listen carefully to the other person; you can't imitate the other person; you can't drown out the other person; you can't be drowned. If you forget these precautions, you will think your concept was flawed; you'll forget that not having a concept, being surprised, was the point. You'll start acting like dicks to each other. There will be fights, and boredom. The music will go flaccid. Like a band in decline, you will become a joke or break up.

At the tollbooth guarding Queens and Brooklyn, the boroughs where I had places to crash, I reached into my wallet for $6.50 and found only napkins: Tom, Myra, Julie 2. The ink had begun to bleed. Tom's nose had melted, and merged with his mouth. Myra's flower now sprouted from her head. Julie 2's hand was reduced to a blot, but her cello, creased in two places, was still a workable instrument. There was a mile-long line of cars behind me. I folded the napkins, put them back inside, and turned to face the brooding man in uniform.

200

12.

The Spanish Show

A month later, I walked west on Canal from the Q train, with a carpetbagger's gait, the Great Black Bag slung over one shoulder, my guitar case strapped around my back. Ominously encumbered like this, I'd have to turn on the charm if I wanted my father and Allison to put me up for a night. But I didn't dislike my burdens, on this particular afternoon. Seven years of experience hauling amps from vehicle to stage to vehicle made my load light. It was time to be in a band again. The lifting, the plugging in. The taping of microphones to half-broken boom stands. The elbowing through a crowd toward the bar with your drink tickets in your hand. The living noise of electricity before a drummer counts 4/4 on rim-bitten sticks.

I was on my way to meet Rachel for dumplings in Chinatown before we descended on Allison's loft together; my father had summoned us for an announcement. Rachel had just taken the Amtrak down this morning, and I hoped she might be persuaded to put me up in Somerville. I had envisioned myself potentially couch-surfing for a matter of years. But being homeless turned out to produce yet more of the already dominant feeling in my life: that of being a bassist without a band. After a month I was in awe of its depressive power—I felt not so much a surfer as a horse thrown off a ship, paddling in the center of an ocean. I was tired of baleful looks from old half friends' girlfriends, who had long grown sick of asking me about my breakup with Julie Oenervian. I was tired of trying to obtain the modest royalty checks that were inevitably sent to the apartment where I'd camped the week before. I was sick of e-mailing Julie from Internet cafés, writing page-long treatises on why we should have a phone conversation. If I could crash at Rachel's for a solid fortnight, I would have time to balance, attain dry land, find true north. I imagined sitting at her clean, circular kitchen table, a hand-me-down from the long-ago-vacated house in Wattsbury, recently showered, wearing a clean sweater, eating oatmeal with sliced bananas.

Rachel was late for dumplings, red-cheeked and slightly wild-haired from the rush downtown from her belated train. She threw her purple L.L.Bean backpack on the Great Black Bag and looked at me with something just short of revulsion.

"Jesus, Josh. You look like one of those old men outside the Stop and Shop who feed cans to the recycling monster."

"Mmmrghmh," I said.

"Seriously, where are you living, what's happened to you?"

"I'm living here, right now." I kicked the bag. This was melodramatic. But I had just been ejected from a *Vice* editorial assistant's couch in Bushwick for being the suspected source of a bedbug infestation. Petulance was my due.

"I assumed— Are Dad and Allison being dicks about letting you crash there?"

"They've got some secret shit going on. For a month they've been telling me they, like, can't make provisions for visitors right now. I feel like they're making a Frankenstein monster."

A waitress came, and Rachel ordered two teas. "They're probably on the rocks," she said. "I think today's announcement is going to be divorce."

"Maybe. But he said something to me in the car last month about her wanting kids, so maybe they're fucking all the time, to get her pregnant? So if I was crashing there it'd be like . . ." I made the descending hand gesture and melancholy dive-bomb sound that in concert signify boner death. "And now she's going to tell us she's having a kid."

Rachel considered. "It's either breakup or pregnancy. Their relationship can go one of two ways."

Our tea came, and Rachel ordered us each a pile of fried dumplings stuffed with shrimp. I promised to pay her back once I obtained a new check for a royalty payment from Argentina that had been mailed to Julie's and had never been forwarded. From Chinatown, we pushed south to Allison's loft, the two extant Paquette/Beckerman siblings. Fog slurped at Manhattan from its perch above the river. Trickles of black water took ninety-degree turns in the sidewalk, leaking from flowerpots set before a furniture store. They made me think of Julie's tears, flowing down the streets of West Hollywood. Tears I had drawn from those beast-stilling eyes. Julie would be happier now, I decided to decide. She'd find a man who would come home from work an hour before her, at 8:00, to help Samson with their babies. A man who would sling down his laptop bag, roll up his sleeves, and take his children in his arms, another Wednesday done. He would pay their teenagers' tuition fees at a wonderful school when she became too old to be a star. If nothing else, Khadijah and I had made this possible. We had weaned Julie off of me.

Funny, how after dire events you could simultaneously rise and fall in your own estimation. Maybe this was how you moved through adulthood—always walking both directions at once, toward redemption and hell.

"It's for the best, bluebird," I said.

"What?" said Rachel.

"Sorry," I said. "Just talking to somebody who isn't there."

Rachel studied me a moment, worried, before she pretended to laugh. "Have you thought of crashing with Mom?" she asked.

"This new guy she met at meditation is living there now. He was on one of their dathün retreat things with his guru. And then he didn't have a place to stay—everybody's losing their jobs up there, it's weird—so now he and the guru guy are both in her house."

"You can hang out at my place a few days, I don't care."

"You should know," I said, "I might have bedbugs on me. I'm not sure."

"Oh, then, no. Sorry." We walked in silence for a moment.

203

"It's supposed to be hard for a person to carry them," I said. "Like, it's usually furniture."

"Then how do people get them, then? It's people coming into their houses. I know people who got them without buying furniture or going to a thrift store or anything."

I allowed myself to stagger ever so slightly, under the weight of my bags, to dramatize my plight. "How is your work going, with that homelessness elimination campaign?"

"Oh God, fuck me, man, fine. You can stay, but you can't take your bags inside, we can figure out a storage-space situation. You can shower at the Y and I'll buy you some new clothes."

She had sounded so much like my father when she'd said *fuck me, man*. The family still had some juice in it.

When we stood before the door to Allison's loft, I took a deep breath and pushed—unlocked again. No sooner had I thrown down my bags than Miles swept around the corner, from Allison's closet. A herder, by inclination, he twisted his cloud-like body as he took the curve, to flank and usher Rachel and me farther. Or so I first believed. But Miles was in fact the one ushered.

His pursuers were two little girls, about five years old. They caught him, briefly, stroked his fur with both hands before he redoubled his efforts to reach me. The girls gave chase, but stopped when they came under our shadows. My father and Allison strolled in from the kitchen, until they realized, simultaneously, that strolling wasn't the right mode, and jogged to the children. My father put his hands on one pair of little shoulders, Allison her hands on the other.

"See, this is the reason we didn't want to have you stay indefinitely, Josh, it wasn't a judgment on you, it's only the contingency of the . . ." Allison indicated the two squirming creatures.

"Rachel, Joshua," said my father, "this is Lucia."

"And this is Victoria," said Allison. She peered closely at the girl after she said her name, as if she would have appreciated some confirmation of her reality. "This is their second day in their new home, and we're still getting used to things a little around here."

I introduced myself. Lucia said hello almost inaudibly, with her hands over her eyes. Victoria hopped slightly with each syllable: "Hell-o."

Allison was calm. "Josh and Rachel are your half brother and half sister," she said, kneeling between them, her hands in her lap. "They're New Daddy's kids, but they have a different mommy." The girls studied us. I studied them back, these children whose sense of the possible had over a period of days been made to expand and expand. But in an instant they were in motion, resuming their hunt for Miles.

My forehead was tight from the chill outside, my hands drawn into my sleeves. But soon I was warmed by the embrace of my father, who, though he didn't smell like weed, seemed softened, eroded by some natural force.

"We decided to adopt last year," he said, as he enveloped me. "We wanted to make an announcement to everyone at the same time, sorry, once everything had gone through. It really hits you a flake, when they arrive. That's an Irishism, 'to hit him a flake.' It means to strike somebody violently."

My father's need to swathe emotional confessions within the sharing of information was tolerable to me, just now. I put my arms around him. "Congratulations, dude," I said into his beard.

"And Boston? Did you and Khadijah dine on falafel?"

"It was kind of a fail. We chewed each other up a little."

Somewhere in a distant corner, Miles, finding no sanctuary, yowled. "I know what that's like," my father said. "It can be fun. Looking back? Right now? That sounds surpassingly fucking fun."

"Where are they going to sleep?" I watched the children pursuing the dog. "I mean it's awesome." It might take me a few moments, I decided, to ingest that the Dad who had been so eager for Rachel and me to grow up and release him had signed on for a second tour of duty. But I suspected that his old restlessness, so uncongenial to fatherhood, had fallen on its embers. He might have less energy for the new children, but they would have more space, more silence.

"Sleep? I'm not aware that they sleep."

It was at this point that Lucia and Victoria stripped the cushions off the couch and placed them on the living room floor.

"This is a ritual they've developed in the last twenty-four hours," my father said. "It's called the Spanish Show. They're both used to Spanish in the home—they're from a family in Washington Heights—and they do a kind of performance in Spanish for us. The rule, apparently, is that when you put the cushions on the floor, Spanish comes over you. It's like speaking in tongues."

"The Spanish Show begin," said Victoria, who seemed to be the director. Lucia took up the call.

"It's just one of life's minor surprises," my father mused.

Sure enough, Victoria and Lucia, evidently by mutual decree, returned to the language they shared and we did not. They commanded Rachel, in this language, to stand on the cushions and impersonate a full cabinet of wonders: monkey, bear, snake, sea horse, dolphin. The Spanish Show was improvisatory. Just as the past came to your mouth unbidden, so did the roles that consumed your body. The girls stumbled across the soft landscape in their white dresses, shapeshifting. I came to see in them something essential: that which remained constant as the poses changed.

"New Daddy has a house in the country where they real bears," Lucia told me, once we'd jumped up and down, hands in armpits, monkeys, perhaps fifteen times. This was the first full sentence that had passed between us. "It not even a house. It a castle. He make it himself." She spun around in a circle with her arms open to signify vastness.

My father leaned against a wall with his eyes closed.

"Dad," Rachel barked. She snapped her fingers in front of his face, and he blinked back to life.

"Sorry," he said. "Two kids is a bit of a project. But so far, they make us"—he scanned the ceiling for a description—"too tired for bitterness and depression."

He made his way to a battered coffee table supporting a splendor of liquor options, and one of his bowls of frozen yogurt, the frozen yogurt half consumed. He poured himself a substantial vodka tonic and put ice cubes from a little bucket into his mouth. Chewing ice was a habit of his I had almost forgotten. It was what he did, when compelled into child care, to wake himself up.

"I mean how do you start to make amends," he pondered to me, "if the way you were raised to think of yourself, it's all become sin? This is one thing you do, maybe." With his free hand, he indicated his children. "I'm going to be working," he said, "till they put me in the ground."

"New Daddy," shouted Lucia. She pointed to my father. "You an animal."

"Quite astute, darling." He put the drink beside a neo-Cubist bust of Allison's father, Bruce, commissioned from a nearby sculptor. He knelt beside Lucia suddenly, so stiff, quite old; he dropped. He put his hands on the floor. "What kind of animal," he asked, "do you want me to be?"

Curious to see how the apartment had been modified for children, I ambled from the living room into what would have been the dining room but now, covered in toys, looked like a tornado-buffeted playground. A puffy sticker of a fire truck adhered to the cheek of an eighty-year-old African mask, which had been torn off the wall and thrown on the floor. Moving on to the kitchen, I pulled myself a glass of water from the dispenser and leaned against the fridge, drinking deep, enjoying the pure martyrdom of homelessness. This theatrical display—the vagabond, slaking his thirst, quivering by the Sub-Zero—would have drawn some attention a month earlier. But my father had other children now. And Julie and Khadijah were, for the foreseeable future, unavailable. So I stood erect, and fixed my hair in the little tin-framed mirror that hung above the sink.

Rachel joined me in the kitchen. "I got the scoop from Allison," she murmured. "It's just so fucking batshit this is actually happening. Allison wanted white international newborns. But Dad held out for local, probably traumatized, nonwhite non-newborns. I mean, hey."

"What about the essays? I mean, Dad used to dream."

"That's what he likes to do. He's given himself to dreams. He's liberated."

"What are you talking about? Liberated how?"

Rachel tapped her cowboy boot against the floor. "I mean from acting on them."

"Linus, stop with the vodka, just do me that favor, okay?" This was Allison's voice, rising from the other side of the Japanese screen that divided the kitchen from the central living space. "If you can be sober when it's cleanup time," she said, "that'll be extremely helpful to me."

"Do you truly believe the janitors of this nation keep it clean in a state of sobriety?" I heard my father ask Allison. "Have you ever spoken to a janitor? Are you so alienated from the masses that this is your notion of how cleaning takes place? Sober?"

"Remember last week, when you cleaned the tub? Maybe I *should* talk to a janitor, because maybe he would clean up without doing ten thousand dollars' worth of water damage, even if he was wasted."

"Maybe you should find a man like your dad, who can just throw out ten thousand dollars and not have it be a thing. Because that's actually what you're saying to me right now, right?"

"You could hear a lark singing in a meadow and you would think the lark was implying that you were poor. You could hear a dog barking and you'd think it was implying, 'Linus, you're a poor loser. Linus, you're a poor loser.'"

"That's what *you* hear when a dog barks. I gave you children—what do you want from me? Am I not an adequate father, despite my unsatisfactory income?"

The sounds of falling silverware and shattering plates issued from the parlor, where the children were, and their parents rushed to see what had happened.

"Asshole," I heard Allison mutter under her breath as they ran.

Rachel went after them. Maybe I should have gone and helped with the emergency, too, but I was very tired, suddenly, overwhelmed. I considered the situation. My father and Allison had been married now for ten years. Given the age of the girls, they would have to hang tough another twelve. Longer than my father and my mother had endured each other. And, when I was a child, my parents, preferring whispering and occasional violence, had traded overtly hostile words like this only on very special occasions: the shattering of Paquette china, the disparaging of my mother's meditation teacher. The life that these girls had been drawn into, the air they would breathe in this largely wall-free apartment—there was no predicting anything.

Lucia marched in and interrupted my reflections. "You hiding?" she asked. "We going to do another show. Grown-ups have to watch."

To express urgency, she tugged on my black Marc Jacobs cardigan, an old gift from Julie, streaking it with the white frozen yogurt that now covered her fingers and much of her person. The commotion, I suspected, must have started when she discovered my father's used frozen yogurt bowl on the coffee table and dragged it to the floor by pulling on the tablecloth.

"Wait," I told Lucia. "Hold still." I squatted, as I'd seen harried parents do in the streets of Los Angeles, and extracted some folded paper napkins from my wallet: Tom, Myra, Julie 2. I soaked them in my glass of water and applied them to Lucia's face and hands.

Acknowledgments

Thanks so much, Brant Rumble, Claudia Ballard, Kyle McCarthy, Linda Baker, Conn Nugent, Annie Baker, Curtis Sittenfeld, Michelle Huneven, Allan Gurganus, Peter Orner, Rachel Reilich, David Gorin, Leslie Jamison, Andy McNicol, Holly S., Elizabeth Cunningham, Lan Samantha Chang, Elizabeth McCracken, Uncle Rory and the rest of the Baker and Nugent clans, especially Jack, Danny, Molly, Isabelle, and Kati. I'm grateful to the Iowa Writers' Workshop, Yaddo, Southern New Hampshire University, Beth's Cabin, and the people at Scribner and William Morris Endeavor I rarely or never see, such as Nan Graham, Susan Moldow, Ian Dalrymple, and my copy editor. And to those who offered affirmation when it was much needed: Rob Spillman, Aisha Muharrar, Amy Williams, Edward Carey, Connie Brothers, Melissa Flashman, Greg Walter, Blake Fronstin, Hanna Rose Shell, Amie Barrodale. And to Khadijah Britton for the use of her name and nothing else.

Printed in the United States
By Bookmasters